What Solomon Saw and Other Stories

———

ISBN: 0692238689
ISBN 13: 9780692238684
Library of Congress Control Number: 2014910948
InkWit, Michigan City, IN

To Tom
With much love and gratitude

Contents

What Solomon Saw

More than anything in the world Lester Johnston wanted to see Libby Tatum's titties. It was an overnight obsession as they had sprouted within the same time frame. One day she was as flat chested as the rest of us; the next she was at Thalheimers department store scooping them into a 34B Maidenform. No training bra for these gals, they could two-wheel on their own.

There wasn't a likable bone in Libby's body. And before she had grown a pair even Lester would dismiss her. Once, when Oliver Jenkins crossed home plate and the ball skipped between Libby's legs and she screamed her usual "damn ball," Lester threw his glove into the dirt and said, "It's always the ball with you, Libby, can't throw one, can't catch one, and it's always the ball's fault."

That was the big brother I looked up to. But today, though he had just celebrated his thirteenth birthday, he had crossed into a camp of idiots. Libby might have been curvy, but she had edges sharp enough to cut glass. She was bossy and made anybody younger or smaller than her feel like they just weren't up to snuff. She couldn't get enough of the word *mature*. "When you're more *mature*, Martha, you'll understand." Or with a bored air, "I guess I'm just more *mature* than most girls my age." A smart-aleck, big-boobed know-it-all was more like it.

As she walked down Elizabeth Avenue, the Maidenform's concentric conical stitching formed two perfect beehives under a too-tight T-shirt and pointed her in our direction. Lester hopped off his bike, stood, jaw agape, and somehow mustered a weak "Hey, Libby" while directing his gaze at the center of her T-shirt. My own jaw was set as I bit the inside of my lip.

"Goin' to the creek?" he asked her.

"No, I'm gonna lay out by the pool." She held up a bottle of baby oil and iodine. "Wanna come along?"

That baby oil might just have well been a key to a motel room.

As he tried to hide his eagerness, Lester slowly got back on his bike and made circles in the street.

"I guess." He blew out air. "Nothin' better to do."

I could have carved better backbone out of a bar of soap.

"Hey, Martha, you wanna come?" she asked.

I answered with a too-quick, too-sharp no, then added, "I'm busy building a porch on the tree house. If y'all get bored suntanning, I'd appreciate some damn help!" I ended just short of shrill.

I watched my brother follow Libby Tatum up the hill, doing wheelies on his bike. School had just started back and I had promised God and Sister St. Hilda that I would watch my temper this year, but I was already cussing under my breath and shooting the finger at their backs.

Until that late summer day in 1960, I'd never thought much about a woman's bosom. When my mother nursed my little brother, David, they seemed a suitable convenience, but when one was whipped out, even in the privacy of our own home, I would wince as David latched on, a lip-smacking little magnet. I had once seen my fat Philadelphia grandmother take off her underwear. When her breasts were finally released from bondage, they rolled down the mountains of abdominal flesh like lava then finally halted. When she saw me, she turned her back so quickly one of the pendulous things swung out like a wrecking ball and knocked the toiletries off the dressing table.

As far as my own breasts, I had what could pass for two butter beans under bee-stung nipples. Nothing more. When I was six, I pulled my panties down in front of Harvey Wade. We did the usual inspection and became familiar with what sat in the saddle, but that was the extent of our research. Other than my grandmother's physical anomaly, what occupied the upper half of a woman's torso was of little interest to me until the day Libby Tatum sashayed down the street with her breasts pointing heavenward. While I was as hopeful as the next eleven-year-old that I would look like the girls in *Seventeen* magazine one day, I was prepared to bind my chest like the Chinese did their feet at the first sign that something was getting out of proportion.

All of this focus on bodies changing put me in a foul mood. I had liked my life before. Ever since I could follow my brother around, he, the Wade boys, and I spent our free time as a company of raga-muffins. We rose each morning and grabbed the first thing out of a drawer—usually shorts and a T-shirt. We blew through the kitchen, slurping down Wheaties, and ran into the woods to begin the day's work: tree-house building, creek damming, and salamander dissection. We knew it was lunchtime when our stomachs said so or when we heard Josephine, my family's housekeeper, holler out the back door. A quick tomato sandwich and we were back for the second shift.

Around four o'clock, Josephine would round us up and, at finger-point, force us into the tub then plunk us in front of a black-and-white television no bigger than a windowpane. When our parents got home, the only evidence of the day's labor lay crumpled in the clothes hamper. The gears of the day slowed as the sun slipped. Josephine's hand would cup each chin as she kissed us good-bye. "Mind your mama, sugar," she'd say. Then she'd walk to the car where Melvin was waiting. Melvin Witherspoon was a housepainter during the week and a preacher at Living Grace Mission Baptist on Sundays. He was the tallest man I'd ever seen and the blackest. Josephine was round and brown.

Once, when my mother came home from the radio station, where she was the only female newscaster in North Carolina, she had a puzzling conversation with Josephine regarding Cassius Clay, the phenomenon who had won an Olympic gold medal for boxing that summer.

"He says he is a black man," Mama said. "Not colored. It's catching on. I have been corrected twice in recent days by reporters that colored people are now black people. How do you feel about that, Josephine?"

"Does this here look black to you?" Josephine thrust her arm at my mother. "All the time and money I spend on bleaching cream, buttermilk-and-cucumber paste? This here is coffee with a bit of cream, baby.

3

This ain't black. Now, Melvin may be black. That's fine for him. But I ain't black. I don't care what no boxer say. Dr. King, he ain't running around calling hisself black."

Too many things were changing: coloreds to black, flat chests to bosoms, a Catholic was running for president, and my brother was becoming somebody I didn't recognize. Even in our North Carolina town we straddled old and new. We lived in a new development built on a swath of land Farmer Eli Peters had sold off right after the war. Mr. Peters had kept most of his acreage, where he still farmed a little cotton, corn, and tobacco and kept some cows and chickens. My father often remarked that we had the best of both worlds—a new house, a city bus stop on the corner, and a working farm for a backyard. A boy of the Depression who'd gone to college on the GI Bill, my father was of the mind that dark times were behind him. He'd married a pretty Yankee girl, and after I was born, he became a Catholic. "Everything changes, Martha," he would say. "It's the only thing you can count on."

Our tree house sat deep in an old willow oak we called Solomon about a hundred and fifty yards from our back door. It was a massive thing, taller than a steeple with branches that spread out half a city block. Solomon was a hiding place to smoke cigarettes, a command center for neighborhood attacks, and a church where you could sit blue and moody. I knew every gnarled limb, which branches would hold me, and which ones were brittle. And I knew a secret knothole where I once found three baby squirrels.

There were remnants of previous hideouts in Solomon. Some had rotted; some had been architecturally unsound. But mine would last. Daddy came out one Saturday and gave it a once-over. He drove long wood screws through the tree's bark and into its belly, pushed hard against his work, and pronounced it sound. I had a basket attached to a rope for bringing up supplies, sandwiches, and jars of sweet tea. My plan was to build a little porch out onto the supporting limb.

In spite of my anger, there I was hauling up nails and scraps of one-by-fours I had gathered from the scrap heap at a building site down the street from our house. Mr. Peters walked by wearing the same overalls he'd worn every day for the past thirty years and the same sweat-stained straw hat. A shotgun was opened and folded over his forearm. Five or six bird dogs pranced ahead of him and sniffed the ground.

"Hey, Mr. Peters," I said politely.

"How do." His reply was barely audible, and he was quickly gone along with his yapping dogs.

Libby moved into our neighborhood when I was six. We had been friends for no more than a month when she told me that she couldn't play with me anymore because I was a Catholic.

"My daddy says it's kind of like coloreds, Martha. You should stick with your own kind."

I ran home sobbing. Not because I liked her, but my head had been turned by the swimming pool her father was constructing in her backyard. When I got home, I told Josephine that I wasn't going to be a Catholic anymore, and I wasn't going to put one more penny in the jar for pagan babies.

"Suit yourself," she said. "But I took you for somebody with more fiber. If I have to be a credit to my race, shouldn't you be setting a good example? People looking to you, Martha. Every Catholic in this town got to shine."

A month later the swimming pool was put on hold as Libby's father was laid off. A week later he was in my father's office interviewing for a job. As he shook Daddy's hand, he made sure to invite the whole family "any ole time, to stop by for a swim." As it turned out, his old company took him back, and my father never had to tell him that he hadn't made the cut. And while Lester and I would take a dip now and then in what turned out to be not much more than a wading pool, my father and mother never walked through the Tatum's back gate.

The Sunday after Libby Tatum had blossomed was the first time St. Leo's Catholic Church was going to have a Sunday evening Mass. We must have been a progressive parish, 'cause we were going to have a guitar player and a folk singer accompany our choir.

Late Sunday morning, my father and I drove to Krispy Kreme Doughnuts. On the way home he almost wrecked the car when he saw Libby Tatum mowing the grass in the first bikini anybody in Winston-Salem, North Carolina, had ever seen. She jiggled from shoulders to cheeks right along with the power mower.

"Jesus, Mary, and Joseph," my father said. "Somebody better tell that girl she shouldn't be mowing the lawn in her underwear." My father's head spun like Howdy Doody's to get a better look. "I better never catch you doing such a thing."

I was delighted my father thought I had such potential.

Minutes later, we were sitting in the kitchen, drinking milky coffee, and dunking our donuts when Lester came in the front door.

"I sure am glad I don't have to go to that hootenanny Mass with y'all tonight," he bragged.

"How's that?" my father asked.

"'Cause I already went, that's why." Lester held high a self-righteous head. "After I finished delivering papers this morning I went to eight o'clock Mass. I wasn't dressed too nice, so I stood in the back, but it still counts, don't it, Mama?"

"Doesn't it," Mama corrected.

"Anyway I have a science test tomorrow and I have to stay home and study."

Daddy said that Lester was a slick planner and suspected that he wanted to play baseball until it got dark. Mama said it was time he exercised some independence and reminded Lester that trust was something that was earned.

That evening, the guitar player had just got started when the church grew uncommonly dark for five thirty. Then in a flash the stained-glass windows lit up and fluttered to dark like Christmas trees. Lightening, thunder, and torrential rain drowned out the guitar, the singer, and even Father Daley's sermon. My father looked down and winked at me and whispered that there was "a real frog strangler going on out there."

Halfway through Mass the electricity went out. It was beautiful with just the altar candles lighting the church. Save for old Mr. Peel who tripped going up for communion and yelled "Goddamn, Mother of Christ," it was lovely having Mass in the dark. Mama hoped Lester had had enough sense to close the windows. David slept through the whole storm cuddled on a blanket in the pew.

As soon as it had come upon us it passed. We came out of church to the sun setting over the slate roof and rivers running down the sidewalks. Father Daley shook Daddy's hand and said that it looked like God wasn't all too pleased about the new time slot. Daddy said maybe He just preferred pipe organs to guitars.

We rode home, dodging broken limbs and flooded viaducts. About two miles from the house the electricity came back on. We watched lamps and televisions pop on one street at a time.

Before we even got out of the car, Lester was at Mama's door, helping her with David's diaper bag.

"That storm was almost bad as a hurricane, wasn't it?" he asked as we walked toward the house.

"You alright?" asked Mama. "You are as red as a beet."

When we got inside, Daddy noticed that not only were all the windows shut but the blinds and drapes were closed as well, like a summerhouse shut up for winter.

"Lester, what's that dining room chair doing in the middle of the living room?"

As Lester went to move it back, he said he'd used it to put his feet on to do sit-ups. I'd never known Lester to be concerned about his abdominal muscles. He wasn't even playing football yet. Things got even more peculiar as the night wore on. I'd never seen my brother so considerate—helping Mama get David down, helping Daddy reopen the windows, even asking me if I wanted to listen to his transistor radio while he studied.

The next morning, before school, Josephine and Mama were leaning against the kitchen sink, sipping coffee, when Mildred Tatum arrived at the front door. Even a glimpse of what Libby might have ahead of her was enough to make me rethink my hatred and consider pity. Mildred was a tall, high-hipped woman with black wires for hair, tamed by a battalion of bobby pins. She was pale; her only makeup, poorly applied blue-red lipstick, was as likely to land on her teeth as her lips. Once, I heard Mama describe her as melodramatic and "on edge." But Mama was being kind.

"Why, morning, Mildred, what brings you by so early?"

"That good-for-nothing tree house, that's what. I am absolutely fit to be tied."

Mildred pulled out a chair without being offered one and lit one of Mama's Salems, also without invitation. Within a minute we were sitting in a green fog.

"My Libby fell out of that tree house yesterday evening trying to get down in the storm so she wouldn't be late to get to the youth social at Redeemer Baptist. She wobbled on a loose board and missed the ladder. Either that or somebody pushed her. The result is a broken arm. My daughter is wearing a cast up to her armpit."

"Mildred! I'm so sorry—"

But Mildred Tatum put up her hand to hush my mother while pulling hard on the Salem.

"Old Mr. Peters heard her holler and came and got her and took her to Baptist Hospital in his truck wrapped in a blanket. My poor Libby, she was worried she might be bleeding and so she quick took off her new Sunday blouse and her brassiere." Mildred drew another lungful into her chest. "Mr. Peters must have got an eyeful when he found her—you know my Libby is developing."

"We had noticed," Mama said.

Mildred shot my mother a look.

"That she is developing into a statuesque young woman," Mama said.

"Well, she was so embarrassed she liked to die. Forest and I were at my mother's for dinner. And, when we got to the emergency room, do you know what? There was a colored boy being tended to while Libby waited. Burned me up. Right there in the emergency room of Baptist Hospital, not the Katie B. where he is supposed to be."

"My, my," Mama said and took a sip of her coffee.

"Anyway, they set the bone, put her in a cast, and gave her something for the pain." She took another deep draw, and because she couldn't speak while inhaling, I shot in.

"What happened to the colored boy, why was he there?"

"Stuck his hand in a lawn mower, crazy boy. His mama was in there wailing like she was in a revival tent, Lawd Jesus, Lawd Jesus!"

"Well, did he lose a finger, or his hand?" I said.

"I don't know, Martha, and that isn't the point." She turned to Mama. "The point is I want that tree house torn out immediately before the next child breaks a neck, not just an elbow. It's unsafe, that's all there is to it, and I want you and Walter to take care of it today, not tomorrow, but today."

Josephine and my mother had maintained their positions throughout the diatribe. David sat in his high chair and chewed his Zwieback. Josephine toyed with her dishrag and shifted her weight from one leg to the other. Lester sank his chin deeper into his cereal bowl and read the back of the Raisin Bran box.

Suddenly Mildred Tatum spun around to me and put her finger in my face.

"And you, Miss Martha, can bring your jaw up to your top lip. It's time you started playing with dolls instead of two-by-fours anyway."

"You can't . . ." I started toward Mildred Tatum, my jaw so geared up I could have chewed glass. Josephine's arm came around my shoulder and gently pulled me to her. Mama slowly pulled out a chair and sat across from our guest.

"Mildred, I appreciate your concern for my daughter's choice of activities, but there are certainly worse things a child can get into these days. I'll call Walter and have him take a look at the tree house when he gets home from work. Now, if you'll excuse me, I have to get to work myself. How 'bout if I drop you off on my way and you can tell me all about Libby's arm."

She stood, and in a single gliding step, my five-foot-two mother had slipped her pocketbook on her wrist and escorted too-tall Mildred out of the kitchen. They left the house and walked toward the Chevy. I stood at the door and heard my mother say as they walked down the path: "What a clever girl, if not a contortionist, to be able to unhook and remove a brassiere with a broken arm. You must be so proud."

When they'd gone, Josephine lifted her dishrag and talked right into it while she wiped the table.

"Well I do declare if that woman don't beat all. Who she think she is coming in here at quarter to eight in the morning, spouting off, and telling us what to do. She right scary, all that hair and lip color."

She took the end of her apron and wiped David's face and hands then went back to the table.

"And how she know if that boy's daddy don't have insurance, or maybe he can pay out his own pocket. That woman burn me up. Always has."

Josephine wiped the bottom of the sugar bowl, put the salt and pepper in the middle of the table.

"And if you ask me?" she pointed her rag in my direction. "Serve that Libby right breaking her arm. What she doing climbing up in that tree house all by herself on a Sunday evening? I don't know about white folks, but colored folks don't have no youth socials on a Sunday. That's Friday night to keep the young'ns off the street. Why wasn't she having dinner with her family or doing her homework? Something don't sit right about this. Naw, sir. Something ain't right at all."

Lester finished his cereal, carried the bowl to the sink, and skulked out of the kitchen. The "something that ain't right" grabbed his book bag and went walking down the hall and out the door.

"OK, buster, you better fess up and fess up fast," I demanded when I caught up with him at the corner. "You don't have any science test. Hell, we only been in school four days. You were in that tree house with Libby Tatum."

I Perry Masoned him right in his face. And what I got was a stunner. My big brother threw his book bag down in the grass, then threw himself down next to it and began to cry. I hadn't seen him cry since he'd cut the tip off his finger the year before.

"I'm gonna go to hell, Martha. I'm gonna die and go to hell or at least spend about three hundred years in purgatory."

This was too good to be true. My brother was actually admitting guilt about something. I was no confessional and truly not up to the task, but I immediately sat in the grass next to him and conjured up a sympathetic face, brows knitted, head cocked.

"What happened, Lester, how'd Libby break her arm?"

"I'm gonna catch hell, Martha, when Daddy finds out, I'm good as dead. I know old man Peters is gonna tell him."

"Tell him what."

Lester drew in a deep breath and blew out the following: "That Libby did a striptease for me and Harvey Wade."

"What?"

"She took off her shirt, on the tree-house porch . . . me and Harvey were standing on the ground looking up, clapping, whistling. She was spinning around to throw her bra and lightning cracked like a bull-whip and the next thing I knew she was on the ground screaming."

This couldn't be! Libby Tatum was a Baptist. People in North Carolina might expect that kind of behavior from a Presbyterian, but never a Baptist.

The image of bossy, know-it-all, Libby, bare breasted, twirling her bra over her head like a helicopter blade, then flying ass over teakettle to the ground was delicious. In fact it has never left me.

"Then what happened, Lester?"

"I heard Mr. Peters calling, 'What's wrong over there?' Harvey ran off like the chickenshit he is. Libby had one arm holding onto the other. I found her shirt in some bushes and wrapped it around her. She was hollering and crying, said she'd told her parents she was going to the youth social at her church. Said if I told anybody, she'd say I pushed her. Then Mr. Peters was there with a blanket. It was raining like hell by then, thunder and lightening to beat the band. You could hardly hear, the wind was so loud, the trees blowing. Mr. Peters hollered that it was dangerous out there in the woods, that we could get hit by lightening, or a falling tree limb.

"When I got home I closed all the windows, put on dry clothes, and pulled a dining room chair into the middle of the living room. I figured if lightening was going to strike, it'd have to travel halfway across the room to get me. That's when the front door blew open and the electricity went out and I just knew God was gunnin' for me for lying about going to church and studying. I said, 'Sweet Jesus, don't kill me. I know I shouldn't have looked at Libby's titties. I know I shouldn't have asked her to show 'em to Harvey and me. I promise I'll go to confession and I'll never look at another girl as long as I live.' That's what I said, Martha. Then I knelt down and rested my elbows on the chair seat and said a Rosary, like Mama does during Lent. I was in the middle of a string of Hail Marys when I realized the storm had passed and y'all were driving up. I was never so glad in all my life to see anybody."

Lester wiped his cheeks with the back of his hands, his nose on his shirtsleeve. He appeared to be calming down, but started up again in earnest.

"But now I know I'm going to get skinned alive. They probably won't let me play football this year, or race in the Soap Box Derby. And what if she tells her mother I pushed her? Harvey hadn't got a bone of gumption in him, so he'll just lie and say he wasn't there. It'll just be her word against mine. I won't have any proof that she's lying. Oh God, Martha, Mrs. Tatum will have me arrested. Do you realize I could end up in reform school?"

We had been such a normal family, and suddenly I pondered having a convict for a brother. I should have felt worse than I did.

Deep sobs rocked poor Lester as I reached over to pat him on the back. I was, for a change, innocent. Something punishable had happened and I had no part in it. My brother's guilt and the image of him saying a Rosary alone in the living room was almost as delightful as what I knew about Libby. Finally, Lester stood, ran the cuff of his shirtsleeve over his face a final time, picked up his books and his lunch box, and walked to the bus stop. He rode sullen all the way to school, didn't even cuss at the public school boys who called us mackerel snappers.

When we got home that afternoon, Josephine told us she'd grab a switch if she caught us in the woods, so we stayed in the house while she ironed Daddy's shirts and folded diapers. A Soap Box Derby pamphlet came in the mail with colorful photographs of cars that had won in years past. I took it into Lester's room, but he turned to the wall.

"Why bother," he said. "I don't think you can race in the Soap Box Derby if you're in reform school."

While Josephine and I folded David's diapers, we speculated on why a boy would put his hand into a lawn mower.

"I bet you a quarter his baseball rolled underneath it," I said.

"I bet you a quarter it was the first time that boy saw such a thing as a power mower. More dirt than grass over in East Winston, baby. That boy was with his daddy mowing the golf course or over at the Jewish church. Colored people be home or in church on Sunday unless they get work. And that's where Libby oughta been, either with her mama or at church."

"Do you think Miz Tatum is a bad mother?" I put my stack of diapers in the laundry basket.

"Naw, baby. But I think she's afraid she might be."

At five o'clock my father pulled into the driveway and stopped to smoke his Lucky Strike with Melvin, who was waiting out front for Josephine. It was a moment they shared Monday through Friday. Primarily they discussed the inner workings of Chryslers, Fords, and Chevys—how to change this, drain that, or reassemble the entire engine. There were also discussions of fish caught and groundhogs shot. They never spoke of work or their families. I ran out the door and rushed at my father with the news about Libby Tatum—omitting Lester's revelation—and what Mrs. Tatum had said about my tree house.

"Martha, where in world are your manners? You leave 'em at school? Now, you say hey to Melvin and I'll talk to you in a minute."

"Hey Melvin," I whined, and apologized for being rude.

"Who say you have to tear out your tree house?" Melvin said.

"That mean old horse face, Miz Tatum, that's who."

My father gave me a hard look.

"Well, I don't care, Daddy. She don't have any right to tell us what to do with our own tree house."

"Doesn't have any right. But Mr. Peter's does. It's his tree on his land. He's always given you children a lot of freedom to roam his property. Best you ask him how he feels about his tree." He turned back to Melvin.

"Well, I guess you're going to have to excuse me." My father took a final draw from his cigarette. "I have to check the architectural integrity of Martha's tree house. You 'n' Josephine have a nice evening."

My father crushed the butt under his shoe and allowed me to pull his long arm towards the woods.

When we approached Solomon, I skipped ahead, but Daddy said he wanted to go up first in case things had jarred loose in the storm. As he started up the ladder, we saw Mr. Peters up on the roof of the tree house holding the longest stick I'd ever seen. Two of his bird dogs were wiggling under the tree, tails beating the air.

"How do, Walter," Mr. Peters called down.

"Evening, Eli, mind if I come up?"

Mr. Peters stepped down onto a limb and offered his hand to my father who was making his way up a ladder of one-by-eights screwed securely into the trunk. It was odd watching the two Gullivers, hunched over, traipsing around my tree house, ducking their heads. They pulled and poked, stomped and kicked like they were checking car tires. Finally, they came down, chuckling that things were safe as houses and that I showed promise as a builder.

"Don't you worry 'bout Miz Tatum, Martha," Mr. Peters declared. "This here tree house is likely to last as long as old Solomon hisself."

Again he looked up into the tree's upper branches.

Daddy said much obliged to Mr. Peters and told me not to stay too long, said supper would be ready soon. He hurried off back towards the house, leaving me alone with Mr. Peters.

This was my cue to thank the owner of my tree, but he barely let me get out a word of appreciation.

"You should be right proud of that brother of yourn, Martha." The old man scratched at his ear and spit tobacco juice to the left of his shoe.

"What brother?"

"Lester."

"Why?"

"Why, he did a right brave thing last night, stayin' with that girl when she fell, lightnin' flashin', tree limbs fallin', and such."

He leaned on his tall stick and studied my face.

"He gave her his shirt, tried to shield her from all them cats and dogs falling out the sky. That fool Harvey Wade run off like a scared hen, but not your Lester. Got me a real bad hip, so it was him carried Libby to my place, cleaned out the cab of my truck, and helped me get her inside. There weren't room for the three of us or I'd a-taken him home too. I told him to stay there in the barn 'til the storm passed, but he said he had to get home and shut the windows, so he run on."

My brother had mentioned none of this. His guilt must have over-shadowed his good deed.

"Lester's afraid Libby's going to tell everybody he pushed her out of the tree house."

"Oh, I don't reckon she'll do that."

Old Mr. Peters who had never said more than "how do" or "nice mornin'" came around and put his hand on my shoulder.

"You come from good people, Martha. I knew your granddaddy, your uncle Jacob and aunt Myrtle. All them Johnstons now buried at the old Salem Cemetery. Solid as rocks, they was. You and Lester are going to turn out just fine."

He reached in his back pocket and pulled out a short piece of rope and threw it for the dogs. They took off into the woods and came back, looking like draft mules, each holding one end of the rope in his mouth. The dogs dropped the rope, sat on their haunches, and looked up at Mr. Peters, panting, tails wagging. He threw it again.

"Whatever happened to the colored boy?" I asked.

"What colored boy?"

"The one at the hospital. Miss Tatum said when she got to emer-gency there was a colored boy who'd stuck his hand in a lawn mower. Doctor told her they wouldn't treat Libby until they were finished with him."

Mr. Peters frowned and shook his head.

"I never saw no colored boy. They usually go on over to the Katie B. Hospital, over in East Winston. Libby was the only patient there that evening. Doctors said unless it was a matter of life or death they couldn't treat her 'til her parents got there. Took us a while to track them down. Nurse called Libby's grandparents; they was the ones who told us that Mildred and Forest was at that new steak house up on Stratford Road, the one that lets you have a cocktail on Sundays. We called the restaurant and they come running. And boy did Mildred Tatum get worked up. She kept hollering, Lord Jesus, Lord Jesus. You'd've thought Libby had been found dead instead of just a broke arm."

I should have been relieved, but I felt even worse. The dogs were back for more. But Mr. Peters put the rope in his back pocket.

"Me and Josephine been worried to death about that poor little boy," I said. "She sure is going to be happy to find out he doesn't even exist. Why you reckon Mrs. Tatum to tell such a lie?"

"Oh, I don't know, Martha." Mr. Peters reached a hand up under his overalls and scratched his stomach. "Sometimes folks want you to notice one thing so you won't see another." He took his hat off and wiped his brow with a red cloth he pulled from his back pocket. "Anyway, I just want you young'ns to be careful. A broke arm can just as soon be a broke neck." He put his hat back on and returned the red bandana. "That's one thing crazy Miz Tatum is right about."

In my world, children didn't often converse with adults who weren't family, and here I was carrying on with a farmer as old as my grandfather who smelled of cow manure and chewing tobacco, earth and sweat.

"Thank you for letting us play in your tree, Mr. Peters. Daddy says it's the biggest tree he's ever seen in all of North and South Carolina, Virginia, and Georgia. Says it must be a good three hundred years old if it's a day."

"It's a good one." Eli Peters ran a hand over the bark of his tree. Two old and rough surfaces touched.

I turned to go, then turned back.

"Hey Mr. Peters?"

"Yup."

"What's the stick for? You goin' fishin'?"

"In a matter of speakin' I reckon I am, but this pole ain't got enough poke."

He laughed and I did too, not knowing exactly what I was laughing at. Mr. Peter's speckled dog nuzzled at my leg. I scratched his ears, then turned.

"Have a nice evening, Mr. Peters," I said.

"You do the same, Martha."

I walked down the path that had been created by generations of children going to play in the giant tree and in the creek that ran beside it. As I often did, I turned around at the trailhead to take a final survey of my tree house and the glory that was Solomon. The September sun was setting, sending glimmers of orange and yellow through the leaves that had not yet changed their color. Then I saw it and knew what Mr. Peters had been fishing for. High up on a brittle branch, perfectly lit by the setting sun, hung Libby Tatum's bra.

The Army Jacket

"We going hunting on Saturday, Daddy?" the boy would often ask.

"You bet your buttons," his father would say, and it would set off a glow in the boy's face. It was better than a promise of going to a picture show or swimming at Crystal Lake.

The boy stood eye level to where a metal button of his father's old World War II jacket should have been. The other buttons, embossed with *U.S.*, traveled up one side and met at the notched lapel. His father wore the jacket on days like this when the weather was cool, when they went hunting. The boy had never seen it buttoned, so the missing one really didn't matter. If it did, he reckoned his grandma would have sewn it back on, or taken one off the sleeve and put it in this one's place.

"You ever shoot you a German, Daddy?" the boy had asked his father once.

He had not. He could tap Morse code like talking English, so the army had given him better things to do.

The boy liked the coat. It smelled and scratched like wool and mimicked its owner, sturdy and used but with a lot of wear and tear ahead. Now, many years after it was issued, the boy wore it often while playing army, with the sleeves rolled up three times and still his fingers barely poked out. There was a hat, too, and pants, but the only other thing his father wore from his days as a soldier was the pair of big, heavy brogans with laces as thick as electrical cords that crisscrossed halfway up his calves.

The boy looked down at the boots now while the two of them, along with his uncle and grandfather, stood at a wooden counter, a display of Hoppe's gun oil at eye level. It was their routine to stop first at Oxton's Bait and Ammo, then at a ramshackle diner up the road for a bite of breakfast. They would make it to Mr. Reed's pastures by nine, where they would shoot groundhogs and maybe a quail or two. They were happy to help old Mr. Reed out. The groundhogs not only tore up his land but left deep holes that his cows would trip in. He'd had to shoot two last year, costing him dearly.

The boy was too young to shoot at anything other than beer bottles, but they'd been bringing him along since he was six. His father would wake him before daybreak, and they'd leave the house in whispers and shiver until the car heated up. They'd stop first at his uncle's, who'd already have two wiggling dogs in the back of the truck. He was newly married and didn't have children yet, just the dogs that were far more disciplined than he was. Then they'd caravan up six blocks to his grandfather's, who'd be standing out front, finishing a Camel and taking a last sip of coffee. He'd leave the china cup on the stoop and crush the cigarette butt on the sidewalk. The four of them would leave the darkened city and meander through the piedmont and be well into the mountains before anyone else in their family had gotten up to pee.

The boy liked these mornings. At first there had been the elevated status of being with the men. He'd even bragged to his little sister that he had to miss Saturday morning cartoons. But now a relaxed confidence had settled in along with a sense of adventure as cornfields and tobacco barns became barely visible as daylight crept into the east. At home, he was a rambunctious boy, curious, asking about every sort of thing. But on the mountain, he respected that things took on a different tone and that answers often came without questions. Until a blast cracked the air, hunting was a quiet time, which suited the men because they weren't much for talking anyway. And for some reason, when he was with them it suited him too.

Two weeks ago his daddy had tucked a small rifle up under the boy's armpit and showed him how to line it up with the empty Budweiser bottle in the distance. It sat up on a rock with a bunch of scrubby bushes on either side. He'd shot the rifle before and the kick damned near knocked him ass over teakettle, but this time he was determined to hold steady. His nose started to run, but he let it, and remembered to squeeze, not yank on the trigger. The bottle was gone before the sound exploded in his ear. The rock sat empty, and his father shouted "Goddamn!" and smiled that half smile of his that stretched to one ear and put a twinkle in each eye.

The boy always felt righteous when his daddy shot beer bottles. There had been a time when his father was a drinker, a real bad drinker. He'd been sober now for a few years, but the boy had memories of him coming home drunk and his mother crying. He remembered when his daddy had been in the city hospital drying out and then had started going to meetings in a church basement. He'd been going to them for a while now and had become friends with some of the other men. In fact, they all got together on the banks of the Yadkin River on Fridays in the summertime. They cooked catfish and cranked out homemade ice cream and watched their kids catch lightning bugs at dusk. Now and again the boy's father would get a phone call and leave in the middle of the night, like a doctor. Later the boy would find out that one of the men had had a slip and his father had gone to help.

Oxton's Bait and Ammo was open at daybreak. The tiny shop was perfumed by cherry pipe smoke. The owner, in dirty overalls, dragged a bum leg from one end of the counter to the other, his pipe clenched between yellow teeth.

"So you're getting out of the gun business, I see." The boy's father looked at the empty racks.

"That big ole place over in Greensboro done run me out of business," Ox said. "Don't pay no more. I'll do just fine with my lures and line, and I'll keep stocking your shells."

"I feel bad leaving you with just one box of those Wingmasters, Ox." The boy's father handed the money over.

"Don't worry about it," the old man said. "I got an order coming in Monday. Y'all have a good breakfast and bag me a bird if you see something fat."

"Will do."

The boy and his father walked out to the car and the caravan made it's way to their next stop: Jack's Spot, the diner on Old Mountain Road.

At the diner, they waited just inside the door, by a tall built-in desk where the cash register stood. A frail, sallow-faced girl wiped crumbs from an oilcloth-covered table and set the ketchup bottle next to the sugar bowl. Her hair was straw colored with dark roots and held in check by a black hairnet that made her look old for her maybe twenty years. Her eyes were rheumy and she had a hint of red lipstick caked in the creases of her lips. The boy noticed that her fingernails were bitten down so low that the thumbs had bled and the two index fingers were covered with dirty adhesive tape.

There were five tables and a counter with six stools. Two of the tables held two men each and the other three were waiting to be cleared. The counter was empty, but plates and coffee cups littered the sticky Formica.

"How do." Jack, the cook and owner, came out from behind the long wooden table that was his workstation and began to clear away the dishes and cups.

"Fine, Jack," the boy's father said. "Fine and hungry."

The cook's apron was stained and he wore an old sock hat with sprigs of gray hair sticking out every which way. Behind him, a stove held four frying pans, a giant pot with grits bubbling, and a waffle iron, batter dripping out the sides. The kitchen walls were milky green with cracks in the plaster traveling up and out in every direction. Whenever they sat at the counter, the boy would follow the cracks like roads on a highway map as they connected grease spots and traversed under church and bank calendars. The 1956 Calvary Baptist calendar had only two sheets left. They were stapled to a cardboard picture of a fire-colored maple that seemed to prop up the mountain behind it. It had been taken at a lookout point up on the Parkway and had ended up in every picture postcard rack in every drugstore in North Carolina. The boy felt a particular pride because his daddy knew the trails of that very mountain like the back of his hand. In fact, they'd be deep within that picture this side of an hour.

The girl moved slowly and sniffled as she mopped the table. She was new to Jack's Spot, or at least the boy had never seen her before. Usually Jack's son helped him in the mornings. But the boy had spied a picture hanging on the wall behind the cash register when they walked in. It was Jack's son sporting a shiny military uniform and a fresh-shaved head.

The boy's uncle and grandfather had just taken their seats. He and his father were approaching the table when they heard gravel flying and a car door slam hard. The cook looked out the dirty window, and in a single motion, he placed one hand on the counter and hopped over it as if it were a pommel horse.

Still in flight, he hollered, "Mary Alice, here come yo' Piney!"

But before he could reach the door, it blew open, and the girl spun so fast the saltshaker flew out of her hand and landed at the boy's feet.

"You a crazy heathen bitch of a woman! What I tell you, Meh'Alice? I said, 'Ain't no wife of mine ever gonna cook taters for a livin' soul but me,'" yelled a tall skinny man who stood in the doorway allowing a blast of cold air to tear through the room.

He wore no coat, just an old tattered flannel shirt over long johns and a pair of worn work pants. His eyes filled up most of his unshaven face and were full of a kind of rage the boy had never seen, not even on the television or at the picture show. The boy circled his small arm around his father's waist and hugged himself into the jacket.

"You get on outta here, Piney," the cook said, blocking Piney's path to the girl. "You know Mary Alice just tryin' to make ends meet. Now go on home, sleep it off, and leave her to do her work."

While everybody in the diner stared at the two men, the boy kept his gaze fixed on the girl. She clutched her rag to her small bosom and backed up against the wall. She had on a dingy flowered dress and a thin blue sweater. She wore a pair of Keds that had once been white with no socks.

"My wife ain't none of your business, Jack Tree. Now you give her here to me."

"Your *wife* ain't mine to give. She done spoke for herself when she lit out on you yestiddy."

Jack wasn't as tall as Piney, but he could easily pick him up and toss him, like a chair, out into the parking lot. While Piney's voice sounded like a wounded animal high on hooch, Jack Tree sounded like a cool pat of butter on a warm biscuit, firm but yielding.

Both men looked at the girl who had backed herself against the wall over behind the counter. Soon every man in the room was looking at her as she grew more pitiful by the second. The boy knew how it felt to wish the floor would open up and swallow you, like standing at the blackboard when Sister Saint Hilda was determined to ridicule and humiliate. They watched her shoulders cave, her head drop, and her eyes close as sobs began to rack her body. Jack Tree started toward her, but she put up a hand. She drew herself up a bit. In fits and starts a mouse-size voice crept out of her mouth.

"Piney, I ain't comin' home no more."

Tears streamed down her cheeks, her nose ran and her chest heaved as she delivered the words. She lowered her hand back to the rag and twisted it in knots as she spoke.

"I'm gonna go live with my momma and I'm gonna work here for Jack Tree 'til I can get ahead a bit, then I'm gonna set out."

Every few words were halted by a sob or a choke, but she kept up, unpracticed and tortured.

"I wanna live me a good, Christian life, Piney, and someday I'm gonna be a man's *real* wife, not a shameful sinner like I been."

The mouse voice gained volume and she ended with her head upright and her eyes wide—scared and pleading but wide.

The angry man stepped forward and jutted his chin and curled his lips in a snarl. He seemed to sober, his venom and fear even more palpable.

"Well, you a sad whore Meh'Alice. You ain't got a snowball's chance in hell of livin' any Christian life."

Then he spit something brown and ugly onto the cracked linoleum floor.

"I'll see you dead before I see you another man's wife." He spit his words and the veins in his neck popped purple under his clammy skin. "I'm gonna run get that gun Ox has been trying to sell me and send you to kingdom come. You see if I don't."

The man didn't give Jack Tree the time or the satisfaction of throwing him out. He was in his car before Jack got the door shut good behind him. The patrons all looked at each other and a hum swept through the room. Mary Alice left her spot behind the counter and bent to wipe the tobacco juice from the floor. When she rose, she straightened her shoulders, went to the sink, ran water over her hands, and then put them to her cheeks. Jack Tree patted her on the shoulder.

"He's gone now," Jack said softly.

And she replied just as quietly, "But, he'll be back. He means to kill me this time, Jack. He ain't never gonna let me go."

"Now you don't know that, Mary Alice."

Jack opened the waffle iron and relieved it of a golden-brown beauty. He cracked two eggs into a pan. He maneuvered the oven open with the toe of his boot, and with his idle hand, he grabbed a potholder and pulled out a dozen biscuits and popped them into a basket.

The boy didn't know what a whore was, but he knew that the girl wasn't one. He couldn't imagine a beaten-down thing like her being anything too bad. He was sure he'd just seen the first bit of gumption the girl had ever shown, and to his way of thinking, it took more guts than that to be bad.

He and his father still hadn't taken their seats. Instead they'd both wandered over to the window. The boy felt his father's big hand caress the top of his head then move down to his shoulder and rest there. They were looking at Piney, who still sat in a car that was old with rust and paint so oxidized the boy didn't even know what color it was or, for that matter, what make or model. His father studied the scene with one hand in his jacket pocket and the other still on his son's shoulder. They could see the drunken man fidgeting with something on his lap. Occasionally he would drop his head onto the steering wheel then let it fall back onto the seatback. The boy finally made it out: Piney was clutching a woman's balled-up flowered handkerchief, pink and violet with lace around the edges.

"Coffee?" Jack Tree held out a cup to the boy's father.

"Much obliged, and a glass of milk for the boy if you would."

"Don't y'all worry," Jack pointed to Piney with his coffee pot, "he'll go home and sleep it off, then come back here around six o'clock smelling like aftershave begging her to have him back."

The boy just looked up at his father.

"Got waffles, eggs, sausage, and biscuits and gravy this mornin'. Whatchu gonna have, little feller?"

The boy would have a waffle; his father ordered sausage and eggs. The others already had their coffee and were spreading butter onto steaming biscuits. When they heard the ignition of the battered car turn over, they looked back out the window. Gravel and dirt kicked up as the car spun off, tires screeching. The other two tables emptied out and Mary Alice came to clear them, this time more quickly, her eyes a little dryer.

"Walter, c'mon and sit down." The boy's grandfather beckoned to his son and, finally, they walked over to the table and sat. But, even sitting, his father continued to survey the outside, and the boy continued to feel his unease.

"Walter, you put that twenty-two dollars I gave you in your pocket?" The grandfather studied his son's face.

The face hesitated for a second, then answered that he had, holding the white-haired man's gaze longer than seemed necessary.

"Good," the grandfather replied, then broke off a piece of biscuit and handed it to the boy.

The boy's uncle poked him in the ribs and said, "Twenty-two dollars. Looks like we gonna have us a fine breakfast this morning. Hope you brought your appetite, little buddy."

The boy and his uncle laughed. His daddy looked out the window as the other patrons got in their trucks and left.

They all left for the mountains dressed rough, but it never ceased to amuse the rest of them that the grandfather always wore a crisp white shirt under his old sweater and woolen vest. He was an elegant old man who'd grown up the son of a Georgia dirt farmer and had found dignity in his white shirts and his post-Depression job in the men's department at Thalheimers. He was white haired with a powerful rectangular face. It was the boy's daddy's face too, and some of it lived in his uncle. They were all tall men, and the boy, though small for his age now, hoped against hope that he would grow to be as tall, to be able to strap a rifle with a sight on it over his shoulder and traipse through wet bottomland looking for birds or deer. But for now his feet didn't even touch the floor as he sat at the table. People often told him that he looked like his mother, who was pretty, red haired, and freckled, but she rose only a whisper above five feet. The boy had higher aspirations.

The sound of the first blast lifted the boy right out of his seat. His father grabbed him around the shoulder and flattened him onto his lap. The other men hit the floor and Jack Tree ran out from behind the counter and grabbed the coffee pot out of Mary Alice's hand. Ducking low, he pulled her into the kitchen and crouched under the counter.

"Stay low," the boy's father said and dragged him into a corner.

He turned a table on its side in front of the boy then crawled into the kitchen. One by one glass panes started popping as Piney shot out window after window. There were three good-size front windows at Jack's Spot, smaller ones on the sides, and only a tiny high one in the kitchen at the back. Each window was double hung with six panes at the top and six at the bottom, and within a few seconds, a sea of glass covered the floor and tables. Not all the panes were gone, but more than half were shot through with enough buckshot to drop a man, and certainly enough to blow a gal the size of Mary Alice clean in half. The boy caught a whiff of his breakfast cooking then burning before Jack slid on his belly to the wall and unplugged the waffle iron.

"Whatchu mean there's no back door," the boy heard his father say in disbelief.

"Jus' ain't one," Jack Tree replied. "I just lock up the front with that there lock when I leave at night."

He looked apologetically at the boy's father and pointed to a nail on the wall where a large padlock and key hung.

"Phone don't work neither."

And the boy understood. They were trapped.

He was huddled in the corner next to a gas room heater, its chimney a low brown elbow angled out through the wall above the boy's head. His grandfather slid over to join him and the boy noticed a dark-red drop of blood billow into the fibers of the crisp white collar. It grew to the size of a fifty-cent piece then held there.

"You shot or cut?" The boy pointed to his grandfather's neck.

"Just cut. It don't hurt." He pulled the boy to him.

"Get out here, Meh' Alice," Piney yelled. "Get out here before I come in and shoot the whole bunch of you heathens. Anybody eat Jack Tree's food is bound for hell."

The empty windowpanes let in currents of cold air, but the boy knew this wasn't why he shook. Fear gripped him, and his grandfather's arm around him was of little reassurance. There was a roaring in his ears that had nothing to do with the rifle blasts, and he could see his own chest thumping like his heart would jump clear out. Just when he thought it was over, another round of blasts began. They were separated by the time it took Piney to slip another couple of shells into the chamber, close the double-barreled firearm, and shoot again. More windows shattered, and now splinters of wood covered the floor as Piney shot right through the walls of the old place. "Get on out here, gal," he yelled before and after each blast.

Four or five minutes had passed since the last shot and the boy chanced a look at his father. He was peeking out over the cash register, trying to see out the windows across the room. And in spite of the chill he was sweating. His right hand cupped the side of his thigh, where the flap pocket of the old army jacket rested.

The silence was broken by an occasional swoosh as the gas heater ignited and flames swept across the grill. Sometimes the boy would hear a rustle outside, first on one side of the building, then on the other. Once he heard a car coming up the road; then his heart sank as it continued on, straining up the hill. The dogs were leashed in the truck. They'd been remarkably quiet, but then they were trained not to react to the sound of gunfire. After another five minutes had passed, he saw his father move toward the door, crouching.

"Daddy, no!" the boy shouted through a whisper.

His father shushed him with a hand and opened the door a crack. He closed it back just as quickly and positioned his back up against it, wedging himself between it and the solid desk where the cash register sat. They heard a thump and saw the door move and his father bounce as Piney tried to shove through.

"Meh'Alice, come on out here. Don't make me do this to you."

He was slurring now, sniveling and yowling as he moved back and forth. They could hear his boots clomping on the wooden porch and periodically a howl as he demanded that Mary Alice come on home so he wouldn't have to shoot her. He'd seem to calm down a bit, but then there'd be another shove at the door. The boy was sure Piney couldn't get past his daddy; he was well wedged in, his legs straight, the strong boots flat against the oak desk, which was anchored with metal L-brackets screwed well into the floor.

The girl cowered behind the counter but inched forward enough so that the boy could see her full form. She shivered like a rabbit cornered yet sweat dripped down into her collar, darkening the flowers and the dingy gray of the cotton. Pity filled his chest. He'd felt sorry for his sister when she was yelled at by the mother superior or by his father, and once, he ached for a drunk, colored man who had been chased off the bus by the driver. As if it belonged to someone else, he watched his small hand inch across the linoleum and approach the tired blue sweater sleeve that held the girl's skinny arm. He patted it, like he would a rabbit. She smiled and the boy saw that she was pretty.

Another volley of bullets shot out the lights in the kitchen. Everyone covered their heads with their hands and huddled into fetal-shaped balls. In a moment it was quiet again.

"Mister?"

It was Mary Alice addressing his father. She was peering out from between a counter stool and the tall desk, on elbows and knees, not a foot from his right boot. The boy could see his father's thick black eyebrow rise up and acknowledge the girl.

"I'm goin' on out thar."

She nodded at the door.

"Piney don' wanna hurt you or your young'n. He don' even wanna hurt me, mister."

She spoke slow and clear without tears or even a throb in her throat.

"I brought this on all y'all. Now, let me pass, mister, and I'll end it."

The boy's father respectfully listened and took a second before he answered.

"No, ma'am. Now you go and stay next to Jack. This'll be over in a minute. What's Piney's full name?"

"Jasper Lee Pinewood."

The boy saw the two profiles staring flat into each other's faces. The girl crawled backward behind the counter.

"Jasper Pinewood?" His father's voice was loud, deep, and clear. The boy had heard this volume before and it usually sent him running to his room. But this time the words came not from his throat but from somewhere deep inside his belly, and not a soul within fifty yards would have doubted that decisive action would follow.

"My name's Walter Johnston and I'm in here with my family—my father and brother and my nine-year-old son. You seem to have us at a disadvantage, Mr. Pinewood."

He listened for a beat.

"Now, I understand you're a man in pain, I've suffered as much myself and I'm prepared to come out there and speak with you—"

Another blast ripped the air.

"Only pain I'm feeling is that son of a bitch Jack Tree kidnapping my wife. Just 'cause his gone and died on him don't mean he can steal mine. Send me out my wife and I'll leave you be."

"I said you *seem* to have us at a disadvantage, Mr. Pinewood."

Again he listened for a moment.

"You about to run out of shells, aren't you? Only gun Carl Oxton had left this morning was a Remington just like mine. If he sold you the gun, he sold you his last two boxes of shells."

"So what if he did?"

"I know how to count, Mr. Pinewood. Law's going to look a lot kinder on you if you walk away without anybody getting hurt. Put your gun down and I'll come out and talk with you. Let me see the barrel lying on porch through the door crack and you standing out front by that blue Chevy yonder. You hear me Jasper Pinewood?"

There was no answer. There never was one. They heard a crash on the porch, which was later identified as a case of Coca-Cola bottles being overturned. But they never heard a word from Jasper Lee Pinewood. After a while the boy thought he heard a car start in the distance and a hum on the asphalt, but he couldn't be sure. He could have just been wishing hard. They waited for what the boy felt was an eternity, and then his father slowly lifted first one boot, then cautiously another, and stood. He looked out a window, then walked closer and surveyed the parking lot, then each side of the building. The boy held his breath.

"Jack, any way you can see out the back?"

"Little winder in the john."

He got up and went to it.

"Don't see nothing," he said when he came back out.

"You got you a car?" the boy's father asked.

"Yup, truck's over yonder." Jack pointed to the side of the building closest to the door.

"Where's the nearest phone?"

"Back down at Oxton's."

"Okay," the boy's father said, all the while looking out one window, then another. "Take the girl and head on down. We'll be right behind you."

Jack Tree and the girl rose, then the boy's grandfather and his uncle. Within seconds the boy was in his daddy's arms, gulping air and crying.

"It's alright, Lester. Everything's going to be fine, just fine." He cupped his son's head and spoke into his hair. "You were right brave back there."

"Daddy?"

"Yup."

"I got to pee."

Walter laughed at the first normal thing he'd heard since they'd walked in the diner. All three of the men joined the boy outside and peed in a bush toward the back of the building. Then Walter lifted his boy and carried him around to the car. The boy kept his head buried in the jacket, not knowing that his daddy had hawked-eyed every inch of the place before he got in the car and continued his survey as they drove off.

They stopped at Oxton's, where he was sitting on an old chair, a bloody rag held to his head. The sheriff and an old woman stood beside him. Jack Tree and Mary Alice were already there. Jack was on the pay phone that stood just inside the door. All the men talked in a circle. After a while the boy's father wrote something on a piece of paper and handed it to the sheriff. The two men nodded to each other and then shook hands. When his daddy returned to the car, he took off the army jacket and laid it on the seat between them before he got in. His grandfather and uncle got in the truck behind them and waited.

"You want me to take you on back home?"

"No!" The boy was crestfallen.

"Haven't you had enough adventure for one day?"

"I want to go hunting."

"You think we could keep this between us then, and not bother your mother with it? Thing like this sure could worry her and that might put a damper on you coming out with us in the future. It's not a lie, Lester. It's just some things men don't talk about."

"I promise I won't say a word, Daddy, I promise."

Walter Johnston put the key in the ignition and the motor turned over.

Relieved that all was settled, the boy impulsively reached his hand into the pocket of the army jacket, saying he wanted to see the twenty-two dollars. His father's hand came down firmly to stop him, but he had already felt the lump, and staring up into his father's face, he pulled an old .22 pistol out of the pocket.

"You had you a gun?"

Never in his life had the boy seen a pistol. Shotguns and rifles of every sort, but pistols were things that cops and crooks carried, not his daddy.

"Be careful, Lester. Put it back."

"You had you a gun the whole time?"

"It's been sitting in a drawer at Pap's store for over five years." His daddy shrugged. "We brought it up here to see if we can get it to fire."

"Is it loaded?"

"Well that appears to be the problem. There's a bullet in the chamber nobody can seem to dislodge. You don't ever want to fire a gun like that. It could blow up in your hand. Could kill you."

The boy looked again at the gun.

"But I brought some reloading tools with me," his father said. "Looks to me to be a good gun. I think we could clean her up and get her working. There's a trick I know with a piece of wire and a rubber band. Want me to show you?"

"I reckon."

Walter Johnston waved to his brother and father to follow. As they pulled out onto the road, the boy knelt over the seat and looked back at the small group standing in front of the store. The old woman was helping Ox to his feet; the sheriff wrote on a clipboard. Jack Tree stood with Mary Alice. As they took the curve and a pine tree moved to erase his view, he saw Mary Alice drop her head onto Jack Tree's shoulder. The man's arm moved around her back and pulled her into him as he kissed the top of her head.

The boy sat and looked down at his chest and was relieved to see it behaving normally, his heart tucked back inside. They rode quiet for a while. He knelt up sideways on the seat, propped his elbows where the door met the glass, and looked out the window at the orange-yellow blur of passing trees.

Walter drove and waited for the boy to ask. He knew the morning's events would in time feed endless hours of raucous make-believe in the boy's room—and that Jasper Pinewood's fate would be rehashed every time they retold the story. Finally, the boy turned on his knees and faced his father.

"If he'd gotten in and tried to kill her, would you'd've shot him—even with that broken gun, Daddy?"

Since he'd put the car in gear he'd been laboring to craft a reassuring reply. Then he wondered if he could answer at all. It occurred to him that he'd never eaten. The black coffee and the events of the morning offered agitation and now lightheadedness. Looking into the round, freckled face that had just sampled its first real taste of fear—still smudged with tears and dirt—a lump made its way into Walter's throat that he couldn't seem to swallow. He took another minute then patted the boy's thigh.

"You bet," he finally said. "You bet your buttons."

Walter allowed that it was a true and possibly a wise reply for it melted the lump and stretched a smile across his son's face. It wasn't that he felt tears in front of the boy were a cowardly thing; he just felt they should be reserved for true tragedy and this just hadn't quite touched that stone. He put his eye on a ribbon of highway that rose into the sky, finally Carolina blue, and pointed to two hawks crisscrossing up ahead.

Oh! Canada

Loretta sat on the couch with her feet propped up on the coffee table. *Texas Heat*, the label on the polish read. The cotton strips between her toes stretched them wide apart. She wiggled ten little chili peppers at the television. For the first time in twelve years she was loved; the gnawing in her middle, finally fed. All day she'd been thinking about Johnny taking care of her. *Nothing says love like a bullet to the head*, she thought. Her Johnny with shoulders wide as a door and a smile that made her get all goofy in the head was doing the right thing. He could touch her cheek and send a charge to the other end of her torso in a second. They had passports and driver's licenses that said Lorissa and John Benson, 441, rue Chapel, Québec. They'd already shipped four boxes of clothes and pots and pans and dishes. In a day or two, they would be Canadian citizens, or at least pretend to be Canadians. Loretta had barely been out of the Bronx. She had gone to see *Cats* when she was twelve, a school trip that left her singing "Memories" for a solid year. Her father took her ice-skating in Manhattan when she was eight. Once, she and Johnny drove up Interstate 87 until the gas gauge was on empty. They filled it up and drove back.

She had a small English-to-French dictionary and was taking a night class at the community college. Every night she told Johnny to *ferme la porte* when he walked in the house and *ferme la bouche* when he talked with his mouth full. She talked dirty to him in bed, phrases she had found on the Internet.

Johnny had an interview—an "in" with the maintenance department at the Château Frontenac. Overlooking the Saint Lawrence Seaway, it was one of the largest and most exclusive hotels in North America. She would convince the hotel that her skills as a hairdresser should land her a job, even sweeping up hair, in the salon. The words sounded so pretty rolling off Loretta's tongue. *Château Frontenac. Québec. Oui, ça va?* She and Johnny had never said a word to a soul about Canada. It drew them closer than a tie and a shirt collar. They started watching hockey. Knew the names of every player on the Montreal Canadians. Knew all the words to "O Canada."

When her phone rang, she hobbled over to her pocketbook on her heels. Across the rear of her jeans, pink satin letters read *Don't Touch.*

Five minutes later she was back on the couch. Her cheeks ran mascara black. Two wet spots grew on her T-shirt, right above her nipples. She goddamn-son-of-a-bitched him for half an hour, and now she traced his name tattooed on her thigh. The *J* of *Johnny* formed the stem of a rose that appeared to grow from between her legs. Five years ago when she stretched out on a table in a back room on the Grand Concourse, she eagerly told the guy with the electric needle, "'Johnny,' I want it to say 'Johnny Forever.'"

"Bastard," she said to the room. "Weak-ass bastard."

She shook her head and broke into another gale of angry sobs. It had started to snow. It would be black dark in less than an hour. She slammed her fist on her thigh then hugged a pillow into her stomach The gnawing, back again, ate away at her middle. A long wet tongue tried to force itself between her clenched teeth. She crossed her legs and then her ankles. Seconds later, she heard a car door slam and looked over her shoulder out the window. Loretta watched Johnny bounce up the steps carrying a pizza box.

"Like he hasn't got a care in the world," she said and grabbed the discarded cotton strips and rubbed her cheeks.

"Yo, Lo," Johnny called from the front hall.

She chewed her nails as she listened to his boots falling one at a time, the closet opening, coat hangers clinking, door closing.

"You hear Ruben Diaz got his car jacked?" Johnny put the pizza on the coffee table.

She couldn't believe he was acting like nothing had happened. Same ole Johnny, sweep everything under the rug.

"Who's Ruben Diaz?"

Johnny rolled his eyes.

"He's the fuckin' borough president of the Bronx, Lo. You ever read the papers? It's been on the news all day."

Johnny walked into the kitchen. He came back with two beers and a wad of napkins. Loretta turned up the volume on the television.

"You TiVo'd the *Idol!* Good girl."

Johnny opened the box and slid a piece of pizza out and into his mouth. Loretta pulled a pillow to her stomach and hugged it. She stared at the television.

"The mulignane's gonna win. Sings like a fuckin' angel."

"She's black, Johnny, why you have to talk like that?"

"Excuse me, Miss I Go To Night School. The *black* mulignane's gonna win."

"You're such a racist."

She picked a *Glamour* magazine off the table.

"I'm not racist," Johnny said with half a slice of pizza in his mouth.

"Then, why you got to call black people eggplants."

"I don't call 'em eggplants. I call 'em mulignane." Johnny spoke to the television.

Loretta nibbled on her fingernails and watched a boy with a pony-tail sing an old Neil Diamond song.

"Slice?" Johnny asked.

"So tell me how it went?" She waved away the pizza. "You want to take a shower or something?"

She turned to face him, propping her heels on the edge of the sofa.

"I don't need no shower, Lo."

"No mess? God, I'd think the chicken market alone would be disgusting." She tested her big toe. "Good for you, Johnny. Your first: nice and neat. That's what I told Benny, I said, 'Benny, my Johnny will do his job and do it well.' So tell me about it." Loretta bobbed her head.

"I don't want to talk about it."

Johnny took another bite, tilted up the longneck, and finished half the bottle. When he put his beer down, Loretta was still staring at him.

"You mind?" he said. "You mind if I don't talk about it? Jesus, Lo. I got other things on my mind. I got to go out in a little bit. And I got to get us out of here tomorrow and on the road before Benny comes asking me to do him another favor."

Benny Saltone had been married to Loretta's older sister, Janine. Five years ago, Janine caught him in bed with another woman after he'd sworn up and down for three years of marriage that he wasn't cheating. The woman he was cheating with had a three-year-old son who looked remarkably like Benny. Still, he continued to hover over the family like Vito Corleone, bringing gifts—cases of wine, a Thanksgiving turkey, a new watch for his ex-wife every Christmas. He got Loretta a job at the hair salon and always had a kind word for her mother. But he made fun of Johnny: "Still working construction? Still pouring concrete?" One day Benny came by in a brand-new leather jacket, soft as butter, black as the seats in his Mercedes. "You want to touch it?" he'd asked as he held out his arm to Johnny. Made Loretta want to smack him. But other times she wished that Johnny would take advantage of Benny's offers to get him work that could put a little money in his pocket. Maybe buy her a nice soft leather jacket. She hadn't cared about any of that since they made their plans for Canada. Now it was all ruined. All dead.

Johnny looked at her like she hadn't heard him.

"You know Benny's running a chop shop at your father's old dealership right under everybody's nose. Cops just can't seem to bust the fucker. Place is always clean when they come by. They just don't come by at three in the morning. Thousand bucks says Ruben Diaz could find his car with one of Benny's goons popping off the VIN plate, choosing a new color in a few hours. I don't want to do Benny any more favors. I don't want to be his lookout, paint cars, pick up a blowtorch. I'm ready to leave your family behind . . . and I ain't gonna miss mine either."

Any more favors. Like Johnny had done shit. He'd pissed her off like this before, made her so mad she could go cold as a corpse on him. When they first met he didn't have the guts to break up with that virgin Marjorie Cappola when Loretta knew he got a bulge in his pants every time he saw her. Marjorie was a classy girl, straight As, committed to the Holy Madonna Society. But the only thing she did for Johnny was make his mother proud. One night Loretta crawled into the backseat with him. She popped her gum as she rubbed his thigh. He kissed her neck and reached inside her blouse.

"Whoa," she said pulling back. "Not so fast." She chewed on a cuticle. "Let's get the rules of the road straight, OK? I can't fuck you 'cause it's against my morals for a first date. And I won't blow you 'cause it's dirty, but I'll pull you off and you can touch me anywhere you like. OK?"

She knew it was sweet talk like that that a boy understood. Soon enough Marjorie Cappola was history. But a week later she saw him talking to another girl in the hall. Loretta wouldn't speak to him for a month. He called her night and day, caught up with her after school and begged her to talk to him. In a last desperate effort, he stood outside her window and sang "You Light Up My Life." It was the worst thing she'd ever heard, but it melted her heart, and before she knew it she was in love with Johnny Barello. Being with him was the first time she felt safe since her father died. He wasn't great looking, had hair the color of dust, but he had a smile that had, over the years, chipped away at the stone in her chest, revealing a girl's heart that had been bruised and battered but wanted bad to beat, even if it had to bleed its way back to life.

Johnny finished two slices before Loretta nibbled at the crust of her first.

"I left my pocketbook in the car."

She got off the couch and walked through the kitchen to the back door.

"Put some shoes on for Christ's sake—a coat, it's snowing out there, Lo."

"I don't need no shoes," she yelled from the back door.

She hurried down the path to the garbage cans. *Please don't let it be there, God. Don't let it be there.* But it was—wedged between the fence post and the dented can, exactly where Benny, minutes ago on the phone, had said it would be. Shaped like a boomerang, the gun was wrapped in the *Daily News*, secured with rubber bands, and much lighter than she imagined. She could hardly feel her feet anymore. She hurried on stumps to the car and opened the door. The snow had stopped. The dusting had only turned the world a paler shade of gray. She sat on the car seat, half in, half out. The chili peppers looked almost black against her blue feet. She pulled a pack of Winstons out of the glove compartment, lit one, and drew deep. She hardly saw the cloud as it left her lips. *Gray. It's the color of the whole fuckin' world,* she thought. *The sky is so low, it's all around you, can't even see the fuckin' street light. Five o'clock in the afternoon and it's dark as an undertaker's suit.* She put the pack back and unwrapped the gun. She slid it into the back of her pants, the way they did it on TV and slammed the car door.

"Fuck you, Johnny," she said to the air. "I'll never forgive you for making me do this."

The smell of sour red wine rose up into her nose. She remembered she'd been drinking beer.

"Mulignane's still in," Johnny said when Loretta returned. He was at the refrigerator, a beer in one hand, his fist offering a bump to hers. "What'd I tell you, baby, what'd I tell you? Oh, sorry." He threw up his hands. "The black chick made the cut." A warm grin filled his face.

No way in the world could she do this. How could Benny even think she'd do it? It was because she flirted with him that's why. Men were so stupid. You rub up against a guy and he thinks you're just dying to do him. One thing she could say for Benny was that he had a pair of cahones big as an elephant's. Everybody knew how Loretta was with a guy with no balls. It could turn her cold as a meat locker. She didn't want to shoot Johnny. She wanted to smack the smile off his face. How could he do this to her? To them? Fuck Johnny. He grabbed at her ass. She slid around him and moved into the living room, sat, and took a piece of pizza from the box.

"You get paid? Benny pay you?" Loretta chewed and swallowed.

Johnny sat and pulled out another piece of pie.

"Later, I'm getting it later. What're you worried about?"

"Why? Why not now, Johnny? How come Benny didn't pay you after work . . . after the *j-o-b*?"

"What the hell is going on with you, Lo? Ever since I walked in the door you been sharp as teeth with me. You on the rag? I leave the seat up? Jesus."

He shook his head, then hunched in for another bite.

She turned toward him and folded her arms across her chest. Her shoulders took turns leveling themselves.

"I'll tell you what's going on, Johnny. I got a call from Benny. He saw Paulie Gocci eating a calzone at Sal's at one o'clock this afternoon. What do you think about that, Johnny?" She didn't give him a chance to answer. "You were supposed to take Paulie out after his shift, remember? Remember what you were supposed to do, Johnny? Take Paulie out for lunch then a little trip to the back of the live chicken market? What's the matter, chicken heads lying around a little too much for you?"

"Benny said that?" Johnny tilted his head. "Benny said he saw Paulie? At one? Today?"

Suddenly, Johnny turned around and peeked between the blinds to the street below.

"Word for word." Loretta moved her hand to her back like she was scratching up under her bra strap. "I can't believe you, Johnny." Tears filled her lower lids; her voice cracked. "Look what you're making me do." She pointed the small black gun at Johnny's chest. "I hate you, Johnny, I hate you 'cause I love you, you son of a bitch."

"Wait, Lo." Johnny put his hands up over his heart and moved to the coffee table across from her. Pizza slid to the floor. "You don't see what's happening here?"

"Yeah, I see. I see you're a fucking coward and I can't be with no coward, Johnny." She choked out his name. Her shoulders shook. "I believed in you, for Christ's sake. I thought we was gonna go to Canada and live new lives. We got jobs waiting, an apartment paid up for six months!" Loretta wiped her nose with the back of her other hand.

"Anyway, Benny says if I don't . . . he'll . . . Oh, fuck you, Johnny, why couldn't you do it?"

In less than a second, Johnny had the gun in his waistband and Loretta's arm pinned behind her back. He yanked her off the couch and pushed her into the front hall. He stepped into his boots and shuffled toward the front door. Then seeing Loretta's purse, he reached back and slipped it off the hook inside the closet door and grabbed his coat.

"My shoes," she whimpered.

"You don't need shoes, remember?"

He pushed her onto the stoop. He checked the street. No headlights coming or going. It was snowing again. Quickly, he shoved her ahead of him. Loretta looked at her toes, ten little drops of blood tripping down the front steps.

"You're so smart, aren't you? So smart."

He moved her down the sidewalk.

"Benny's trying to get you to do his dirty work and you don't see squat. When'd I ever let you down, Lo? When?"

Johnny pushed her toward the back of the car and clicked the key. He held one thick arm around her tiny shoulders, trapping her arms, and with his other hand, he steered her head with a grip on her hair that she felt beneath her skull. He pushed her face under the popped trunk. Paulie Gocci was curled there like the letter *G*, a clear plastic garbage bag taped neatly around his neck, not a speck of blood on the yellow blanket beneath him. Her mouth hung open, but no sound came out. Her heart was beating like it could fly out of her chest and bounce on top of Paulie Gocci.

"You think I had trouble with this?" Johnny kept his hand on her hair and turned her head to face him. "After what he did to you? It was him that did my uncle Bubble, you know. You think I don't know that?"Loretta's eyes softened. She looked at her man like he was the Holy Redeemer. She smiled through her tears. Johnny's grip on her hair felt like love.

"Somebody shoulda taken this little scumbag out years ago."

Johnny pulled her head back and slammed the trunk, and with his hand still gripping the thick clump of hair, he directed her around the car, opened the door, and shoved her into the passenger seat.

"This is the thanks I get?"

"I'm sorry. Johnny, you know I—"

But he had shut the car door and was walking around to the driver's side.

"I thought Benny was going to take care of getting rid of the . . . of Paulie," she said.

"Well, he didn't. He left the little fucker lying in the dirt in the back of Mayo's Market."

Johnny pulled out into street and headed up to Gun Hill Road. As he made the turn, he looked in the rearview mirror. A series of *fuck*'s flew from of his mouth.

"What?" Loretta said, turning.

They could both see Benny Saltone's Mercedes pull up in front of their place. Through a gap in the houses, they saw Benny and some guy get out of the car and walk up the front steps.

Johnny drove two blocks toward Christopher Columbus High School, pulled around to the rear of the building. He put the car in park and turned to Loretta.

"Gimme your phone." Johnny held out his hand.

Loretta reached in her back pocket and handed it over. He took his own phone out of his coat, opened the door, and stepped out of the car. He stomped on both phones, smashing them into the street. Then he tossed the pieces behind the dumpsters. He got back in the car and drove. He constantly checked the rearview mirror.

"I work construction, Loretta, 'cause I don't want to mess with this business."

"I know, baby." Loretta hiccupped and shook out words. "You know I wasn't . . . I couldn't . . ."

"I don't even know what I know." Johnny pulled the gun out of his belt and slid it under his left thigh. "Right now I just know I got to get a body out of my trunk and lose this car."

"We still going to Canada, Johnny?" She said it with no more force than a baby.

"We're getting outta here, Loretta. Beyond that, I don't know what I'm doing."

Twenty minutes later, Paulie's body was transferred to the trunk of Loretta's mother's black Buick, and the Taurus was tucked neatly into her mother's garage with the keys in the ignition.

Loretta had eased in and out of her mother's house unnoticed. The blue glow of the television and her mother's laugh sent a shiver up her spine.

"Everybody does not love Raymond," Loretta mumbled as she tip-toed down the back stairs. She tossed a pair of boots, sweatshirts, jeans, hats, and gloves into the Buick's backseat and climbed into the vehicle.

"You get the license plates?" Johnny said as he backed the car out of the garage.

"Why'd you need my mom's old plates?"

"We're going to have to lose this car sooner or later. Anyway, I don't want to fuck your mother. This ain't her fault." He stared out the window.

"She'll have your car."

"Ah, my dad will fight her tooth and nail for my car. Cheap bastard. We'll leave this somewhere in Yonkers, maybe closer. You get some money?"

"Only three hundred in cash. I got the bankbook though. And Johnny?"

"Yeah?"

"Tomorrow's Saturday. Banks are only open 'til two on Saturdays. You got the passports?"

Johnny nodded and patted his left chest.

"You got mine too? You're not going to leave me stranded are you?"

He reached in his pocket and pulled out both their Canadian passports, their driver's licenses, and an electric bill for 441, rue Chapel, Québec. She pushed them back into his hands. They headed to the Major Deegan, then on to the Cross Bronx Expressway.

"Why are you Benny's dirty work?" Loretta suddenly asked.

Johnny said nothing.

"Why, Johnny? Why would Benny want you gone?"

"So, now you're asking questions. I thought you were the shoot-first-ask-later type." He looked at her and shook his head.

"So why?"

"He thinks I know something."

"Like what?"

"This ain't my field, Lo. I'm in over my head here."

Johnny was quiet while Loretta slipped heavy wool socks over her jeans and pulled her boots up to her knees.

"I knew something was wrong, right from the start," he said. "I drove to the dealership at noon and Paulie's brother, that douche bag Al, slides out from under a car and tells me Paulie already walked up to the chicken market. Every Friday, like clockwork Paulie goes to get chickens for his ma, same bat-channel, same bat-time. Suck-tit gaffones still living with their mommy."

Loretta pulled her legs up onto the seat, hugged them, and looked out the window. The South Bronx was pitch black. The occasional light flickered. Crack pipes and flashlights, a gentrified block here, another one there.

"I got to the chicken market and drove around back." Johnny went on. "God, the smell. Week-old blood. Shit. I walked around front. There's Paulie, paying at the counter, that ponytail all wild, looking like that freak on the *Idol*. The Korean gives him a plastic bag with chickens wrapped in white paper. Funny, the blood pooling into the bottom of the bag almost made me gag. Paulie sees me and slams his hand to his forehead. 'Fuck,' he says, coming out the front door. 'We was suppose to grab a bite. Sorry, man.' I told him I'd give him a ride, and he pulled a gym bag up onto his shoulder, the chickens in his other hand, and walked with me. He didn't like I'd parked way in the back, said the noise from the tool and die shop back there gave him a headache. I said for a tough guy, he sure was a pussy. He said fuck you and walked around a stack of crates to the car. I must be the biggest wimp in New York 'cause he didn't suspect nothing. He gets around the driver's side and I says, 'This is from Loretta, asshole.' The slamming of the punch press next door made it sound like a pellet gun. He just dropped, like his knees buckled, caught it right in the left eye. I didn't even shake."

Johnny snorted, raised and lowered his shoulders.

"Can't fucking believe it, fucking headless chickens in a plastic bag make me want to puke, but popping that prick made the world smell clean."

Loretta's heart was frantic in her body. She put her hand to her throat and begged her pulse to settle down.

"All the sudden Benny's behind me," Johnny said. "I smelled his cigar before I saw him.

"'You was late,' he says.

"'I was early,' I tells him.

"I got the bag and the tape from my car. Benny goes behind the crates and starts going through Paulie's gym bag. He's says *fuck* a hundred times, goes through Paulie's pockets. I'm thinking this ain't right. This is supposed to be business, you know like Tony Soprano. You shoot then you fucking leave. But Benny starts throwing things around and cursing, saying, 'You little fuck, what'd you do with it?'—to Paulie, not to me. Benny even reaches down Paulie's pants then opens his mouth and feels around up under his tongue.

"'Christ,' I say. 'What's going on here?'

"And Benny turns on me. 'Paulie give you something? He say something?'

"'Paulie didn't say shit,' I says.

"The little prick's shit is all over the ground, loose change, slips of paper, his wallet. Finally, Benny finds Paulie's keys in the side pocket of his gym bag. He tosses them up in the air, catches them, flashes me a shit-eating grin, and turns to leave. But he comes back, grabs the chickens, says, 'Hey, punk, don't you know you're supposed to leave the gun and take the cannoli.' Then he turns around and leaves.

"A few seconds later, I'm slipping the bag over Paulie's head and I feel this thing in that wad of hair. I'm thinking it's some kinda ponytail thing. I yank it out."

Johnny reached into his shirt pocket and handed Loretta a diaper pin like a large safety pin, the closure covered in a light-blue plastic with a yellow duck stenciled on one side and the letters *M&T* on the other. A little blue key was dangling off the end, a locker key like the ones they had at the bus station. It had the number 117 stamped onto one side.

"What's it to?" she asked.

"Got me."

Johnny reached deep into the front pocket of his jeans and dumped what he had recovered from the scene of Paulie's death into the well between the bucket seats.

"The only smart thing I ever did in my life was not tell a soul about heading over the border," he said. "I got this no-pay job shooting concrete into the buildings, so I sign on to get paid to do the one thing I been dying to do for ten years anyway. Benny thinks I'm a piece of meat. Thinks he's going to get him a made man."

Johnny glanced at Loretta but shifted his eyes back to the road.

"He knew there wasn't a chance in hell you'd pop me. But he knew you'd be mad as hell. He was banking on us being in the middle of a hell of a fight, your prints on the gun. He comes in and does us both, gets what he thinks I have, and poof, it's a murder-suicide of not-so-epic proportions."

Loretta reached out a hand to touch Paulie's things, a couple of coins, a few small bills, but she was shaking so hard, she couldn't actually pick anything up. She stuffed her hands under her thighs.

They turned off the Henry Hudson onto Riverside Drive. She looked up into the apartment buildings towering above them like canyon walls, drapes open, lamps in windows, people passing back and forth, looking out at the lights across the Hudson River. She used to dream of having a place like this or up on Pelham Parkway. It was almost in her grasp to be working in a place that looked over the St. Lawrence River in Quebec, watching the snow float outside a window.

"Loretta, you know what the safety is on a gun?" Johnny broke the spell.

"What?"

"Next time you want to shoot somebody you take the safety off. OK?"

Loretta knew exactly what and where the safety was on a gun. She knew how to slip the little lever down or up with her thumb. Her uncle had brought a gun to the house six months after her father died.

"Neighborhood's changing, Agnes," he said to her mom. "You got to protect yourself, your kids, capische?"

The handgun, a .22, stayed in her father's old closet along with the clothes her mother could never bear to give to the Salvation Army. Nobody ever touched it except Loretta. She took the bullets out now and then, cleaned the barrel with oil like her uncle showed her. But before she put it back in the shoebox, she'd aim it at Paulie Gocci's face, which hung like a hologram floating in the middle of the room. Each time she pulled the trigger, but it never put him out of her head.

She looked out the window again and began to cry, softly, freely. The image of Paulie Gocci's face on hers when she was just fourteen, a virgin, breasts the size of anthills, loomed. After her father's funeral, he came into the room attached to the garage where she sat crying on the old sofa her father had used as a refuge when her mother's nagging drove him out of the house. He would read to Loretta here when she was little—all the Madeline books.

"I want to live in Paris when I grow up," she had told her father, but he said Paris would be too far from him.

"You can live in Quebec," he told her. "It's right up in Canada. It's just like France, only closer."

And when she was older, as her father worked on a car or at his workbench, she practiced her numbers on the same sofa: *un, deux, trois, quatre, cinq, six, sept, huit, neuf, dix.* After her father was buried, it was to the old sofa that she stole away from all the people in the house and especially her older sister and her mother's keening wails.

"You OK, kid?" Paulie had asked. He said that he'd come out to grab a smoke and saw her through the window. "Here."

He pulled out a flask and gave her a drink of something strong. In seconds, it warmed her and made her feel giddy. Paulie had worked with her father at the Chevy dealership in the parts department. Her older sister thought he was cool, all that hair like a rock star and enough gold around his neck to drown him if he fell in the East River drunk. He was a wiry thing. During her mother's pinochle game, she once said Paulie looked like Frankie Valli.

"Yeah," one of the other women added. "But he has feet like Michael Jordan!"

They all howled. Loretta didn't get it.

Two more long pulls of the stuff in the flask and she was giggling and loopy.

"Everybody needs a little snort in a time of loss," Paulie said. "You're never too young to learn that."

Then he was running his fingers up her skinny thighs, moving onto the sofa, making it bow in the middle.

"You gotta leave, now, Paulie," she said, but he was pressing her onto her back, pulling at her stockings, his fingers pinching and prodding. She'd pushed him and tried to yell, but barely a whimper made its way past his chest on top of hers.

"There, there," he said as he licked at her throat, his hands holding both of hers above her head. "Good girl," he said. "You're a good girl, Loretta."

The first black dress she had ever owned was pushed up above the bra that was too big for her. What felt like a fist forced its way up and into her body. Finally she let out a scream, but Paulie sealed her mouth with his own, his tongue fighting with hers, until she bit down hard enough to taste his blood. Paulie was off her and out of her in seconds.

"Little bitch!" he hissed.

There was a knock at the door.

"Paulo, Paulo," came a whine in Italian. "Paulie boy, you in there? I'm ready to go now. You take me home. Now, Paulo."

Paulie zipped his pants and opened the door. His short, black-clad mother stood in the doorway like an old crow surveying the room. She curled her lip in disgust at Loretta's crumpled form on the couch then threw her hand at the room and turned. Loretta lay huddled on the couch, her legs pulled up; she hugged her dress over her knees. The pantyhose she had bought at the drugstore lay torn and twisted on the black oil stain in the middle of the garage floor. The room spun. She tried to read the spines of the books on a shelf above her father's tools:

Madeline and *James and the Giant Peach.* Then she closed her eyes and buried her head in the pillow.

Years later, when her mother caught her in the same place with a boy's hand up her skirt, she called her a little slut. She yanked her out of the house and drove her to confession. When she told the priest about what Paulie had done when she was just fourteen, he said that God wants us to take responsibility for our own actions, not lay them at the feet of others.

She didn't notice at first, but slowly, as she and Johnny made their way down the long right hip of Manhattan and each tear left her body, she began to uncoil. When they hit Midtown, she wiped her cheeks with the sleeves of her sweatshirt.

She wanted Johnny to ask her if she was okay, to reach over and pull her under his wing. But he continued to look at the road before him, checking the rearview mirror every few seconds. She looked again at Paulie's things in the compartment between them.

"I can't figure the diaper pin." She pulled the thing from the tangle of coins and keys. She ran her finger over the duck and *M&T* stamped into the plastic fastener. "Paulie sure as hell ain't hiding a kid somewhere, and anyway, nobody uses these things anymore. Everybody uses Pampers."

Just after midnight, Paulie Gocci's body improved the vertical load of a building going up just off the West Side Highway. Loretta didn't watch, but she imagined the concrete coming up over his pants, soaking into his clothes, making its way over his nasty face. She could see his wide nostrils filling with gray sludge, his evil, fat cock, now no bigger than a thumb, stilled forever.

Loretta and Johnny found a motel near LaGuardia. It was the first time they were in a bed together that they didn't touch. Johnny had been the first boy who treated Loretta like a lady. He would grab her and tickle her like an older brother, then pick her up, take the stairs two at a time with her straddling him, and, laughing, deliver her to the bed like she was made of glass, and they would make love as if floating on silk and feathers. He could spoon her, his hand on her belly, and make the touch of Pauli Gocci, her father's death, and her needy, nagging mother disappear. He and the priest in the confessional were the only ones who knew about Paulie Gocci. Johnny told her once that he wanted to shoot Paulie and set Father McCarthy on fire.

When they woke, it was snowing again, heavier than yesterday. Every time Loretta looked at Johnny, he looked away. The blade twisted with each failure to hold her gaze. The only thing he said to her was to dump her contacts and wear her glasses. Nobody had ever seen Loretta in her glasses except Johnny. They showered separately and looked for a breakfast joint before driving back to the Bronx.

"There's a McDonald's," Johnny said.

"But there's a Starbucks." She pointed across the street.

"You and your Starbucks," Johnny said. "What is it with you wanna-be yuppy chicks always wanting a latte?"

"They got good coffee and clean bathrooms."

At Starbucks, Johnny grabbed a *New York Post*. Loretta read from it as they drove to the bank, sipping their coffee and nibbling on croissants.

"Ruben Diaz says it was his wife's car that was stolen. A black Mercedes, looks like Benny's."

She held the paper out and showed Johnny a picture of Mildred Diaz leaning against the car her husband had bought her for Christmas.

Loretta wasn't familiar with Parkchester, but it had a Republic Savings on Metropolitan Avenue. She usually went to the branch on Tremont Avenue, near her house. Parkchester was safer and closer to Manhattan—where they would go next to the Royal Bank of Canada to make the deposit before heading north.

"In and out, Lo," Johnny said. "This ain't all that far from Paulie's mother's place."

"Oh please." She turned the rearview mirror toward her and stuffed her hair under her cap. "Who's going to recognize me?"

Loretta hadn't left the house without full makeup—foundation, shadow, mascara, and lips the color of candy—since she was fifteen. Her hair, thick chestnut waves that draped over one shoulder, was stuffed under a black fleece cap. With her face naked, she looked like a scrubbed boy with glasses. She wore a gray City College sweatshirt over a turtleneck and tight jeans stuffed into tall black boots.

Johnny gave her a cursory glance.

"Your own mother wouldn't know you this morning."

Loretta hurried into the bank, darting her eyes around the room. She walked to the counter that held the deposit and withdrawal forms in little slots and began to fill in her account numbers. In the teller line, two women with kids in strollers were in front of her, chatting away, sipping their own Starbucks. Five years ago, there wasn't a Starbucks to be found in the Bronx, now they were popping up here and there, just like in Brooklyn. The women were dressed in running shoes, slim Lycra pants, and bright hoodies. One of them turned to pick up a toy that had fallen out of the stroller. Any other day Loretta would have never noticed it, but on the breast of the woman's light-blue hoodie was a diaper pin with a key attached. It was a pink pin and the key, light blue, was identical to the one in the change dish of her mother's car. It reminded her of the locker keys at Jones Beach that she'd pinned to her bathing suits as a kid.

"Excuse me," Loretta said.

Both women turned. The other one had the same diaper pin and key hanging from a zipper.

"Those pins are so cute. There a Y around here?"

"Moms & Tots," one of the women answered. "Right next door."

"Moms & Tots," Loretta echoed and smiled. "Oh, I see the little *M&T* there on the pin."

"It's a place to get your ass back in shape after one of these turns you to marshmallow." The woman pointed at the sleeping infant in her stroller and laughed.

"You know, aerobics, weights, machines," the other one said. "And they have babysitting and Mommy & Me. Fifty bucks a month, unlimited classes."

"I've been looking for something like that," Loretta said. "I just had a baby myself. I'm having a bitch of a time losing those last ten pounds."

"You just had a kid?" one of the mothers said. "My God, you look fabulous."

The woman moved up to the teller. When it was her turn, Loretta cashed out her account. She put five one-hundred-dollar bills into her wallet along with a cashier's check for six thousand dollars.

"Johnny, never in a million years are you going to believe this."

Loretta slid into the car. She told him what she'd learned as she tossed her pocketbook into the backseat and snatched the diaper pin and its key from the compartment between the seats.

"What the fuck would Paulie be doing at some baby daycare place?"

He started the car.

"Moms & Tots," Loretta corrected. "Wait, Johnny, where are you going? I need to get in there."

"We need to get out of here before somebody sees us."

"Nobody knows this car and anyway, like you said, I look like a nerdy twelve-year-old boy."

"This is not the time to go pushing me, Lo."

"It's easy, I just go in, flash my key, say I forgot something in my locker, and I'm out. How hard can that be?"

"What if they ask for a membership card?"

That stopped her.

"Then I say I'm just checking things out. I say I just had a baby."

She opened the door and stepped out of the car.

"Fifteen minutes, I'm not waiting, Lo!"

Loretta walked in the door and was met with the sound of crying and cooing babies. She took off her glasses and wiped off the snow. The lobby was full of young mothers angling their strollers into a long hallway with cubbies on one side and room to park on the other. A woman at the desk was busy talking to one of the moms from the bank. Loretta moved down the hall, hoping it was the way to the locker room. Through a glass door on her right, she saw ten or more women bouncing toddlers on little trampolines. She hurried past and found a door with *Locker Room* painted on the glass in pink and blue candy-cane letters. She felt for the diaper pin in her pocket and walked in. The room was surprisingly empty. She could hear the shower running in a room farther back and a toilet flush. Her heart raced as she moved down the row of lockers starting with 001. The numbers grew as she rounded a corner onto another bank of lockers with long benches between them. There it was: number 117, an upper locker at the end of a row. She could see into the shower room as a woman with a huge pregnant belly wrapped a towel around her head and walked toward her.

"Hi," the woman said and moved past her toward the other bank of lockers.

Loretta's hand shook as she lifted the key and put it in the lock. She swallowed and turned the key. A resounding click released the inner hardware and the locker opened. A soft pink bag sat on top of a large package of Huggies and baby wipes. She grabbed the bag and closed the locker, taking the key. As she turned to leave, the mother from the bank, now free of her baby, was slipping off her boots and putting a key into a locker.

"Oh, I see you came to check it out. Good for you."

"Yeah, looks nice." Loretta hugged the diaper bag.

"You got a girl, I see?"

"Yeah, a girl." Loretta nervously laughed.

She hurried past the mothers and their babies leaving the trampoline class, past the lobby and out to the car. She tossed the bag at Johnny and tore off her hat.

"A diaper bag?" Johnny unzipped the thing and rummaged through it. "Nothing else?"

"Well, a pack of Huggies and baby wipes back in the locker. That's it."

She went through the bag. Bottles, baby shampoo, a rattle, a newborn sleeper, a hat, socks. Johnny had taken his car key and ripped the lining of the diaper bag, felt in and around the entire thing. Nothing. He opened the baby shampoo, smelled it; he cracked the rattles, opened the empty bottles. Nothing. He tossed the bag and its contents into the backseat and finally looked at Loretta.

"We're on the wrong track," Johnny said. "Maybe Paulie did have a kid, or got some girl knocked up and was supporting her. Benny was looking for something else."

He put the car in gear and pulled out into the constant stream of Saturday shopping traffic.

"But you say he grabbed the keys and left. He was looking for a key. And the only key Paulie had hidden was this one. How many keys were on the key chain Benny took?"

"I don't know, three, not counting his car key."

"So, let's figure one or two keys for the house, one for the shop, the car key . . . even if there was one more, Benny had plenty of time to check them out, see whatever he was looking for wasn't there, before he called me. There's something in that locker. Something Benny wants."

They were crawling toward a yellow traffic light when a woman came down the street pushing her baby. She stopped near the car and leaned into the stroller then pulled a baby wipe out of her diaper bag. She scrubbed the little boy's hands and face with the wipe, tossed it back in her bag, and moved on.

"I gotta go back."

Loretta opened the car door as the light turned red.

"No you're not!" Johnny slammed on the brakes. "We're going to the Royal Bank of Canada on Fifth and I'm depositing the check in your pocketbook under the name of Mr. and Mrs. John Benson of Quebec, the fucking name I bought for five hundred bucks two weeks ago."

"I just know there's something in that locker. I missed it. I know it's there. Please, Johnny, pull into that space there." She pointed to an empty spot across the street, got out of the car, and slammed the door.

At Moms & Tots, the woman behind the desk said, "Our last class for the day just started. We don't accept latecomers for prenatal."

"Sorry," Loretta said, dangling her key in front of the woman. "I just left something in my locker. I'll be right back."

She raced down the hall as the woman said something about wet floors and the cleaning staff. Loretta hurried to the lockers, past a woman in a uniform running a vacuum cleaner around the first bank of lockers. The woman didn't hear her over the noise. When she was in front of locker number 117, she slipped in the key and opened it. She quickly removed the Huggies and baby wipes and put them on the bench behind her. She felt the sides of the locker, examined the hooks, and inspected the inside of the door. The vacuum became louder, drew closer. She stood on her toes and felt the top of the locker. Nothing. The vacuum was behind her now. She turned to grab the diapers and wipes—they were gone! The vacuum was running but unattended. Loretta looked around to the other bank of lockers. There was no one. She ran into the showers, looked in every stall. Empty. She checked the toilets, no one.

"Who took my diapers?" she said to the empty room.

Finally, a form came from out of a utility closet. It was the cleaning woman. Loretta was two heads taller. She bent to talk to the woman who kept her head down as she straightened the hair dryers on the station in front of the mirror.

"Did you take my diapers and baby wipes?"

"No speak English," the little woman said and moved past her toward the locker room.

And though Loretta had only seen her once in her life, at her father's funeral, she knew it was Paulie Gocci's mother.

"Did you take the diapers?" Loretta grabbed the woman by the shoulders and spun her around. "The diapers and the baby wipes. I left them right here on the bench."

"I don't take nothing!" The old woman bit off the words and sneered at Loretta. "You need diaper, ask desk."

Loretta had gotten so used to seeing the little blue keys on the women, pinned to their sweatshirts and tank tops, she hardly noticed that the cleaning lady had one pinned to her uniform. She looked closer at Mrs. Gocci's diaper pin, reached over, and, just as her hand was slapped away, saw that it had the numbers 117 stamped on the key.

The woman narrowed her eyes and stared up at Loretta.

"You and Gianni," she said over the drone of the vacuum, pointing her finger at Loretta in recognition. "My Paulo . . ." The woman turned her pointed finger at her own neck and drew a line with it across her throat. "My Paulo, he's going to take care of your Johnny."

Despite the chill that then ran down her spine, Loretta pushed past the woman and lurched to the closet. Surprisingly, the door opened. Sitting on the floor amidst mops and brooms and cleaning equipment was the package of Huggies with the baby wipes on top. She scooped them up and shoved the old woman to the floor.

"Your Paulo's no longer *up to the job*."

Mrs. Gocci struggled to get up. As Loretta made her way past the front desk, she heard, "Ladro, thief!"

Loretta ran out to the curb, clutching the pack of diapers and the wipes to her breast. She kept her head down as the snow flew into her eyes. She hurried across the street, reaching her hand out for the car door. But when she made it to where Johnny had parked, it wasn't her mother's car in the space. An old man was getting out of a Volkswagen.

"Oh my God," she said out loud, looking up and down the street.

Mrs. Gocci was coming out of Moms & Tots, she looked one way, then another, spied Loretta, and hobbled across the icy street as cars honked.

Loretta ran up the block and around the corner into the parking lot of the Stop & Shop. She headed straight to the back of the lot and huddled between two cars, poking her head up to look for Johnny . . . for Mrs. Gocci. The little crow turned into the parking lot, running stooped over on two bowed legs. Loretta duck-walked through the parked cars to a stack of pallets that separated the Stop & Shop from the building next door. She put the diapers down, tore off her City College sweat-shirt, and stuffed it under one of the pallets. When she picked the diapers and wipes back up, she thought of ditching them and coming back for them later. *What's in there?* she wondered. *Not drugs, it's too light for bricks of cocaine or marijuana. Could be LSD or ecstasy.* She imagined taking an X right now, the whole world going pretty.

Fat snowflakes collected on her glasses. She pressed her head into the pack of diapers and pinched her eyes shut. The image of her father teaching her to skate in front of the big tree at Rockefeller Center filled the black behind her eyes. Just the two of them. She was eight. He pulled her wobbling self behind him around the rink. "That's it, Lolo. You got it. There you go, sweetheart." He released her hand and she was sailing on the little white skates, the world finally in balance, snowflakes as big as rose petals falling and melting on her tongue. Freedom, she remembered feeling. Was it that long ago that she felt free?

Mrs. Gocci stood at the entrance to the grocery store, looking inside, eyeing each person that left with a shopping cart. Just when

Loretta thought she couldn't squat with her ass in the snow for another minute, now having to pee, she gasped and swallowed hard. Benny Saltone rounded the corner along with his goon and was embraced by the little old lady. The old bitch pointed into the grocery store; she waved her arms around. Benny, wearing only a sweater, rubbed his arms then patted the old lady on the back. He nodded his head as he bent to hear her and finally walked with her into the Stop & Shop, leaving the goon to stand guard.

Sweat poured down Loretta's back while her frozen fingers clutched the diapers. She had no money, no cell phone, no Johnny, and she had to pee so bad she thought she was going to explode. It was then that she smelled coffee. A door opened at the back of the building next door. The smell of fresh brew poured from the place. A Starbucks! And through the back door she could see a hallway and a ladies' room. In a single move she slipped through the railing of the stoop that separated the parking lot from the building. While a kid in a Starbucks cap dumped boxes into the dumpster, Loretta looked back at the entrance to the grocery store where the goon was stomping his feet and chewing on his knuckles. She shot up the steps, through the rear door, down the hall, and into the ladies' room.

The relief, even in her panic, was sublime.

"Oh God," she said, hanging her frozen ass over the toilet. "If I ever get out of this, I swear to you, I'll go to mass every Sunday for a year."

She stood and washed her hands, smelled her pits, and remembered that they had no deodorant this morning. She ripped off her turtleneck and tank top, opened the baby wipes and pulled one out of the pop-up lid. Sweat continued to pour from her body, but at least it was masked by the *new, powder-fresh, aloe-infused formula* of the wipes. She was flushing her fifth wipe when she struggled with the pop-up canister. She opened the lid and gasped.

"Holy shit!" Loretta said and pulled out a stack of soaking-wet one-hundred-dollar bills.

She couldn't grasp how many there were. She sat on the toilet seat and stared at the limp images of Ben Franklin, who seemed to smile back. She turned and looked at the jumbo pack of Huggies. She zipped open the package. At first glance there were diapers, thirty of them. She pressed one, balled it up, then finally ripped the no-leak lining from the outer plastic layer. Twenty one-hundred-dollar bills wrapped in a paper band fit nicely in the crotch of the diaper. It took her what seemed to be an eternity, but after the first few, she was able to open each one, remove the bills, close the little clamshell diapers, and stuff them back into the package. A series of knocks on the door fell on deaf ears as she worked. Finally she put her tank top back on and lined her midriff, breasts, and hips with the money. When she slipped her turtleneck over her head, she looked at her boxy form in the mirror. From the neck down, she looked like her barrel-chested father before he died.

She took a single Ben Franklin and walked to the front of the coffee shop. She was about to order, ready to explain that she didn't have anything smaller, when she noticed a Gap across the street. She threw a glance over at the Stop & Shop. The goon was still stomping his feet on the snowy sidewalk, his shoulders up to his ears. He pinched a cigarette between his thumb and finger, brought it to his lips, and drew hard. She walked across the street between two other women—three girls out shopping on a Saturday.

The first thing she bought was a gray-and-yellow messenger bag that she slipped across her shoulder. She passed by the racks of things in her signature pink, sequins, and glitter. As she sat on the bench in the dressing room transferring the money into the bag, a blizzard of thoughts concerning whether Johnny was dead or alive flew at her. She pushed them away, trying to focus on the moment, but the idea that Johnny was in the trunk of Benny's Mercedes froze her on the bench. *But I have the diapers—the money,* she thought, *and that's what they want. Benny ain't going to kill nobody 'til he gets what he wants. He screwed that up yesterday with Paulie, he's not going to make the same mistake twice.* She was ripping off her sweater for the second time in the last few minutes when she stopped and sank against the wall. Maybe Johnny just left. He saw his chance and took off. He could be headed up I-87 by now, the money safely tucked into the Royal Bank of Canada, a debit card in his pocket. *Oh, God!* Her heart sank. *Oh, God! Well, fuck him.* She ripped the turtleneck over her head. *He does that to me*, she thought, *I'll somehow make my way to Quebec and track him down.* Her mind was busy with how she would use the cash in her bag to get to 441, rue Chapel, Québec, the home of Lorissa and John Benson, names they had chosen so they didn't have to learn new ones. Lo was Lo. Johnny was John. *Fuck him*, she thought, stomping to the checkout counter. She saw herself ringing the bell on rue Chapel and slapping him as soon as he came out on the stoop. *Why'd you leave me, Johnny?* she would say. *Why'd you leave me?*

She left the Gap in a navy peacoat, a light-blue sweater, charcoal hat, and scarf. She'd never been so subdued, and as she glanced at herself in the glass window, she thought, never so classy. So French.

Loretta held tight to the strap of the messenger bag that contained her old sweater and close to ninety thousand dollars. She glanced across the street, relieved to see that the goon was finally gone. She sighed and watched her breath form a cloud as she took her place among the collection of Saturday shoppers. She had taken no more than three strides when a cop car came flying down Metropolitan Avenue, weaving between cars, its horn whooping. Sirens came from the other direction as well. She turned to see two more squad cars screech to a halt in front of the Stop & Shop. In seconds, six cops were surrounding a parked car, throwing somebody up against it. Shouts and growls and grunts came from across the street. "What the fuck, what the fuck!" A crowd was gathering as traffic halted. Cautiously, Loretta walked toward the scene, craning her neck to see above the heads and shoulders. *Oh God*, she prayed. *Don't let it be Johnny.* If Benny sent the cops after Johnny, she'd find him and his goon, cook their livers, and make 'em eat 'em! At the bus stop, she stood on a bench and looked across the street. Benny Saltone and his goon were spread-eagle, one draped over the hood of the Mercedes, the other over the hood of a squad car.

"Holy shit," she said, her gloved hand at her mouth.

"What's going on?" some guy was saying behind her.

She ignored him and watched while the cops cuffed Benny.

"Looks like somebody's getting what they deserve, right Lorissa?"

The guy moved into the street.

The voice registered and Loretta looked down to see Johnny standing on the curb below her, staring up.

"Oh God, oh God!" She threw herself into his arms. "You bastard!"

She pounded him on the back as he pulled her to the sidewalk. She held onto him as the squad car doors slammed behind them. She heard a cop say, "Show's over folks, go on back to your business, show's over, move on along."

"Show's over," Johnny whispered into her hat. "Take a nice long breath, Lo. Show's over."

"Wait a fucking minute!" She pulled back and held him by the shoulders. "How come you're wearing Benny's jacket?"

"You want to touch?" Johnny held out his arm and winked at her.

"No, I don't. And where'd you go?" She grabbed his arm and walked close to him. "You know we missed the bank. It's after two."

"We'll go to the bank on Monday. In Quebec." He led her to her mother's car parked on the corner.

"Oh God, Johnny, I was so scared," she said when they were in the car. "I thought . . . I thought you left me." She dropped her hands into her gloves as he pulled out into traffic. "You coulda left me, Johnny. Nobody would have blamed you."

He reached over and squeezed her knee.

"If I'd bolted, you'd of tracked me down like a dog." He reached for her hand and brought it to his lips and kissed her fingers. "Wouldn't you, Lo? Wouldn't you track me down?"

"Yeah, baby, you bet."

He had seen her run out of the Moms & Tots with Paulie Gocci's mother on her heels. He watched for a few minutes then saw Benny and the goon pull up and park. He pulled out and circled the block. On his third pass, he got caught in traffic right next to Benny's car.

"Shit, I thought any second he could come out and I'd be fucked," Johnny said. "Then I noticed something. You know how Benny's always putting his Ray-Bans up under the windshield when he parks his car. I always thought it was 'cause he was such a show-off. All of a sudden, I got a good look in the windshield. His car don't got a VIN number.

The glasses always hid the fact that the car was stolen—not that it should surprise anybody."

Johnny drove toward the expressway.

"So?" Loretta ran her fingers up and down the sleeve of Johnny's jacket.

"So, then I see the back window is open. Snow falling right into the backseat. And there's Benny's coat. I don't know what got into me, but I threw the car into park, bolted, ran around, reached in the back window, grabbed the coat. I was moving through the intersection in less than ten seconds. But, guess what else, Benny's phone was in his coat. Cracked me up. Benny won't wear his coat in the snow so it won't get ruined. He'll fold it all nice and neat in the backseat but leave the fucking window open. That's when I noticed the Starbucks. I knew in my bones you were in there. I pulled over and parked so I could see the street. Then I called the cops."

"You what?"

"I called the cops. I told them I'd just seen my stolen Mercedes parked in front of the Stop & Shop, fourth meter down from the corner. 'The dealership next to Mayo live chicken market up near Gun Hill Road?' I says . . . 'It's a chop shop by night. The service manager, Benny Saltone, he's inside the Stop & Shop.'

"'Your name,' the dispatch says?

"'My name?' I yell into the phone. 'My name is Ruben Diaz,' I says. 'I'm the borough president of the fucking Bronx. Now go get the little shit who stole my wife's car.'"

Loretta stared at her Johnny. A warmth spread from her ears down to her toes.

"What the fuck got into you?" She laughed and smiled at her man.

He smiled and ran his fingers down her cheek.

"So I see you kept a little money." He pulled her hat off and ran a hand down the lapel of her coat. "Where'd you stash the diapers and the baby wipes?"

Late that night when they crossed into Canada, the customs agent asked them if they had anything to declare.

"I wish," Johnny said and popped the trunk for the man to inspect.

The agent looked at the passports and tapped the car on the roof.

"Welcome home," he said. "Drive safe."

"Merci," Loretta said. "Je suis contente d'être à la maison."

Johnny looked at her as they moved across the border.

"What the fuck did you just say?"

"I said we're glad to be home."

Lorissa Benson opened the window a crack and breathed deep until the smell of sour wine became the scent of the night air rushing in the window; the pressure of a hand at her throat became the touch of her own fingers feeling her pulse. She moved over and put her head on Johnny Benson's shoulder. The memory of everything in the rearview mirror moved to a different place. Not the back of her mind, but somewhere deeper. A place, she prayed, where the pain would settle and someday make her wise.

Rich as Pluff Mud

My family sold off a grand piano in 1964 when I was eight. It had lived in our parlor, they said, since my great-grandmother was a girl. There was also a little spinet that stood in the dining room. And though it was held up on one end by two volumes of *The Encyclopedia Britannica*, it was the one we learned "Chopsticks" on and where my mother played Chopin. Still, watching the big gal leave the front room brought everybody out onto the piazza in mourning. My great-aunt and grandmother twisted their floral handkerchiefs, and Mamie, who traded cooking and cleaning for a back room to sleep in, dabbed at her eyes with the tail of her apron. My brothers and I stood mute while three colored men, who had wrapped the black Baldwin in brown blankets, swung it out a window using ropes and hoisted it between two porch pillars before they lowered it onto the brick walk and loaded it onto the back of a truck. We waved as the truck rounded the corner onto King Street as though we expected three or four ivory keys to poke through the canvas flap and wave back.

"Are we poor, Daddy?" I asked when the truck was gone.

"Certainly not." My father reached out a long arm, pulled me to him, and cupped my chin. "We are as rich as pluff mud," he said, running the other hand over a rotting post. "And don't you ever let a soul tell you any different."

I was not reassured. Though the smell of his aftershave and the feel of his wrinkled linen suit cradled me as ably as my mother's lap, "rich as pluff mud" didn't make a lick of sense. The black, oozy earth of the barrier islands, thick as toothpaste, has surely claimed more flip-flops than the ocean itself. Two hundred years ago it spawned Carolina Gold, the rice that fed America and half of Europe. But the rice is long gone. In its place grows *Spartina* grass, home to clapper rails and blue herons, snow egrets and marsh wrens. They forage among the reeds and leave their droppings to mix with the swamp rot and ocean floor. On any given day the surface winds will pick up and propel the scent of the mudflats right into Charleston Harbor. The tourists hold their noses, appalled that the tip of the peninsula, home to some of the most historic architecture in America, stinks. But when you are a native, it simply smells of home. Breathing in the scent of pluff mud is such a powerful link to memory that the first summer I drove home from college, before I made it past Calhoun Street, it hurled me back to a time before I could talk.

My father was in the habit of calling up old idioms at the drop of a hat. And, while I rolled my eyes, I knew it was his way of infusing us with what would have to suffice for charm and culture. Carlton Barrow Winslow III, with darned elbows and shoes resoled every winter, was heir to a rotting piece of real estate, no matter that it sat South of Broad and had seen the history of the nation unfold. His dignity resided else-where. I was pregnant with my first child before I understood what he knew—that something rich bubbles up from deep within the marsh and that we take it in with each respiration. It salts our blood whether the mud sprouts gold or simply reeds for birds to peck at.

Everybody knows Libby flirts. But flirting with an ugly man whose wife is fat and pregnant and not all that sure of herself in the first place is just asking for trouble. Libby had just had it with all that whining is all—Addison can wear on you. I keep thinking it began the day Addison told everybody she was expecting her third child. We were all at the Porter-Gaud fall fund-raiser. It seemed strange to all of us that a school that cost an arm and a leg begged fingers and toes from the parents of kindergarteners. Addison had a toddler on her plump hip drooling something orange onto her shoulder while her four-year-old hugged her thigh.

"When are you due?" Margaret Fuller asked.

"Mid-April, a month before Dalton turns two. I'll be feeling like the devil himself, breast-feeding and planning a birthday party for a swarm of rug rats."

She closed her eyes and shook her head. With Addison, it's often difficult to tell whether she's bragging or complaining.

"A third is always nice," Libby said, not looking at Addison but painting a pumpkin on the pink cheek of a red-haired girl. "You'll have a spare."

Addison winced at Libby's profile. "A spare?"

Libby finished off the pumpkin with a green stem and leaf.

"Sure, you've got a girl and a boy and now you'll have a spare!" Libby turned and smiled her gorgeous smile, squinting as the late October sun formed a halo behind Addison's head. The halo dissolved into the sunset as Addison rolled her eyes and spun away.

———

Addison is one of those people you've known for so long you don't know why you like them, or even if you do, like a cousin you're stuck with. Libby, I chose.

Addison Légare, as she was known when we were children, was from an old Huguenot family that had probably come to Charleston before the Swamp Fox. Their gardens were lush with azaleas and roses. Ours grew dirt and vegetables. Her piazzas had pale-blue-painted ceilings with twirling fans while mine sagged and were often supported by the odd two-by-four. But Addison and I ran wild in the same backyards and played dangerous games on the seawall, oblivious of the dollar difference between us.

I don't remember when her mother died—we were five. But the day a man came to Ashley Hall in a long gray car left its mark. The man entered our senior assembly with the headmistress and I knew. I had lost my own father years before. You never forget the sudden awareness that the people coming toward the group are coming to you. Before words are even spoken, you know in your throat they are carrying death on their lips.

Addison's father had taken a small pearl-handled pistol that looked more like jewelry than something that could kill and put it inside his mouth and squeezed the trigger. He'd left a mess of course and a spineless note apologizing to everyone, especially Addison for not being there to see her graduate. He also would not present her at the Saint Cecilia Cotillion or walk her down the aisle one day. He'd endured enough, he wrote, and could not stand another minute being such a failure. Fortunately the failure left her a few million and a house that was the envy of us all. But Addison was an orphan and even a weak father beat the hell out of none at all. She had a distant aunt and, thanks be to God, a maid, and a gardener, who along with a group of lawyers kept Addison, body and soul, together. Jackson McMahon took on the job three days after he graduated from The Citadel. Their wedding was lavish with yards of organza and shining swords and epaulets.

I should also mention that Addison had me. There were weeks it seemed she never left my house; so hungry for family, she ate mine up with a ladle. It was there she grew fat—and fiercely loyal. Addison clung to us like molasses to biscuits.

Libby had deaths to mourn too, though no black hats and umbrellas came with mourners in tow to linger back at the house after. She and her husband Adam had been going through the fertility wars and appeared to be losing. "Surely marrying a man named Adam should help," she told me once.

During their attempts at in vitro, Libby had been shot up with enough follicle-stimulating hormone to produce eggs aplenty for the entire neighborhood: up to fourteen one month. But nothing stuck, and month after month there was a bloody reminder of the barren wasteland she called her body. Adam saw none of that. Barren or not, she was the most desirable thing he'd seen since the day he met her in New Haven ten years ago. He vowed he would do whatever it took to make her happy. He said he'd take her to China and get her a perfect baby girl if that's what she wanted. It wasn't. He'd get a surrogate mother. No. Libby wanted to be fat and pregnant and suffer a long and painful labor and stare into the face of a baby that held the blueprint of the two of them in every cell of its little body. The fact that Addison Légare McMahon could do that very thing so easily, and announce it so casually, and be so goddamned annoyed by it burned a hole in Libby like a cigarette that stayed lit until it came out the other side of your hand.

In the meantime, Libby's design firm cranked out logos for Charleston's finest, including the Porter-Gaud School. All the swanky shops and real estate firms turned to Libby Gordon Designs for eye-popping looks. Even the grand hotels that wanted to be old but smell new sought her out for business cards and logos to bring them into the proper century.

Years ago, Addison, Libby, and I drove down to see Newpoint, the new development that we'd all been reading about just across the bridge from Beaufort on Lady's Island. Adam said it was the best project he had worked on in years. As we entered the deeply shaded streets, we hushed. The homes mimicked ours, the Single Houses of Charleston, with tall front doors that led not into the houses themselves but into long side piazzas that overlooked gardens more manicured than ours. The black-green shutters, like the leaves of the magnolias that brushed against them, offered sharp contrast to white and gray clapboard. They were brand spanking new but looked as though they'd been there for generations. The farther in we walked, the larger the homes and the live oaks became, until those on the marsh were so grand, they took you back to a time when women wore hoops. Homes with columns that rivaled old Rome looked out across the sea grass and waved hello to their grandmothers on the Old Point in Beaufort. They said, *Thank you for all that you have taught us—but do come see our shiny new kitchens and twenty-first-century plumbing!*

We had lunch in Beaufort afterward and strolled around the Old Point streets, watching the tourists gawk at the houses where movies like *The Big Chill* and *The Prince of Tides* had been shot.

"Why, you just can't compare the two can you?" Like a museum docent, Addison swept her hand for us to take in the quaint eighteenth-century town. "Feel the difference." She went on. "You can smell it for God's sake."

"The pluff mud?" asked Libby. "I can certainly smell the pluff mud."

"No. It's old brick and cypress," Addison droned. "It's the oil in the cypress that keeps our houses impervious to insects and rot. It's why they last forever, you know."

We didn't.

"Can we leach the oil and drink it?" Libby asked. "I'd like not to rot."

Addison ignored her.

"Don't get me wrong." Addison looked over to the new houses that sparkled across the bay. "I'm flattered they want to look like us. But you've got to admit it's a theme park!" She looked apologetically at Libby. "I know they're Adam's bread and butter, sugar, but would *you* want to live there?"

The week before Christmas, Libby and Adam arrived a little after nine at Bob and Catherine Livingston's party. She walked in and had every head in the room turn twice. She's tall, almost six feet. But if my bangs were cut that blunt and short, I'd look like one of my kid's Playmobiles. I'm an unremarkable-looking woman, myself. Everything about Libby deserves a remark. She has skin the color of bisque with wide-set black eyes and a mole just under the right one. She rarely wears makeup. Doesn't need to. But this night her lips were Christmas red. Her eyes were perfectly smudged a midnight blue, and her hair was pulled up in a topknot held by two lacquered chopsticks with hand-painted, red-tinseled ornaments bobbing off the ends. She wore a long black jersey pencil dress that fell to the floor and a red sash on snake-slim hips. Every woman in the room wanted to kill her. Every man wanted to stand next to her, at least for a little while—if their wives would let them.

Catherine and Bob rushed at the late arrivals and offered them drinks. "I like them," Libby once told me. "They're so pretty, so George Clooney and Gwyneth Paltrow, but neurotic and smutty." When Catherine was expecting Jack last year, she was one of the few pregnant women Libby actually enjoyed being around.

"I'm sure I'm having twins," Catherine had said one day last summer, looking at her naked body in the mirror at the club.

"You just had an ultrasound," Libby said.

"Yeah, but look at my ass. I'm a fucking medical anomaly. I'm carrying the other one in my ass! Have you ever seen such a huge ass?"

Libby had not. Catherine had gotten so bottom heavy that Libby wondered if she would be able to lift her legs into the stirrups when her time came. That was the only time Catherine ever referred to her body for the rest of her pregnancy. Instead she deluged Libby with information on fertility doctors, Chinese herbalists, and more. "We're gonna get you pregnant, girl, if I have to fuck you myself!"

When Catherine's baby was born, the two women had a moment in the hospital, stretched out on the narrow bed together with Libby holding the tiny thing. They both cried. They didn't say a thing. They just cried. Libby was pumped up with enough hormones to make a stud horse in Savannah hard, and Catherine's milk was coming in. A male nurse walked through the door and did a three-point pivot and walked right out.

But here it was just two months after baby Jack was born and Catherine looked like a million bucks. The ass weight had migrated north, and every man in the room, including her own husband, couldn't keep his eyes off the low-cut sequined thing she wore that offered hope of an escapee.

"You going to keep those things in your hair, Libby, or you going to hang them on my tree?" Bob handed Libby a glass.

"What things?" Libby smiled then walked off to mingle.

She had trained herself for parties like these. She was a master evader of the taboo, the snippets of conversation, or even single words that stabbed and made her flat-as-a-pancake belly feel like a vast, empty cavern. If she moved fast, words like *breast pump*, *epidural*, and *Lamaze class* wouldn't make it past her eardrum. Instead they hung in the outer ear barely past her earring then evaporated quickly along with the pain. Surveying the crowd, she thought it appeared as though everyone was of childbearing age. And just when she and Adam had decided to take a break from the death-of-the-month club. What a pity. Still, she would make the best of it.

By the staircase, Libby saw Jackson and Addison McMahon splitting into the crowd. Neither one looked especially happy. Libby put herself right in the path of Addison's husband. Jackson Dalton McMahon IV was an unfortunate-looking man. Almost boy-like in physique, he was short with a small, round belly and a neck that seemed to slide into his arms. Tonight, he wore a tuxedo, well padded so he at least appeared to possess shoulders. He had hair the color of cellophane with eyelashes you only saw when the sun caught them just so. His gray-blue eyes were kind yet unremarkable, and when he smiled, thin lips betrayed a neat little row of small teeth that looked as if his big ones had just never arrived to push the baby ones out.

"Merry Christmas, Jackson." She offered her cheek then made sure her lipstick left a pretty red imprint on his.

"Same to you, Libby. You look lovely."

"And you? You look different, Jackson." She held his shoulders at arm's length. "What is it? Your wife is the one who's supposed to be glowing, but you? What have you been up to?"

Jackson put his hands in his pockets and rocked back on his heels.

"Just working out a bit more, watching what I eat, that's all."

"Well, good God, Jackson, it's made all the difference in the world!"

"Why, thank you, Libby. You're the first one who's noticed."

"I notice more than you think, Jackson." She said it so sweetly, so softly, and so close to his face that the blend of her perfume and the Kendall Jackson rose into his nose and up into his head in a wild rush.

"Where's Adam?" Jackson sobered.

Libby made her lovely face fall.

"Now, Jackson. Asking a woman who's trying to make time with you the whereabouts of her husband could spoil things for both of us."

Jackson blushed and laughed.

"Libby you're a sin just waiting to happen."

"I try." She took a long sip.

Neither one of them saw Addison approach. She slipped her arm around her husband's.

"Hello Libby," she said as cold as Canada, wiping the lipstick off her husband's cheek.

"Addison," Libby declared mockingly, "you have caught us red-handed, or cheeked, as the evidence suggests. I should move on."

"Perhaps you could start with your own husband," Addison said through clenched teeth.

"Oh, I licked him up one side and down the other before I left the house." Libby smiled sweetly and sashayed into the crowd, leaving Addison fuming and Jackson struggling to bring his color down to its usual parchment pale.

Later, Libby found a waiter with a tray of fresh salmon on lovely little puff pastry rounds. It turned out that he was a freelance photographer she'd worked with. They were chatting about an exhibit they'd done on preserving Gullah, the old slave language and culture still familiar to parts of the southeastern seaboard.

"It's disappearing right along with the old money," the photographer said.

"Sweetgrass baskets and Uncle Remus stories," Libby said. "Pretty soon that's all we'll have left."

Suddenly the slow, nasal voice of Addison McMahon erupted from behind. "Lord, I don't know. I can't keep a thing down. Nothing tastes good anyway."

Libby stole a glance. She wondered how anyone could get so fat, pregnant or not, if they were puking all the time and had so little appetite. Then she noticed Addison was holding a plate with a dozen shrimp tails in one hand and a plate with only crumbs remaining in the other.

"I told Jackson I thought we should wait, but you know him. He wants to have everybody out of college before he turns fifty-five." Addison laughed and the woman she was talking to smiled politely. "Of course it doesn't occur to him that it's going to be me and Seeley doing all the work." She put her hand on her lower back and arched forward, grunting. "Lord, three kids under five. What in the world was I thinking?"

"Seeley?" The woman asked.

"Oh, Seeley's been in Jackson's family for years." She handed the plates to a passing waiter and reached for more shrimp. "Her mama was Jackson's mama's maid. Why, do you know that her grandmother—Tulip, they called her—was born right under the back stairs at the house on South Battery?"

The woman did not know.

"Anyway, Seeley came to work for us when Dalton was born. I just couldn't manage without her."

Libby had heard enough. She took one more salmon puff, had her glass refilled another time, and walked out onto the porch. It was cool and, fortunately, full of men. Men talking from deep down in their bellies, lying about golf, scratching their balls, smoking cigars, and having the good sense not to stop just because she walked onto the porch.

"Libby!" Ty Weller called. "Pull up a railing, sweetheart."

He took off his jacket and draped it between two posts like he'd done it a million times because certainly he had. Libby wiggled up. She'd gone to a dance or two with some of the South of Broad boys when they were dating down. But she met most of them after she and Adam had come back to Charleston after college. They bought a Single House without a single thing to recommend it except its location and bone structure, and set about a solid year of gutting and renovation. They joked that their house had more pedigree than they did and that was why they were welcome into this Charleston circle where the men had no first names, just a string of last names that had been collected over generations.

Jackson McMahon made his way out onto the porch and produced a large cigar. Jackson grew up South of Broad in the house that he and Addison will occupy as soon as his parents "move on," as Addison puts it. A hundred years ago Portia Hall was in dire need of a coat of paint and its residents in need of a good tailor—as great a badge of honor then as its' restored beauty is today. For decades after the Civil War, to be well dressed and painted would have meant consorting with the occupying army, and no Charleston family with a shred of dignity would ever have stooped so low. Today, we are happy to consort with anyone who can improve the bottom line. Jackson, for example, hired my husband Peter's firm to restructure his portfolio, which pulled the McMahon honor out of mothballs and returned Portia Hall to its original splendor. Now, on Wednesdays, tourists visit the first two floors and peek into rooms over velvet ropes. Ty had gone and married money, a gal from Houston, pretty as a picture, who had a daddy with more oil than George Bush. Ty's mama taught her how to set a table and softened her vowels. Lucky for Ty, she was a quick study.

"Jackson, my man." Ty stood at attention. "I understand you've gone and spread your seed again. A hearty congratulations!"

Jackson smiled, then looked down and lit his cigar.

"The improvement is that his seed is spilled within his own wife this time." One of the others barked up.

Jackson chuckled lightly while the others howled. He took two quick puffs then checked the tip of his cigar. Seeing that Jackson wasn't going to bite, the men moved on to other nonsense, and within a moment or two, Libby and Jackson were being ignored.

"They're monsters," Libby said, shaking her head.

"They're having a good time."

"At your expense."

"Not at all."

He leaned against the railing. She leaned against another. A pillar the size of a man formed the corner and connected the two.

"Cigar smoke bother you?" He attempted to blow the smoke out toward the garden.

"I rather like it."

They sat quietly for a while. Two sets of French doors were fully opened onto the porch. It had been sixty-five degrees in the afternoon, one of the frequent surprises of the Lowcountry in December. Libby stood and kicked off her shoes. In her stocking feet she was still a half a head taller than Jackson McMahon.

"So if Addison comes out here, is she likely to run me off the porch?"

"Oh, you're a big dog, Libby. You can handle it."

Libby always saw Jackson trapped like a bug under glass, a big fat piece of Baccarat or Waterford, but trapped nonetheless. Was the arrangement made in a dark-paneled room when Jackson and Addison were babies, she asked me once, or did he come along and save the poor thing? I always saw it the other way around. Addison was the first girl who paid him any mind at all, and before he knew it, the deal was sealed with calla lilies and trumpets marching them down the aisle. I figured out a long time ago that the invisible between people is never ours to reason. Jackson and Addison might just worship each other—each baby conceived in fits of erotic passion, Jackson lost in the pink folds of Addison's fleshy torso.

The waiter came by with a fresh chardonnay for Libby and gave Jackson something dark with a cherry.

"What's that?" Libby asked.

"A Manhattan," he said.

"Um, never had a Manhattan—are they sweet?"

"Sweet and tart at the same time. A little like you, Libby." He loosened his bow tie and let it hang freely.

"You going to eat the cherry?" She eyed the thing floating in his glass.

"It's all yours." Jackson lifted the candied cherry by the end of its stem and passed it over to Libby.

"I can tie this stem in a knot with my tongue, you know." Libby popped the cherry into her mouth and chewed.

"I heard that." Ty Weller turned. "Is there a time limit?"

The other men turned as well and so did a few of the women who had wandered out onto the porch to escape the closeness of the crowded house.

"Now isn't that just like a man!" Libby rolled her eyes. "Gentlemen, in matters regarding the tongue, speed should be reserved for explaining why you're late for dinner with lipstick on your shirttail."

Laughter rippled. Libby raised an eyebrow and walked toward the center of the porch and spun to face them.

"Now, I could very easily tie this cherry stem in seconds, but it will most likely take a full minute. Because, like all things involving the tongue, the trick is not in the pace of the oral digit, but in its dexterity, or more to the point, in the quality of the knot . . . if you catch my drift."

More laughter. She had every eye on her. And though she was loaded, she didn't show it. Only Adam, or perhaps Catherine, would have known, and they hadn't made it to the porch yet, but others had. The crowd was growing and Libby was well aware she was the show.

"Mr. McMahon will inspect the stem in question to determine that it has no bends or creases to aid in my endeavor."

She handed the cherry stem to Jackson who moved into his role as magician's assistant seamlessly. He carefully turned the object over in his hand.

"I pronounce that the stem is as it was when it left my glass, sans cherry." Jackson slightly bowed his head in Libby's direction.

"Gentlemen and ladies, if I could have complete quiet please."

Libby spread her arms and bobbed her head. The tinseled ornaments shimmered in the moonlight. She placed her feet hip-distance apart, blew on her hands, then shook them out, drawing giggles from the crowd. Then, like a sword swallower, she tilted back her head and directed Jackson to hold the cherry stem above her mouth. Slowly, she opened, and on cue, he dropped it in then placed his hands in his pockets. Polite applause rippled through the crowd.

From inside the house, the trio began their second set and Libby used it to her advantage. As she worked the thing in her mouth, she ignored the catcalls from the growing throng as more and more partygoers moved onto the porch. Shining Catherine, wearing Bob's arm draped across her collarbone, came out with Adam in tow. Libby slowly danced around until she stood behind Jackson. Then she peeked over one of his shoulders, then the other. She looked down at his lapels, swirling her tongue and pursing her lips. Then she gathered the ends of his tie, and with all the skill of a king's valet, she looped and overlapped, crossed and flapped, and finally tugged the perfect bow into place on Jackson's narrow neck, somehow managing to slip her long leg into the crook of his left arm, the hand of which remained in his pants pocket. And while everyone had their eyes on Jackson's brightly flushed cheeks and perfectly tied Criswell and Barton, slowly, one by one, they began to applaud. The occasional "bravo" and whistle rang out as those assembled noticed that held tight between her beaming upper and lower central incisors was the snuggly knotted cherry stem.

"It was well choreographed, I'll say that," Adam said cheerfully on the walk home.

"Me or her slapping the hell out of me?" Libby asked.

"Well, both actually. I mean you have to hand it to her, baby. She created a hell of a finale."

"She hit me! In public!"

"You were draped all over her husband."

"You didn't slap *him.*"

"Yes, but I'm not humorless, or pregnant." He took Libby in his arms and began to dance. "Anyway, men don't slap other men; they slug them. If I'd coldcocked Jackson McMahon, I never would have gotten you out of there."

Adam Fred Astaired his still-drunk wife across King Street and twirled her in front of Banana Republic, their reflections mingling with the mannequins dressed in holiday wear.

"One more question," she said. "Why didn't she slap *him?*"

"Oh God, Libby! Women slap their husbands all the time. Nobody's ever going to forget the day Addison McMahon slapped Libby Gordon, especially her husband! I can promise you that."

"Did I make an ass of myself, Yancey?"

She looked over Adam's shoulder at Peter and me. We danced behind them, though not nearly so well, but, then, we weren't nearly so drunk.

———

I saw Libby the day before I met her. Our backyards connect, and though they are long and deeply shaded, I could see her scraping paint off a porch pillar. Her long strokes produced snow in July as a hundred years of paint flew into the air around her. Less than twenty-four hours later I met her, in a manner of speaking, in the recovery room at Roper Hospital.

I'm a nurse. When my third child started preschool, I went back to work part-time. I needed the touch more than the money. I saw Libby before I saw the chart. Her long form under the sheet was shaking badly as she was wheeled through the double doors. I pulled two hot blankets from the warmer. Jerome, the surgical aid, pushed her into place and plugged her IV monitor into the outlet.

"She's the ectopic." He shook his head. "Bad. Almost bled out."

"How many units?"

"Two, I think. Here." He handed me her chart.

"Is Dr. Pell with her husband?"

"Yeah, he be here directly."

I laid the blankets on her, tucking them up to her neck. I moved the bag of O negative onto another IV pole and re-hung her antibiotic on the same pole as her fluids. Then I went to the chart. I'd seen her name on the board and gotten briefed in report: Elizabeth Tatum Gordon presented at three this morning with abdominal and shoulder pain. Women with ectopic pregnancies never connected shoulder pain to a possible pregnancy and why should they? The fact that blood was filling the abdomen and sending some code to a distant body part was lost on most women, as if someone were tapping you on the back to tell you something was wrong with your foot. Oh, if only they had told you earlier, like a day or so.

A day or so earlier Elizabeth Gordon was scraping paint off her porch, not knowing that an embryo had snuggled itself into her fallopian tube weeks ago, some blockage cradling it there instead of allowing it to tumble freely into her uterus to make a proper home. I bet ten dollars that she'd always been irregular. No vaginal bleeding gave her any warning. The chart revealed that large clots had been removed, indicating she'd been hemorrhaging internally for days, and that the seven-week-old fetus, who had broken though the walls of his temporary home, had been male.

She was lovely, amazingly white, but exquisite with a rope of dark hair. That's when I connected who she was. I flipped to the front of the chart. Our street numbers were almost the same. I'm odd; she's even. She's on Limehouse; I'm on Greenhill. We're back to back.

"Elizabeth?" I began the barrage my patients so resist. "You're out of surgery, Elizabeth. Can you open your eyes?"

Under "Elizabeth" someone had scribbled "Libby" on her chart. "Libby," I tried again in my clearest, loudest postsurgical voice.

"Libby, it's time to wake up. Libby?"

Finally, lead-heavy eyelids lifted a centimeter or two and a deep groan came out of her long, narrow chest.

"Are you having pain?" I asked.

"Where's Adam?"

"I'm here, baby. I'm right here."

I turned to see a tall, sad-faced man. Where she was light, he was dark—tan and blonde and remarkably present for a man who hadn't slept in over twenty-four hours. I stepped aside, and he moved in, took her face in his hands, and told her exactly what had happened.

"We were starting a baby, Libby. And, don't you worry, we're going to get better at this. Shit, we weren't even trying."

Adam had been in Chicago the night before Libby dropped cold in the bathroom. If it had happened while he was sleeping at the Westin, no one ever would have heard her hit the floor. That thought would haunt him for months.

I work in recovery so I can get my fix without getting attached. But Libby was different. She went from recovery to a surgical intensive care unit, then onto a gyne floor. I followed her progress and visited throughout her stay, something I had never done. It was my way of being the welcome wagon. We became friends quickly. My trips through the back hedge to check in on her created a dent and eventually a hole. Now there is a latticed arch, alive and dense with wisteria.

———

I had the presence of mind to take a handful of Advil before I went to bed so my hangover was bearable the morning after the party. I came downstairs to make coffee and saw Libby sitting on my back porch reading my newspaper, a cup of Starbucks in her hand. She stood as I opened the glass door, put her right running shoe over her left, spread her arms out like Christ on the cross, and dangled her head in shame.

"I doubt they're going to draw lots for your clothes, Libby, nice as they are." I opened the door and she walked in.

"How horrible was I?" She sat at the island.

"You were drunk and showing off. Adam still sleeping?"

"He's running."

"What's wrong with you people? Don't you have the decency to throw up in the morning? Hell, Peter's up there feeling like George Foreman beat the shit out of him."

"We're younger than you."

"Don't remind me." I pressed the button and the pot began to brew.

We settled in a couple of chairs with an ottoman between us and picked up sections of the *Post and Courier*.

"I'll send an apology," Libby said. "I'll messenger a note and flowers tomorrow."

"Not flowers. She did slap you. You behaved badly and she got to slap you for it. Case closed."

"You're the one who's always saying how sad she is, how I should cut her a break because he's all she's got. Him, her trust fund, and her perpetual fecund state!"

"Well, she is sad, but I don't think you should grovel."

"They're powerful people, Yancey. They could affect Adam's business and my business too. And what about Peter? Just because you've known Addison all your life doesn't mean Peter's safe."

"Lineage without the loot," I told Peter when I met him. Instead of him marrying in, I'd always seen it as me marrying out. I liked being bundled with Libby and Adam and Bob and Catherine, the nouveau upwardly mobile who rub elbows with Addison and Jackson but see them for who they are. The new blood invigorates and has created an outer circle of the South of Broad set. I live in an old tree, but I straddle the ring closest to the bark. It lets me live in both camps.

For a century and a half, Charleston didn't care if you were rich or poor as long as you could trace your family back a proper number of generations. But soon enough the money that was growing off trees in the rest of the country came south for a visit and decided to put down roots. To many, the wrinkled green stuff smelled like jasmine, so they sold off their homes and moved elsewhere. But, the likes of Addison, Jackson, and Ty held tight to their inner circle just as Old Europe clings to names like Rothschild. I went off to college with loans. They went around the corner to The Citadel or the College of Charleston; a few ventured out as far as Columbia for law school. In time, some of us filed back in and diluted the pool with our mixed marriages and new friends. While it's more likely that the remaining pure are invited to our parties than we are invited to theirs, they don't ignore us. Charleston still worships her ancestors, but she has finally come to rely on the occupying army.

Still, Libby's warning didn't fall on deaf ears. A strategic whisper and the country club you thought you were going to design in Kiawah might just go to some other firm. We were symbiotic whores, unlikely to pull ourselves up by our bootstraps and do right.

"What will you say in your note?" I asked.

"Don't worry, I'll compose something pathetic and clever."

Christmas came and went. The school pageants were adorable. Even the weather did us a good turn and dipped into the low forties. Libby and Adam had wisely gone to St. Croix, far away from toddlers tearing into presents. Everyone told the story of Bob and Catherine's party. They all mentioned Libby's long leg in the crook of Jackson's arm and the cherry stem clenched in her teeth. But of course it was Addison's chubby little windmill, which came out of nowhere and sent tinseled ornaments flying, that was the talk of the town. Every time I saw that fat little hand meet Libby's porcelain cheek I had the most peculiar feeling. Anger and, strangely, admiration knotted in my stomach and I didn't have a hope of untangling it.

Soon after they returned from St. Croix, Adam took Libby, Bob, and Catherine to a barrier island in a johnboat to see an old Gullah church he wanted to photograph. It had been built by a group of freed slaves in the 1800s. Adam admired its simple lines and squat spire.

He hoped to reinvent it on the Outer Banks in a new urban village he was designing. They'd bundled up in polar fleece and made their way up the salt creeks. When they got to the island, Adam killed the engine and they used a stick to pole around. Libby saw something bright red bobbing just under the surface of the tea-colored water. She reached in but it evaded her grasp. It reminded her of something, but she couldn't bring that to the surface either and looking at it under the rippling water made her dizzy.

"How you even know they's a God?"

The voice of a little boy cracked the clear, cold morning. He'd come out the back door of the church and posted himself on the top step. They poled the boat out of sight and watched the mother face her son down as he sat, arms crossed, lip out.

"I don't. That's why I pray." She pulled the boy up by his elbow, spun him around, and sent him up the step with a swift wallop to his butt. "Now get back in that church!"

The back door slammed and the island grew silent once more. The four of them grinned at each other.

They maneuvered the boat around to the front of the church. It stood proud amidst angel oaks and leafless myrtles.

"Hell of a thing its still standing," Bob said. "Not much protection out here. Imagine how many hurricanes it's weathered."

"It's the cypress," Adam said. "Our houses too. Withstands rot and God's wrath."

Dragged by seaweed, the lure bobbed up again, red in the brown water. This time Libby saw the maraschino cherry floating in Jackson's drink. She swung her head over the side of the boat and threw up her breakfast. Catherine's concern shifted to a wicked smile.

"Don't get all excited," Libby said. "Sometimes puke is just puke."

Bright and early the day after New Year's, I got a call from Addison inviting me to bring Marian, my youngest, over to play with Eve Marie.

"She's been begging to see her ever since school got out. I'll let Seeley make them a tea party and we'll have one our selves. How's that sound?"

It sounded phony, but Marian was driving me nuts so I agreed.

While Addison was eager to move into Portia Hall, the house she lived in was wonderful. Daily, the tourist carriage drivers pull their horses up in front and point. Some Revolutionary War general lived there or died there or philandered there—I never remember which. It was also, however, where Addison's father fired the derringer into his brain. While the Board of Architectural Review kicked and screamed, the room was removed. Now a balcony looks down into the kitchen. Even so, Addison says she's heard that muffled shot and seen her father's desk suspended above the kitchen like a hologram. Once she ran to Portia Hall and curled up on a brocade sofa. When she awoke, a tourist was pointing from behind the velvet ropes.

"I had been dreaming," she said. "I'd jumped off the seawall and changed into a long sleek mermaid. I swam all the way out to Shem Creek. I popped my head out of the water and yelled at the tourists who were eating on the terrace at Vickery's. I screamed that they were eating my children, but no sound came out. I screamed air. I swam back and pulled myself up onto the seawall. My long beautiful fin split back into my short fat legs."

Addison didn't have an ounce of humor, but she had tons of bitter.

When Marian and I arrived at Addison's for our visit, Seeley opened the door wearing a crisply pressed gray uniform and white collar. Eve Marie was sitting grumpy on the bottom step sporting white tights and a tartan dress. Marian and I paled: she in the same karate costume she'd been wearing since Christmas and a pair of red high tops; my own costume was unremarkable.

"Miss Addison taking down the tree," Seeley offered.

I made my way through a series of rooms to a brightly lit, paneled den where Addison was wrapping ornaments in tissue paper and placing them in large white boxes from Condon's, a Charleston department store that had closed its doors decades ago.

"Seeley's going to bring us some tea and croissants," Addison said brightly.

If I didn't know better, I would have sworn she'd started on Zoloft the day after Catherine's party, but Addison would never compromise a pregnancy.

"How was your Christmas?"

Addison took a porcelain Joseph from a crèche and wrapped it in tissue. I reached for Mary.

"Good. Yours?" I asked.

"Well, you know we had the Junior League at Portia Hall this year—a lot of work, but just beautiful. I wish you'd join, Yancey."

"We go through this every year, Addison. I just don't have the time." She stuck out her lip and picked up a shepherd.

"I'm not saying your work isn't for a good cause, but you don't work every day, and we provide a community service too."

"I don't work for charity, Addison."

"Well, you certainly don't need the money."

"Addison . . ."

I was about to tell her that I loved my work. I needed it, that it fed something in me my family and friends simply couldn't satisfy. I was saved by Seeley coming in with a tray. We sat and ate our croissants, sipped at our tea like ladies.

"So, tell me what you got for Christmas," I said.

She put her cup in its saucer and lifted her right hand. On it sparkled a ruby the size of Texas with five or six diamond sisters in attendance.

"My, my Addison." I smiled and took her hand. "Jackson should behave badly at parties more often!"

A vacuum sucked air from the room. Why didn't I just say how lovely! She withdrew her hand and became icy. I tried again.

"I was just teasing, Addison. It's a beautiful ring."

"It was not Jackson who behaved badly at Catherine's party, Yancey. It was your drunken friend! Oh, I got her little note. A hand-painted poinsettia on the front, forgiveness begged in calligraphy on the back." Her head bobbed with each syllable.

"She *was* drunk and she did misbehave." I took a long sip of my tea.

"She was shameful!" She stood and walked to the tree, pulling the remaining ornaments and wrapping them in tissue. "She embarrassed Jackson to no end. She's obviously a very insecure woman. Why she's not happy with her own husband, I don't know. He seems like a perfectly fine young man, handsome, well bred, an excellent architect. I just don't know what her problem is." She moved around the tree, finding the last of the ornaments, pulling bits of tinsel. "I think it's time Libby Gordon settled down and thought about having children instead of worrying about her figure and wearing skintight dresses and flirting with other men. If she's not careful, she'll miss her fertility window altogether. You're a nurse. You should tell her that."

I was speechless. Libby's infertility wasn't a widely discussed subject, but I was stunned that Addison knew nothing about it.

"It would be far more meaningful coming from you," I said. "Why don't you call her so you can have a heart to heart."

I stood, steaming, calling out to Marian. But before I made it out of the room, the girls came prancing in to show us the bears they had dressed in clothes from the layette.

"Where's the pretty lady?" Eve Marie asked me.

"Who, honey?"

"The pretty lady who painted pumpkins on our cheeks." She smiled and leaned into my thighs.

"That's Auntie Libby," Marian said. "She lives at her house through our back gate."

For Addison's jaw to clench tighter would have meant the fossilizing of teeth.

After going on about how adorable the bears were, I told Marian that we had to go and she didn't fuss. We were gathering our things, making awkward good-byes when a tall black man came in along with Seeley to dismantle the tree. As they were lowering it onto its side, Marian called out at the last minute, jumping up and down.

"There's another one! There's another one! It's going to break! It's going to break!"

The man reached up and picked an ornament off the tree and handed it to Addison. She held it up by its hook and slowly spun it around. I didn't say a word, but I immediately recognized one of the hand-painted ornaments that had hung from Libby's topknot the night of the party. If I'd seen him on the way out the door, I would have slapped Jackson McMahon.

———

Late last August, Peter and I were walking home from dinner at Magnolia's on a sweltering night. I commented that it seemed strange that everybody had gone to bed so early.

"How do you know they've gone to bed?" he said.

"Everybody's turned their lights out."

"They're just not here, Yancey. They're back home."

"What do you mean back home?"

"Your year-round population's gone from about ninety thousand to forty since Hurricane Hugo, honey. Hell, half my clients live 'from off,' as you say. Even Boyd Brixton calls his 'the place in town' and that sprawling camp out on the island home. We're a dying breed, baby."

I looked around at the gracious houses and suddenly yearned for the days when the paint peeled and the verandas sagged but the rooms glowed whether it was August or December—before the Yankees came a second time.

Nelson Algren loved Chicago, his beautiful woman with a broken nose. I wondered if I didn't love Charleston more before she had her nose jobs. My grandmother called Charleston a woman of gracious dignity who didn't need makeup to show her good breeding. Well, now we show you everything, even our phony Restoration Hardware. I like my granite countertops, but I miss knowing my neighbors are here because this is home, not a pied-à-terre for some Chicago tycoon.

———

I worked the three-to-eleven shift after leaving Addison's, but I no sooner got my things in my locker when Jerome rushed in and pulled me into a corner.

"They's a lady downstairs asking for you. Say to come get you, and to hurry."

"Who?"

"Don't know, but she sho' is something!"

He smiled wide and talked nonstop as we walked to the elevator.

"She come in the emergency a while ago. I got pulled to work down there today. Her hand all cut up. They's this new nurse down there from New York. Don't nobody like her. Anyways, she going on about this old man. The nurse, that is. Saying she going call for a psych consult 'cause he be talking out his head. 'Bout that time your lady, the one who be asking for you, come tearing out from behind her curtain. She start going after that nurse, screaming at her, saying, 'You stupid Yankee bitch, you don' know shit! You don't know a thing. That man ain't crazy. He Geechee, he talkin' Gullah!'"

Jerome's eyes were the size of cake plates.

"Yeah, she something else. Your lady is. New York try to calm her down, saying, 'Now, that ain't none of your business, you just sit back here and wait for the resident to come in and stitch up that hand.' But your lady? She won't have none of that. She keep on at New York.

"'You don't even know what Gullah is, do you? Y'all come down here, buy up everything, then leave. Come back, get a suntan, then leave again! You don't bother to know a thing.' She yelled it, shaking her bloody rag in that nurse's face. That's when she spy me. She figure I know, and 'course I do.

"'Would somebody tell her?' She yell at the whole emergency room. She crying by then, black eye shit running all down her face. But Miss New York done gone and called security. That's when your lady ask for you. So I figure I better hightail it on up here."

Libby had cut herself good with an X-Acto knife years ago, but since the world had gone digital, she hardly ever mocked-up presentation boards for clients. She'd become all wrapped up in Gullah culture when she worked on that piece for the College of Charleston, but I couldn't imagine that she spoke the language or understood it. Hell, I hardly understood what they were saying and I had grown up with it.

We arrived on the ground level and were rounding the corner. I saw the security guard sitting outside the curtained cubicle.

"Thank you, Jerome," I said. "Will you let them know upstairs that I'll be back as soon as I can?"

I peeked inside the curtain and gasped. There sat Addison McMahon with a pimple-faced resident stitching a long circular cut that rode along her life line and another up under her ring finger. There was blood and mascara on her chubby cheeks and more blood all down the front of her white maternity blouse. A blood pressure cuff was Velcroed to her left arm. At the foot of the gurney pieces of the Christmas ornament lay on a gauze pad along with a pair of tweezers and the beautiful ruby ring. I introduced myself to the resident and reached for the chart. She'd told the admitting clerk that she slipped and caught her fall on a table where a box of ornaments lay. I dampened a piece of gauze and wiped some blood from her other hand.

After she was bandaged and the doctor had left, I found Miss New York and vouched for my friend. She released the security guard. I called upstairs and told the charge nurse I'd need someone to cover for me. I gathered Addison's belongings, but before I helped her off the gurney I whispered, "Addison, why didn't you just throw it across the room?"

She stared and hissed at me through her teeth. "Because I picked it up and squeezed real, real hard instead! Why are you asking?"

"We got a psych consult coming," I said. "You don't want to waste that!"

Finally she laughed and just as quickly began to cry. I reached over and wiped the tears and mascara that flowed and didn't seem to stop.

"Addison, Libby doesn't want your husband," I finally said.

"No?" She choked back sobs.

"No." I smoothed her hair away from her face. "She just wants your children." I screwed up my face and crossed my eyes like I did when we were girls.

"I'm sure you're going to explain that on the way to the car." She hiccupped and slid off the gurney like a small elephant.

"I will." I pulled her sweater around her shoulders. "I promise to tell you everything on the way home."

———

I suppose I am rich. I live in a place that anchors me by people I've known as long as I've known my name—along with a hearty breed of new pioneers—in this old, settled world. Peter says I collect spirits, not necessarily kindred ones. He's right. They grow into and out of me like gnarled wisteria winds its way around a porch rail. I am as disinclined to prune the old branches as I am to snip the fresh blossoms and put them into a mason jar on the back porch.

Speckled Bird

There was an old woman who lived in a stone house in what is now called the Carolina Preserve, an area between Asheville, North Carolina, and Greenville, South Carolina. Today, it is home to some of the most beautiful golf courses and real estate in the country. Until the late 1960s, it was a poor area, home to the descendants of the Scots-Irish, the Daniel Boones who had settled the land before America was a nation. It was said that the woman always kept a canvas suitcase packed for travel by her door. When her husband first noticed it, he asked her where she was going. She replied that if he ever hit her again, she was packed and ready to light out. The suitcase never left its post, but it remained ready to be taken by the handle and swooped out the door. This is the story of Bailey Rose Abernathy Dunham.

I was still a brand-new mother when Harlan started pushing and poking at me to have another. I should a-knowed he'd be hell-bent to catch up with his brothers, that first one being a girl and all. Both Dillon and James Lee had them a boy. Dillon's wife, T. Ellen, said he wouldn't leave her alone. Even when she had that first one in bed suckling in the night Dillon would come up behind her, nuzzling his pecker in like a runt pig. "He wants to give Patton a little brother," she said. "Wants to call the next one Ike." T. Ellen went over to Pickens and had her baby doctor give her a diaphragm. "What Dillon don't know won't hurt him," she said.

After supper the day I had found out I was pregnant with that first one, I told Harlan we was going to have us a baby. He didn't say nothing. He reached over and ran the back of his knuckles down my cheek, then broke out in a grin wide as his face.

"Come on." He pushed back his plate and went to the little door in the side of the mantle and pulled out what looked to be an old army sock. "Come on," he said again, grabbing hold of my hand and pulling me out the house.

We walked up to the stone footbridge over Potter's Creek. It was a cool fall evening, leaves dancing yellow and red all over the Carolina mountains, pretty as a picture postcard. Harlan lifted a half dozen Budweiser bottles from a barrel he kept on the side of the path. He lined them up on the bridge wall, took my hand again, and led me thirty yards through deep meadow grass before he stopped and pulled that sock out of his pocket. A pretty little black pistol slipped out into his waiting hand.

"Where'd you get that?" I asked.

"In the war." He opened it, held it up, and looked through the barrel.

"That ain't your service revolver."

"This here is an Italian gun," he said, sliding what he called a magazine into the handle and slamming it shut. "It's called a Beretta. It's a 9-millimeter. Lighter, easier to use. Holds seven bullets, fires 'em fast, you'll see." He put the gun in my hand and turned me to face the bottles.

"I don't like this, Harlan." I turned back to him and offered the pistol back. "I know how to shoot a gun. Let's go back and have a piece of cobbler. It's got blackberries and white peaches."

"You know how to spray bird shot all over the yard if a possum gets in the henhouse. Things are different now. It ain't just you and me no more. Now, come on, look right over yonder, straighten out your elbow, aim, and squeeze."

Ten minutes later I'd killed more than a dozen beer bottles. I'd satisfied Harlan that I could take care of me and the baby if a raving lunatic happened up the mountain.

I teased him that night, saying "Nothing says love like a 9-millimeter Italian handgun." He laughed and rubbed my belly like it was a magic lamp. "I know," he said, "you'd rather have you a washing machine from the Sears and Roebuck."

By the time my little Gracie come, guns and washing machines flew right out my head. I was full up. Then come Harlan saying "Come on, baby, my mama had one barely walking and one on her hip. You can do it."

"Lord Jesus," I said. "Let me catch my breath."

I didn't care what Mama said about it being my Christian duty to welcome marital love from Harlan. Two months on, I was still sore as raw meat from having Gracie. But I reckon I rolled over to the wall one too many times. When Mama come by the next day to help me with the washing, she took one look at my cut lip and said, "Just wait 'til I tell your daddy, girl."

"Don't tell him," I begged. "Please don't tell him, Mama."

She just swung that big old basket up on her hip and marched out the back door to the washing line. You could never quite figure Mama's mind when she got her feathers up. She wore a hard line across her mouth, whipping them diapers in the air then stabbing them on the line with clothespins. She was still mad when she left me folding the washing. Didn't say bye, didn't say boo.

At six o'clock that evening, my daddy come up the road carrying his strap. Every third step he spit out a cheekful of Red Man, lips hard and sharp as a bent blade.

Harlan looked at me and hissed, "Can't keep your mouth shut, can you?"

He turned and faced the road and drew hisself up tall and straight on the top step. I admired how he was ready to take my father on like a man. Finally the old man would meet his match. But Daddy moved right past Harlan and yanked me up out of my rocker by the arm.

"What'd you do to get that lip, gal? You sass him? You turn him away?"

"I didn't do nothing," I said.

"Yeah? Well maybe that's the problem. You never did do much."

When I got married, I reckoned I'd felt the last of my daddy's strap, but he lowered it onto my back three good times. The first one sent me crumpling to the porch floor. I felt it cut through my dress, felt blood seep up through the cotton. When that next one fell, I felt my dinner move up into my throat, and by the third I smelled it on the porch floor. My heart broke right there that Harlan didn't grab ahold of Daddy's hand. But then, it had been the back of his own that got this started.

"That first one is from me so you don't ever bring shame on this family again." My father bent over me, spitting words like a snake striking. "The second is from Harlan. And the third one?"

I was on my hands and knees staring through the cracks of the floorboards. That yellow dog with the dirt-red belly was curled up under the porch, shaking worse than me. I couldn't see my daddy's eyes, but I knew they was shooting hellfire right through my back. If them eyes could kill, I wouldn't of made it past my third birthday.

"That last one's from Jesus," he said, "who you have defied and sinned against. Don't do it again, gal."

When Daddy stopped yelling, I pulled myself up to sitting like a rag doll, legs straight out, arms flopped at my sides. I leaned my head against the doorjamb and sucked the blood that dripped from my lip. Harlan had his eyes on my daddy, who was already marching down the road, slapping his strap on his thigh. Harlan rocked back on his boots, then took the porch steps in a single leap. In no more than thirty strides he caught up with my father at the fork. I watched as them two stood eye to eye for a good minute or more. They was both big men, well over six feet and rock hard in the middle. Their arms was big as legs from slinging axes and running saw blades through two-hundred-year-old trees. My daddy put his hands on his hips, spit on the ground, then laid a hand onto Harlan's shoulder. He nodded his head two or three times, then turned and disappeared round a row of tulip poplars that lined the road. Harlan had done all the talking.

I don't remember my daddy ever talking my name. He either called me *girl*, *gal*, or *sister*. They say he kicked the bedpost the night I was born. My grandmaw sent him out the room, told him to sober up and go get the preacher. Said she wasn't sure if we was going to have a christening or a funeral. Though it stopped, Mama had lost a good bit of blood and was woozy, fading in and out. They say I looked poorly too, spitting out whimpers instead of a good howl.

Grandmaw Bailey had some Catholic in her and held to baptizing young'ns soon as they come out. She'd a-died if a baby she birthed, especially her own daughter's baby, ended up in the land of Limbo. It was a place, she said, where babies waited just outside heaven to be let in at the end of days. They didn't suffer, she said, but waiting to see the face of the Lord kept them in a yearning state.

When he come back with the reverend, Daddy walked in the house, head down and sober. Mama was sitting up in bed, pretty as a picture, me at her breast. Grandmaw fixed her up with some chicken livers and greens along with a hot cup of blackstrap tea. They say I pinked up right along with her. Daddy was so comforted his wife was still alive he named me on the spot after Grandma Bailey and his dead mother, Rose. He was changed, he swore. Mama always said she married a man who could be mean as a snake one minute, talk sugar and rose petals the next. They say I screamed the whole time the preacher blessed me and dunked me, stark naked, in the washbasin. Daddy finally took me and walked me around the room, saying "So who you hollerin' at Bailey Rose Abernathy? Who in the world got you so mad?"

That was a story my ma and Grandmaw Bailey told all throughout the years. But what I recollect was me getting quiet whenever he come in the room and leaving soon as I said how-do. I broke a thermometer one time and searched forever for the little balls of mercury that slid in between the divan cushions. I learned to be just like that, fast at slipping out and hiding the who of me. My father never heard me sing, never saw the songs I wrote and hid in the shoebox under my bed.

On my wedding day, I heard him tell Mama, didn't I think I was something now I'd married up? Dunhams owned the better of the ridge. Some of Harlan's brothers didn't cut timber, got enough from working their land to make do. My daddy's envy had more to do with Dunhams being happy people, kind folk, not mean to outsiders and coloreds. I caught a look at him when I flung my flowers at a gang of giggling girls. *I'm done with feeling your strap*, I thought. Only hand I was ever going to feel on my face again was Harlan's reaching up to pull me to him, his finger tracing over my bottom lip.

After being hit by Harlan and my daddy in the span of twenty-four hours, I saw my mama's life laid out before me. Just like her I walked around the next day like a mouse, made sure Gracie didn't fuss. We was both little bits of liquid silver sliding under cushions, muffling who we was. The candle on the mud cake was my daddy's strap laying me low. I was right down with that yellow dog cowering in the red dirt.

That night, after I done finished giving Gracie her early feeding, I laid in the bed on my stomach, choking back my hurt. There was a knocking in the front room as Harlan poked at the fire, a thump when he threw on another log. He turned on the radio, then went out on the porch to smoke his Lucky Strike. Roy Acuf's "Great Speckled Bird" come out the speaker, leaked through the crack under the bedroom door, and bathed me in God's love. It was a song that could rock you to sleep or send your soul to soaring.

She is spreading her wings for a journey
She's going to leave by and by
When the trumpet shall sound in the morning
She'll rise and go up in the sky

The moon and a cool breeze come in through the curtains. I let it all, the silver light, the night air, and a hundred years of grandmothers, untie the knot in my stomach. It sent me floating down the Whitewater under a canopy of chestnuts with mountain laurel and barrel moss climbing up the riverbanks. Stars fought through the leaves and the moon hit the water. My hair floated around my head like a black fan. I breathed in earth, pine, and honeysuckle. Now and then I would catch the smell of my own milk as it leaked from my nipples. My soul was at work.

When He cometh descending from heaven
On the cloud that He writes in His Word
I'll be joyfully carried to meet Him
On the wings of that great speckled bird.

I looked over at my baby sucking on her fist. It's a funny thing that something can grow inside your own body and not be you. They cut that cord and this pink, wiggling thing has its own name. How old was I when my daddy hit me the first time? Had I spilled my milk? Crayoled the wall? Gracie released her fist and yawned. She turned her perfect face, whimpered, then settled back into sleep.

I wondered how far the hundred and thirty dollars under the newspaper that lined my underwear drawer would take me. Who was I kidding? I thought myself back to the water and floated in the ripples, pushing myself away from mossy rocks with the tips of my toes. I was drifting, catching the shirttail of sleep. *I could be one of them mothers whose husbands hadn't come back from the war*, I thought. T. Ellen knew a gal worked the hosiery line up in Winston-Salem at Hanes. I could even string tobacco if I had to. There was always jobs stringing tobacco. I kept fighting to get back in that water.

Roy Acuf's saw blade and guitar faded 'til the radio clicked off. Harlan's boots dropped just outside the bedroom door. The door opened and the floorboards creaked as he moved across the room. His belt slipping through them loops and his zipper going down sung dread and retied the knot in my middle tight as a shoelace. God's grace comes and goes quick with me.

He sat on my side of the bed. I felt the sheet pull back and the night air hit my bare skin. I pretended to sleep and prayed to Jesus Harlan wouldn't want me to prove that I'd learned my daddy's lesson.

What I got was a cool cloth, lightly pressed on my skin, and Harlan whistling that song. He lifted the cloth and blew his tune onto my back, cooling my welts, drying my scabs.

"This here was a day gone wrong," he said. "Your daddy oughtn't a-done that. I ought not a-done that. You're a grown woman, birthed a child."

Gracie stirred again in her cradle. Harlan reached his long leg over and pressed the rocker onto the floor.

"I gone off to fight Hitler and come back whole." He went on and blew across my back. "He won't touch you again. He's done with that." Harlan brushed my hair away and rubbed my neck.

We had spent our wedding night in this house. For married people, the mill had white-painted clapboard homes, but they was only passing on the outside. They was nasty once you walked in the door, with rusted water coming out the pipes and winter air seeping through cracks in the walls and up through the floors. This here was an old place on Harlan's daddy's land, but it was built of solid timber and rocks big as your head. After Harlan's uncle died, a black bear they called Squatter moved in and tore up the place. Soon as Harlan asked me to marry him, his brothers and father helped him run ole Squatter off, throwing rocks and firing guns into the air. Then they come up here every evening after work to get it ready. They wouldn't let me see it, but I heard about every crossbeam they added, the new windows, the hot water heater, and the cast iron bathtub it took five men to hoist into the house. After we left our wedding breakfast, me still wearing the prettiest dress I'll ever own, Harlan carried me in this house and laid me down on the bed. Felt like we didn't move from that spot for a month. It was the first time he touched me that wasn't a sin.

One day we had run up onto the top of the ridge that looked out over the Jocassee Gorge and in the bright sunlight, we took off our clothes and lay naked to the sky. Both Harlan and me only talked when we had something to say. But them first months seemed like we ran our mouths like chickens, wanting to know the how and why of every scar.

Harlan got up off the bed and come back with the jar of salve. He sat and spread it gentle-like on my welts and put the jar on the table. I turned and sat up in the bed. Harlan smelled like fresh-cut lumber, sweat, and tobacco—and Unguentine ointment on his fingers. He peeled off his socks and sat in his army underwear. His sunburned chest, without a hair on it, caught the light and warmed the air around us.

"Harlan?" I crawled through a tangle of sheets toward him. "Don't hit me no more."

He looked at the floor between his knees and shook his big head, slow and shameful. When he lifted his chin, he reached out and touched my cheek, then rubbed his thumb over my lip. The sigh that come out of Harlan was all the I'm sorry I needed. But he said, "Shame on me. Shame on me."

I crawled closer, straddled his middle and locked my legs around him. He pulled me into his big arms, careful not to touch my back. I kissed him light on his eyes, his lips, and down his throat.

"It hurts down there where the baby come out," I whispered. "But I can still make you happy."

I took his face in my hands and kissed his mouth. My hands roamed his chest and belly. He moaned as he moved onto his back and let down his drawers.

Later, when we was lying curled into each other, our breathing back to normal, I said it one more time. "Please don't ever hit me again, Harlan."

He reached behind him and patted my leg.

"I'll try, baby. I sure will try."

In a minute he was snoring.

Since he come back from the war, sleep come hard for Harlan, but once he fell off, he was gone. Even Gracie's wailing wouldn't cut through. I gathered a change of clothes, a dozen diapers, and my grandmother's Bible and packed them in a canvas bag that I sat by the front door. Then I took Gracie to the rocker, opened my nightgown to feed her, and put my feet up by the fire. My tears flowed right along with my milk. And along with me, that yellow dog was a-whining, then barking over by the chickens. He did that when the leaves was falling and the wind was up. Brittle things breaking made him jumpy. Not me. I was so tired, I drifted off. But that dog set to howling like a deep-throated thing. The chickens got to squawking, making a racket like I never heard. I was about to get up and call for him to get in the house when I could a-sworn I heard my name screeched like a nasty rattle deep in a throat. *Bailey. Bailey Rose.*

Couldn't be, I thought. My daddy wouldn't have the nerve. Wouldn't nobody else come up here, dark as pitch, without a streetlight for five miles. The dog let loose another long growl and a string of deep barks, and I was on my way to get Harlan. But I stopped. *Last thing I need is him flying off 'cause a raccoon's in the chicken coop,* I thought. "Bang on a couple of pots," he'd say. I moved back to rocking, then realized the dog done stopped. I shifted Gracie to my other breast and leaned back into the pillow at my back. She'd no sooner latched on when I heard a god-awful thing. Wasn't no dog. Sounded like something wild, hissing *Bailey! Bailey Rose!*

I pulled my nipple out of Gracie's mouth and laid her on a blanket by the rocker, then turned off the lamp. She didn't like it and started up.

"Shh, baby girl," I said. "I'll be right back."

I buttoned up my nightgown and walked to the window. I didn't see nothing but black, didn't hear the dog, just some ungodly thing sounding crazy. Sure as Jesus is rose up that's the sound of my drunk daddy's low raspy hissing laid in with the wind and the thrashing tree limbs. *Bailey Rose!* I'd felt the last of his hand on me. My heart banged in my chest; I could hear it in my head and feel it shaking my throat. I looked at Gracie crying and wiggling out of her blanket. I went to the little door in the mantle and grabbed the Italian gun. My hands was sticky from my milk, but I pulled back the safety and opened the front door. It was cold enough to see my breath but that was all. No moon. A dark curtain draped over the whole ridge. The forsythia bushes, a lighter shade of dark, was a-shaking and scraping the side of the house.

The moon peeked out for a second and reflected the only light thing in the yard: that yellow dog laying at the bottom of the steps, his belly opened up from his neck to his hind legs, blood running down the stone path, puddling into the fall roses. I caught sight of his chest rising, then the moon hid itself again. I set to go to him when a roar come through the forsythias and there my daddy was a-coming at me. He smelled of spoiled meat. I backed up toward the door. I peeked in the house and could barely make out my baby wiggling on the floor, crying. There weren't no moon no more. It was shapes, some lighter 'n others. Everything seemed to be moving and for a second I couldn't make out the old man from the cypress tree. I managed to reach back and shut the front door. Soon as I did, he stumbled toward the house, made way for the steps. It was a black man, or my daddy covered in coal dust. In a breath, he sprung for me, showed his teeth. I put that gun in his face and squeezed the trigger just like I done up on Potter's Creek. I squeezed it again and he dropped. He fell so hard it shook the step

I stood on. I walked down, closed my eyes, and shot my father three more times. *What's got you so mad, Bailey Rose Abernathy, what in the world got you so mad?*

"Dunham," I screamed. "Bailey Rose Dunham's my name. I ain't no kin to you!"

I had killed, taken life, but then I was dreaming. I felt nothing, so surely I was asleep. I lifted my nightgown and walked around the blood. I put a bullet in that yellow dog's head and dropped my hands.

Next thing I knew, Harlan was at my side, Gracie in the crook of his arm. The smell of crushed pine needles and the smoke from the fireplace filled up the night air.

"Well, I'll be goddamned," Harlan said.

I knew he was looking at me, but I kept my eyes on the dog.

"That bear's been gone for well over two years now."

"Squatter?"

I spun around. Harlan's flashlight shown on blood and white chicken feathers stuck in that monster's teeth, a whole dead chicken in one of his paws. He lay there on his back, spread out like he was ready for skinning. A rush of relief that I had not shot my daddy come up from my belly, followed just as quick by dread that I ain't. My baby let out a sob and my knees began to buckle. Harlan dropped the flashlight, and in a swoop, he bent and pulled me up with his free arm. I draped myself over his shoulder like an old woman's shawl.

"I only counted six shots," he said as he carried us up the steps. "No matter how bad you want to," he whispered, "don't put the last one in me."

I put my hand on his rough jaw, pinched hard, then patted his cheek.

"I'll try baby, I sure will try."

Girl Interrupted at Her Music

They had met when they were juniors at Syracuse.

"The first thing I noticed about you was this." David Steele dug his fingers into her mass of black curls, kissed her again, and pulled her on top of him.

Nora's hair fell like a curtain around their faces "And the second?" she asked.

"How you glide instead of walk. It's like you move on ice."

The same feet, leaden now, drag from room to room and clomp down stairs like an elephant's might, though surely over the past three years she has lost twenty pounds. But today, Nora Kanter Steele moves up Sixth Avenue as though someone were pushing her from behind, shoving her through crosswalks and against the rush of business suits and shoppers. She spins through the revolving doors of the glass and granite building near Thirty-Eighth Street and takes the elevator to the eleventh floor. At the end of the hall, the CryMark Labs logo is pressed onto the glass door—periwinkle blue, a hopeful color—cool rather than cold. Over the past two days her rage has been replaced by a seething determination, a vivid red on the color wheel.

At the desk, she provides her name, shows her driver's license, and is given a form by an attractive blonde who never makes eye contact and quickly moves away to answer the phone. Nora is about to provide permission to destroy three embryos, the final remnants of her marriage, the last hope that she would ever be a mother, yet she is met with the casual coolness of a bank teller. Somewhere, behind the swinging doors to her left, down a hallway, in a circular vat, is proof—suspended in a fog of ice and magic—that she had once been loved.

She sits with the clipboard on her lap and watches the questions and blank lines swirl. She remembers to breathe, and suddenly the image of David the morning he left for the fertility clinic to provide his *sample* appears on the page like a hologram.

"So, who should I take with me: Miss April, or Miss September?" He stood in their small Brooklyn kitchen and allowed the two center-folds to unfurl.

Nora looked from one to the other. "September," she said. "Except for the face and body, she's a dead ringer for me." She moved past her husband and opened the refrigerator. "She does have good hair."

"Her hair is why she made the cut."

"And Miss April? Why'd you pick her?" Nora poured a glass of orange juice and leaned against the counter with a smirk on her face.

"Her legs. She has long legs, like you." David folded up the maga-zines and reached for his suit jacket. "I'll call you after." He moved to his wife, dug his fingers into her curls, and put his mouth to her forehead. "See you at two."

At two thirty, David held her hand as she lay on her back, her heels cradled in stirrups. With each pinch, she bit her lips and looked up into his dark eyes. His black eyebrows crossed and relaxed. His entire face mirrored hers, softening then smiling when it was over. They had five eggs harvested and fertilized—two implanted and the remaining three frozen.

They had read all the pamphlets, were familiar with everything they ever wanted to know about cryopreservation—especially postthaw embryo survival rates. Dr. Olivet recommended implanting at least three, but Nora and David insisted that two would do. After all, this was the twenty-first century. Science was on their side. They finally felt lucky.

"Take care of those baby buds," David said to Dr. Olivet before she left the operating suite. "Don't mix us up with some blonde couple."

The next day, Nora lay on the sofa with her legs up on a pillow. David came into the room, his cell phone to his ear. He flipped the phone shut.

"That was Mom. She wanted to say, for the hundredth time, that she hoped we'd change our minds and drive up to the cabin." He winked at Nora. "I said we had other plans."

Nora had learned early on to enjoy David's family in small doses. "They can be a tough room," he often said. Barbara Steele was sixty-three and looked fifty. She sprinted up and down the stairs of her lovely home in Westchester County, played tennis three times a week, and biked every weekend. At the cabin in Maine, a rambling, gray-shingled cottage that overlooked the ocean, she jogged the beach every morning at daybreak. "She's something, my Barbara," David's father, Carl, would say and wrap a meaty hand around his wife's shoulder. "Gave birth to four kids without anesthesia and was back on the tennis court in a week. Now that's a woman!"

Barbara had tried desperately to win her only son's affection. All Nora Kanter had done was smile and cradle a cello between her thighs. When David brought her home, their last year at Syracuse University, they were full of private jokes and spent hours studying, with a hand or a foot always reaching, touching. The cello went where Nora went, and when she played, David would lie on the floor, his hands behind his head, eyes closed. "That was lovely, dear," his mother would say, bounding into the room with her tennis racquet. "Anyone ready for a cocktail, glass of wine?"

When they married, his parents begged, even tried to bribe him to leave his software engineering job in Brooklyn and join his father's investment firm. But in the mornings when the two of them left their third-floor walk-up, kissed at the corner, and made their separate ways to work, Nora to the Brooklyn-Queens Conservatory to teach cello and he to his lab five blocks away, they thought their life practically perfect.

After Nora lost her second baby and the fertility bills began to pile up, David agreed to take the train into Manhattan and learn the high-wire act his father performed effortlessly. David needed a net. The only consolation was that Pamela, Nora's roommate from Syracuse, worked with his dad. Pam was a southern girl, a music major who decided at the eleventh hour to switch to finance. "Girl has to make a living," she said. She had a lousy track record with men and often ended up on the sofa with David and Nora, engrossed in old movies, passing a quart of Häagan Dazs between them. Pamela was petite with red hair as short as a boy's. She had a locker-room vocabulary and earned the disdain of Barbara Steele the first time they met. "This house is fucking huge," Pamela said in the foyer of the house in Westchester. But she was brilliant, and Carl hired her on the spot. She also played a passable violin. She and Nora performed duets at luncheons and small receptions. Occasionally, Barbara hired them for events at her club. "That was lovely, ladies," Barbara would say before the applause had ended. "Now, is everyone ready for a cocktail, glass of wine?"

Nora and David told Pam about the in vitro but not his parents. When Nora had lost the last baby, Barbara was in orbit around her daughter-in-law, whose own mother had died years before. She misread Nora's politeness for permission to mother her. David called his mother's attentiveness sm-mothering.

"You need to get your mind off it," Barbara had said as she arranged the pillows where Nora curled into the sofa corner. "Working out more would do you good. Why, I exercise all the time, always have, and I never had a miscarriage." Barbara passed a pillow to Nora. "How about tennis?"

Nora had managed a smile and pressed the pillow to her flat stomach. She ran her hand over the mound it made.

Pam, on the other hand, had taken Nora shopping and to the Met. After they cried together and shopped for shoes, they stood in front of their favorite Vermeer. *Girl Interrupted at Her Music*, painted in the seventeenth century, features the intense gaze of a woman in a red coat and white cap. She looks up at the viewer as though someone has just entered and halted her session. Her teacher, or lover, who stands behind her, continues to look down at the sheet of music. Knowing full well the association of music with love, the full-length portrait of cupid hardly visible in the background, Nora and Pam pooh-poohed the art historians and upon each visit crafted a new circumstance that had provoked the girl to turn.

"Her father," Pam had said. "The music teacher has a hard-on under all those robes and her dad just wants to make sure she isn't going to reach across and give him a little squeeze."

"A likely scenario, but I'm not buying it," Nora said, not taking her eyes off the painting.

"No?"

"The music teacher's wife has just burst into the room." Nora cocked her head and squinted at the little painting. "She's brandishing an early, rather crude but effective, firearm. What you are looking at, Pamela, is the last breath Vermeer's little vixen took."

"My, my, but aren't we dark today? A far cry from the girl who once said it was trick-or-treaters."

Having enjoyed a weekend with her husband at home in New York instead of with his parents in Maine, Nora awoke on Tuesday morning to find David up and dressed.

"I didn't think you were going in at all this week," she said.

"Pam's going to give me her SIMEX tutorial."

"Simex?"

"Singapore International Monetary Exchange to the uninitiated like yourself." David pulled her out of bed and slid his arms around her. "Meet me for lunch?"

"Sure. Call me when you're ready for a break." She kissed him on her way to the bathroom, but he pulled her back and kissed her long and wet and sweet.

"Mrs. Steele?" the blonde in the lab coat comes out from behind her glass partition and stands before her. "Should I take that?"

Nora has only filled in the date: April 20, 2004.

"Do you have a bathroom?" Nora asks, placing the clipboard on a chair.

"Down the hall to the left. You'll need a key." The unsmiling woman goes back to her desk and hands Nora a key.

Nora rolls the plastic chain in her hand like a rosary while she walks to the ladies' room. As she sits on the toilet, she continues to run the thing between her fingers. *Ice cubes. Tiny ice cubes linked together like pop beads to form a key chain. Somewhere between clever and creepy, she thinks. Frozen sperm, frozen embryos, the possibility of what so many want so much mocked in plastic.*

Nora and David were lucky to find their apartment on Henry Street. It was sunny with high ceilings and a back porch they shared with a ginkgo tree. One of the gingko's limbs leaned on the rail like a neighbor's elbow, showing off fan-shaped leaves, then littering them in the fall all over the porch and onto the terrace next door. They strung lights on the tree at Christmas and Chinese lanterns in summer.

All that Tuesday morning Nora felt pregnant. Her nipples were sore and tingling. Of course it was too early, but the discomfort was bliss. She did the breakfast dishes, showered, and answered e-mails. A few minutes before nine, the phone rang. It was David.

"Something hit the North Tower." He was calling from his cell phone. "There's paper flying all over the place, like confetti. Is the TV on?"

"Are you okay?"

"I'm fine," he mumbled.

"What are you eating?"

"Cookies. It's Pam's birthday. We forgot." He swallowed.

"She's coming for dinner, remember?"

"Oh, yeah." Nora heard David take another bite. He spoke with his mouth full. "So, anyway, about ten minutes ago we hear this huge pop. All we can see is smoke and a bunch of paper flying around the windows. We headed down to the sky lobby, but they said everything was cool, so we came back up. Is it on TV?"

"I'll bet it's a traffic helicopter."

Nora moved into the living room and turned on the television. Matt Lauer and Katie Couric, minus their morning smiles, shared the screen with images of the World Trade Center's North Tower. A black gash opened a corner near the upper floors. Strips of polished steel bent away now like shredded tin. Thick, gray smoke poured up its facade, then billowed out over lower Manhattan, dirtying the perfect sky. She told David what she was seeing. When the camera panned out she shifted her gaze to the South Tower, trying to gauge David's floor.

"It's bad," she said. "I don't think it was a small plane or a helicopter. I think you should come home, David." She stood twisting a dish towel. "Please come home."

"Walk with me." He did this often from his cell. She was Tinker Bell sitting just inside his ear.

She listened as he spoke to others: "Hey, Pam, grab your laptop. Nora says this looks crazy."

Seconds later she heard Pam: "Should we meet you on seventy-eight or in the lobby?"

"No," he said. "I'm getting the codes from Dad's office. You go. I'll call you."

"Talk soon." Pam's voice grew faint as the elevator doors shut.

"So much for having a day without the old man, huh?" He was talking to Nora again.

She imagined the route from the elevators to the south side of the building. She paced between the kitchen and the television.

"Hey, Jackson? You leaving?" David had ducked his head into an office.

"I'm right behind you," a man said.

"Are you there yet?" Nora stayed in the curve of David's ear as he walked.

"Yep."

She never tired of being in Carl Steele's vast office with its view of New York Harbor and the Statue of Liberty. It was where the Steele family watched the fireworks in July—looking out, instead of up, at the bursting blooms of light.

"Matt Lauer says it was a commuter plane," she said. "But I don't know; the hole is huge. I don't like this. Just leave now, honey." Nora was pacing with the portable phone glued to her ear.

"Jesus, Nor, I can't leave without the security codes. You don't understand about this shit—it'd take forever if we have to relaunch everything. Dad'll kill me. As a matter of fact, I should call him. Let me call you right back."

"No!" she screamed at him. "Do not hang up that phone! Screw your father, screw the passwords. Just come ho—"

"Come on, Nora!" He cut her off. "This is the problem. You don't really get it. No wonder my father feels like you're not in my corner. You're not in his."

"That is not fair, David." She blew out a sigh. "This is not the time. Just get out of there. Nobody needs you to be a fucking hero, not your dad, not me. Nobody."

Katie Couric was speaking to an eyewitness on the phone, an NBC employee who had dropped her child off at school and saw the plane hit. The woman was back home now watching the towers from her lower Manhattan window. The woman was a pro, but you could feel the anxiety in her voice. The camera zoomed in. Even a novice like Nora knew it wasn't a commuter plane. The hole was huge.

"Okay, okay!" David said. "I got 'em. Relax."

Nora sighed into the phone. "I'll meet you at the subway."

They would go for coffee and bagels at the little place with the television on the wall. He would bring Pam.

The next thing he said was a sound, more animal than human, more gasp than groan—half scream, half wail.

"Turn it off!" He was yelling so loud she jerked the phone away from her ear.

"David?" She swung her head to the living room.

"Oh, baby!"

"David?"

"Nor—"

Her name was lost within a giant, sucking roar, swallowed into nothingness. Looking at the phone, she held the silence in her hand.

"David? David?"

She looked at the television where an orange-and-black fireball engulfed the South Tower.

"Oh my God," Katie Couric was saying. "Oh my God."

Nora didn't remember fighting through the throngs coming the other way out of lower Manhattan. And she would never be able to distinguish between her own memory of watching the South Tower fall and what she later saw on television. Staccato images of walking home under the towering arches of the Brooklyn Bridge would come and go over the following months. The floodlights had caught particles of ash and dust swirling like snow on the hot night. Was it dark, or the air so char covered that it seemed like night? She was part of the leaving masses, covered in ghoulish white powder, eyes darkened with tears and mascara or soot. It was only the blood she clearly remembered—dark and red that cried down her chalky inner thighs.

Nora takes the ice cube key chain and walks up Sixth Avenue to Bryant Park. She gets coffee from a street vendor and sits behind the library. Children traipse in and out with mothers and nannies. Their squeals and giggles sting. It's a bright spring day, as brilliant as the one that flung her world into space three years ago. She prefers cloudy days. But today she endures the sun, hides behind large sunglasses, and moves her café chair under a tree.

At David's funeral, among a sea of black-clad mourners, Nora had crumpled onto the wet grass as she left the church in Scarsdale. She was rushed to the emergency room. "Don't tell my family there was a baby," she said to the doctor before he pushed the vial of Valium into the IV. Three days later, after the D&C, she was found despondent, wandering around the hospital nursery. She spent three weeks in Lenox Hill's psychiatric unit. Carl and Barbara visited often, their grief and anger emblematic of an entire city.

By the time Nora was discharged, Barbara and Carl had set up a foundation in David's name. Barbara had been quoted in the *New York Times* about addressing the needs of victims' families.

Nora saw a therapist twice a week but refused to attend the recommended grief counseling groups. She visited Pam in the burn unit at Presbyterian, but when she came home, she crawled into bed and stayed there for days. She took Zoloft and stared at the cello gathering dust in the dining room.

For six months, Barbara called daily with little pep talks, lines of inspiration, and updates on the foundation. Every time she stopped by the apartment she brought something to, what she called, brighten things up a bit. There were red and blue silk pillows plumped onto the linen sofa. A colorful brocade throw was draped over the arm of the gray tweed chair. An Oriental rug was delivered one day. "For the dining room," the note read. Slowly, over time Nora and David's soothing, neutral apartment became a museum of color.

"The book I read on the process of grieving said introducing colorful items into your home and wardrobe promotes healing." Barbara lifted a heavy jade Buddha from a box and placed it on the coffee table. "I got one for myself. I find it remarkably soothing."

Nora managed a smile as her mother-in-law moved from the Buddha to fluffing pillows. She cared little for the expensive additions, however colorful, to her home. She noticed only that the rooms seemed smaller when Barbara was there. She had no opinion about whether that was a good or bad thing.

One day, in her typical uplifting tone, Barbara got Nora's attention. "By the way," she said, "we had no idea you tried in vitro."

"Pardon me?" Nora sat up on the edge of the sofa.

"Medical bills, insurance statements, everything that would have gone to the office comes to the house now."

"But, those things are private."

"I'm sorry, Nora. I opened it not thinking. I'll drop it off tomorrow and the co-pays from Lennox Hill. They're all paid."

"You didn't have to do that. I can pay them." Nora pulled a blue pillow to her middle.

"Why didn't you tell us?" Barbara said. "David never kept things from us."

"We didn't want to get your hopes up."

"So, that was the D&C? No?"

Nora nodded her head.

"And you couldn't have told me even then?" She drew herself up and lifted her chin. "I can handle disappointment, Nora."

Of course you can, Nora thought. *You can handle the end of the fucking world and the next day plan the postapocalyptic repopulation process.*

Nora took a deep breath. "I wasn't so sure I could handle your handling it." Nora could barely hear her own voice.

"What is that supposed to mean?"

"That you handle things so uncommonly well."

"You make it sound like a fault instead of strength of character."

"Is that what it is? Having character?" Nora snorted a short laugh. "How very Jackie Kennedy of you."

"You know, Nora, we are all you've got and our arms are open to you. But if you keep pushing us away, one of these days we might just stay away. I don't think you really want that. David would be furious."

The unspoken *If you had only come to Maine, this never would have happened* was a bullhorn in Nora's ear. Her own *If you hadn't dragged him to work downtown* was just as loud.

While Barbara continued her work promoting the concerns of victims' families, Nora huddled in her apartment. She left only to get coffee and groceries and to see her therapist, a hand-holding, back-patting older woman full of platitudes and good will. Nora decided she didn't need a grandmother so she quit, reducing her trips to the outer world to the market and her morning visit to the Starbucks around the corner.

The appeals from David's family to join them for holiday dinners and weekends in the country fell on deaf ears. But on a Wednesday in March, a year and a half after David's death, Barbara stood at her door with something she couldn't ignore.

"This came in the mail." Barbara's saccharine demeanor was gone. In its place was a stern line for a mouth. "Go ahead, open it. I did. It's a bill. From a lab. One of those places that freezes . . . things."

Nora took the envelope.

"You are a very foolish and selfish girl, Nora." Barbara moved into the living room, draping her coat and scarf over a chair. "Over a year he's been gone. We've all suffered. But you?" She spun to face Nora. "You suffer when you could have joy. You could have a child. David's child. I thought that's what you wanted. I know it's what *he* wanted. And he'd want it for you now. For all of us."

Nora saw Barbara's tears, but for the life of her, she couldn't move from her spot in the front hall. Each time she thought about the baby buds and imagined going through the process again—without David—a searing pain moved through her. When she imagined an actual child growing inside her and David not feeling that delicious anticipation, not seeing their little girl or boy being born, she was sucked into a hole so dark and deep it could trap her for days. She'd trained herself to avert her eyes from strollers on the sidewalks, newborns strapped to their parents' chests, their little legs dangling.

"We're worried about you," Barbara said. "Worried sick."

Nora managed to walk past Barbara and opened the door.

"You are still depressed."

"Why is it that sounds like an accusation when you say it?"

"Perhaps because you choose to remain in this dream state. What do you do all day? Sit around playing cello in your pajamas, attaching some romantic notion to mourning and melancholia?"

A firing pin pulled in Nora's middle. Words boiled up from her throat and came out at a register she had never spoken.

"Dream state?" She turned so fast her hair whipped and slapped her in the face. For a moment she thought how satisfying it would be to slap Barbara, to push her. "You think I've constructed some sort of fantasy here?"

The clarity of her rage was like a head dunk in an icy pool. It stung but created a certainty she hadn't known since her world collapsed.

"Reality is in every cell of my body, every day. Every fucking day." Nora moved toward Barbara, felt her eyes grow mean and cold. "I see him in the morning, when I have my coffee, when I brush my teeth, when I carry out the goddamn garbage. He's standing there talking to me on the phone in Carl's office." Her hands were fists at her sides. "I can't tell you how many times a day I slip behind his eyes and watch . . . as a million pounds of death comes roaring through that window." She stuck her chin in Barbara's face. "He saw that plane." Tears soaked her cheeks; her nose ran onto her lips. She choked out words. "How many times a day does that black ball of fire slam into your gut? Does it spread out into your arms and fingers? Does it sear into your bones like lava, then blow out the top of your fucking head?" She saw her spit spray as she shrieked the words.

Barbara was grabbing her coat and gloves. "You need help, Nora. You are in much worse shape than I realized."

Nora folded her arms to cradle the stone in her middle. She lowered her voice. "You are clearly better at this than I am. You can channel your rage into your exercise and your committees. It's all I can do to keep mine from consuming my very soul."

"You need medication." Barbara threw her cashmere shawl around her shoulders. It billowed after her down the staircase.

"This is me taking medication." Nora let out a loud sardonic laugh that echoed in the stairwell. "Can't you see how well it's working?"

Back when Nora and David were falling in love she had marveled at the easiness of it, the world changing, body and soul of it. They would hold a sliver of space before their lips touched for long seconds, so close only a filament could slip between them. This is the holy land, she said once. She had loved the mystery of making love, moving into and around each other, at times being of each other, then detaching like separate planets to either side of the bed. If she could find just a bit of that holy space now, she would grab it and press it to her middle like a bandage so it could staunch the pain that oozed so freely from her heart.

In time, Nora canceled her landline, screened her cell calls, and rarely checked her voice mail. When she did, it was often a call from Barbara. "Just checking in to see how you are, dear. Carl and I hope you're giving some thought to our discussion." What Nora believed to be a relationship ender was a discussion?

New words had become part of the American lexicon: *Ground Zero, Bin Laden, 9/11, Taliban*. They tumbled out of the mouths of news anchors and across kitchen tables as easily as *Senate race, New York Yankees, garbage strike*. For Nora, the cloud that rose up from lower Manhattan, the ash of buildings and bones, didn't waft out into New York Harbor and make its way east over the Atlantic. It had become her prison and her refuge, her cushion and her curse.

When David's sister, Carolyn, came in from California, Nora was hopeful she would finally have a sympathetic ear. They had liked each other when they met. They had enjoyed girl talk and shopping for bridesmaid dresses. She teased David as any sister would and rolled her eyes at her controlling mother, telling Nora more than once, "Don't take Mommy too seriously. She's an acquired taste."

Nora agreed to meet Carolyn for lunch. On the way to the restaurant, she caught a glimpse of herself in a store window. She had forgotten to brush her hair, the black drawstring pants were, in fact, her pajamas, and the coat she was wearing was an old suit jacket of David's, the sleeves of which hung over her fingertips. It was a wet October day in 2003. Her flip-flops sloshed through the dirty puddles.

Carolyn did a poor job of hiding her shock when they embraced, smiled, and nervously chatted about the kids and her husband. They had been wonderful after David's death. Carolyn stayed in the guest room until the day of the funeral, making sure Nora ate a little each day. Carolyn had flown back and visited Nora at Lennox Hill and held her hand and cried with her more than once as she struggled back. Most importantly, Carolyn had gone to visit Pam at the burn unit at Presbyterian and brought Nora a note. The message read: "*Girl Interrupted* has just noticed it is Vermeer with the boner!" Nora's sudden outburst of laughter sent Carolyn running for the nurse.

"Are you seeing anyone?" Carolyn asked after their ice teas arrived.

"Seeing anyone? You mean a therapist or a man?"

"A guy."

"Oh God, no. I'm not ready for that. Christ, I haven't even thought about it."

Nora noticed a distinct sigh of relief from across the table. She frowned at her sister-in-law.

"I think Mom and Dad are worried you'll meet someone. You know, a rebound kind of thing. I mean they don't begrudge you, none of us would . . ."

"You can put their minds at ease." Nora put her straw in her tea and took a sip.

"I guess what they're really worried about is that you'll remarry and you know . . ."

"No. I don't know."

"Well, move away, not see them anymore."

"I don't see them now."

"Well, that's part of the problem, isn't it? They're concerned about you. You're a beautiful woman. You will marry again and have children, adopt perhaps."

Nora looked at the perfect blonde hair that grazed her sister-in-law's white collar. A black velvet blazer, without a single piece of lint, hung over her slim shoulders.

"I would think they would be happy for me if that happened." Nora shook her head, deflated at the meeting. "What the fuck is it with your parents?"

"I know they're difficult, but . . ."

"Let's be frank, Carolyn. They don't like me, never have. Why do they give a shit if I get better, meet somebody, and adopt a bunch of babies, or cats, for that matter."

"Please, Nora. They're just worried you'll forget about David's, you know, embryos. Surely you can understand that."

Nora leaned in. "David is dead, Carolyn. He doesn't have embryos. He doesn't *have* anything."

Carolyn, looking hurt, reached out to touch Nora's hand. Nora pulled her arm back and let the waitress place her salad in front of her.

"They just want you to be happy, to be okay. Not like this. They have dreams, like all people their age, to be grandparents."

"They are grandparents. They have your little darlings." Nora spoke through her teeth.

Carolyn ignored her. "David was their . . . shining star. You know that. They . . . I don't know, Nora, they just miss him so much, and to know his child is out there, or the possibility of his child . . ."

Nora shoved her plate across the table. The entire restaurant turned as it crashed to the floor. She stood and glared at her sister-in-law.

"Tell them they're wasting their time. I'd fucking kill myself before I'd have a child right now. David's child or any child."

People at the surrounding tables wiped pieces of lettuce from their shoes. The waitress came over and asked if everything was all right.

"No!" Nora yelled into the crowded room. "Everything is not alright. This woman is not right." She pointed at Carolyn. "This woman is bothering me."

Nora fled toward the door. She heard Carolyn apologizing to the waitress and the surrounding patrons.

"She's not well," she was saying, "lost her husband…my brother…in the towers."

"Leave me the fuck alone!" Nora screamed as she swung the door open. "Get the fuck out of my life."

On the sidewalk, she wiped her running nose on David's sleeve and blindly ran down the street toward the subway. She bumped into a man coming up the steps. "Jesus!" he recoiled and spun away from her. She turned and saw him wipe the sleeve of his jacket with a gloved hand.

As she stood on the subway platform, she looked down at her dirty toes and allowed the black to overtake her. As each train screeched to a stop, or an express train thundered past, she heard explosions, David's guttural moan, *Oh, baby, Nor—*. She stood close as a dozen trains passed. With each one, she inched her rubber soles closer to the edge of the platform. *How easy it would be to step off just as the next express train reaches that post there, two back. There would be no time to break—I could just close my eyes and slip, slip, crumple onto the rail.* But she didn't have an Anna Karenina bone in her body. She was a coward, or perhaps less lost than she thought.

When she walked into the apartment, she stood at the French doors to the terrace and looked at the ginkgo tree as its first leaves loosened and flipped into the air. The rain had given way to sun and cotton clouds. She tossed David's suit jacket onto a chair, peeled off her shirt, untied her pants, and let them drop into a pile at her feet. She stood naked as a torrent of leaves fell from the tree, covering the porch, the little bistro table and chairs, the plant stand and empty clay pots. Strange that she hadn't noticed how she smelled, like dirty sheets and BO and stinking hair.

An hour later she had showered and shampooed, pulled on a pair of black leggings and a soft cashmere tunic the color of flushed cheeks.

"It makes your tits look great," David had said as he reached his arms around her middle and nuzzled her neck outside the dressing room the day she tried it on.

"Here at Barneys," she said, "they don't let you put things back on the shelf after talk like that." She looked around, then pulled him into the dressing room.

They had made love silently, breathlessly, amidst skirts and sweaters and a saleswoman asking if she needed any help.

"I'm good," Nora had panted. "I'm good."

With memories of David's touch fresh in her mind, she coiled her wet hair and clipped it at the back of her head, then dialed the number of a therapist Pamela had seen years before and made an appointment for the following week. She opened the French doors, moved a dining room chair into place, and reached for her cello.

It never ceased to amaze her how quickly the ginkgo shed its leaves. The first would drop one morning and by evening the tree was bare. It happened all over New York, the little leaves sticking in windshield wipers, carpeting sidewalks and front stoops. They fluttered now into the room, so pretty as the sun caught the fan-shaped leaves, sending a dappled carpet of them into her dining room. She cradled her instrument between her knees and let her cheek rest on its neck.

"I am so lonely," she said into the room. "I am so lonely."

Like Monet at Argenteuil, greens and golds collected around her toes, the endpin of her cello. They fastened themselves onto her sweater and covered Barbara's beautiful rug. The bow made its way across the A-string as the torrent of tiny fans swirled around her shoulders. The rich vibrato of a Bach sonata seeped into her body and filled her, for the moment, with the only kind of healing she knew.

What had begun as a searing pain that the body's own opiates dulled, for survival's sake, in time allowed loneliness to break through and then finally a need to fill the void that even music couldn't touch.

By February she needed air. She walked along Pierrepont Street late one snowy afternoon. Flakes as big as doilies fell on her nose and lashes. She stepped into an empty salon and got her eyebrows waxed. When the beautician was done, a stylist came up behind Nora. She took a lock of Nora's hair.

"Do you mind?" the stylist asked.

"No." Nora sat and the woman wove her hair into a thick, beautiful knot at the base of her neck.

"Voilà!" the woman said, securing the knot with a tortoiseshell clip. "You can be anything tonight. A flamenco dancer." She clicked her heels. "A woman of mystery." She draped Nora's scarf over her head, brought it around to cover all but her eyes, then patted her shoulders and let it fall. "You will break hearts."

"How much do I owe you?" Nora stood and reached for her purse.

"Nothing." The woman walked her to the front of the salon. "You already paid for your brows."

"No, please."

"It's my shop," the woman said, lifting a pink rose from a vase at the door. "Happy Valentine's Day."

When spring came, Pamela called. They hadn't spoken since she got back from South Carolina where she had recuperated at her parents' home. She was back in Manhattan and working again for Steele and Associates, now six blocks from Ground Zero. They met for lunch, then strolled the galleries in the Met. Over their meal, they had bantered and caught up on small things. When they approached their Vermeer, they sat on a bench in front of the tiny painting.

"You don't even see them," Nora said, pushing away the thick bangs that Pam had grown to camouflage the scars on her forehead. Deeper, red ones crisscrossed up her arms, hidden now by long sleeves.

"No more pixie cuts for me."

"It's so last season." Nora patted her friend's fringe back into place.

"I flew back from Charleston," Pam said.

"Were you a wreck?"

"The security freaked me out, but the flight was fine. My father, now he was a total wreck." She laughed. "But, I had to do it. I can't be a prisoner. None of us can." Pamela moved closer and took Nora's hand.

"Are you here to counsel me?" Nora asked. "Did they send you to perk me up?"

"No. I wanted to see you. To see how you are."

"And how am I?" Nora turned.

Pamela cocked her head and studied Nora's face. "I don't know." She smiled. "You were his rock, you know."

"Me?"

"Absolutely. He was amazed by how you dealt with everything, with the miscarriages, his parents, your students. We all were."

Nora smiled, warming to the memory of her husband. "He was the strong one," she said. "And the funny one. God, I miss how he made me laugh."

"They've hired a lawyer." Pamela had turned back to the painting. No expression, just words. "And a private investigator."

"Who? What for?"

Pam turned. "They have all your medical records. There's a file."

"A file about what?" Nora leaned closer and studied Pam's face.

"Barbara brought this to the office, left it in Carl's office." She passed a xerox of a clipping to Nora. "I found it after everybody left yesterday." *Grandparents Seek Custody of Frozen Embryos.* "The case in the clipping—it's the mother who is deceased. The father remarried, had kids with the new wife. The wife's parents want the embryos."

Nora looked at Pamela's neatly clipped fingernail as it tapped at the headline. She removed her sweater, loosened her scarf. Slowly she allowed a pent-up breath to leave her chest.

"They've all begged me to go through it again. Even Carolyn came in from California."

"I heard about that," Pam said. "Barbara said, 'Nora thinks mourning becomes her.'"

"How pithy. Though not one of my finest moments."

Nora hung her head, putting the tips of her fingers to her lips. When she lifted her head, Pamela was staring at her, biting her lower lip.

"What?" Nora asked. "What now?"

"Carl has a website bookmarked. Family Creations. Very professional, quite legal, all aboveboard."

Nora looked confused.

Pam leaned forward. "It's a site to locate surrogate mothers."

"Oh, give me a break. This is crazy," Nora said. "And use my embryos? They can't be that nuts!"

"Nobody is questioning *their* sanity, Nora."

"What are you saying?" Nora moved to face her friend head-on.

"If they can determine you're unfit, a danger to yourself . . ." She swallowed hard. "They have a lawyer who's been successful in the past. And there's something else you should know. Carolyn had a tape recorder with her when the two of you had lunch. They have photos of you looking pretty awful and statements from a couple of your students, the doctors at Lennox Hill, and the therapist you saw after, the one you stopped seeing. The head of your department at the conservatory said he was grateful you quit before he had to let you go. He said you were unstable, that you threw your bow across a practice room on more than one occasion. Students were afraid of you."

Nora stood and moved to the little painting. She bit at her thumb. The girl in the red coat looked directly at her. They studied each other's faces. *Who just walked in on your life, little one?* Nora asked the girl.

"I'm better now." Nora turned to Pam and offered a weak smile. "I eat two apples a day and I shower. And I play. Every day I play for two, three hours . . . and no more requiems. Bach and Mozart. I haven't played Beethoven in years." They both chuckled. "And I'm seeing Dr. Salvo. Remember her, the therapist you saw when that asshole broke up with you?"

"Which asshole?" Pam stood and took Nora's arm.

Nora knew that she had separated from the world. But she had not broken from herself. She had been imprisoned as surely as if she had been tried and convicted and led off to a cell. Yet she had been the jailer, and it was she who was doing the releasing. She was still unbelievably lonely and empty, but in recent weeks she had begun to beg for healing, and in the begging, she felt the cracks begin to mend.

"I feel like I'm pieces of this old earthen jar," she said as she and Pam left the museum. She pulled her scarf around her neck when they got outside. "If I get them all glued back into place, I can fill myself up again and stop leaking me out."

They stood on the stone steps looking out on Fifth Avenue. The buzz of the Upper East Side hummed around them.

"If you ever want to do it," Pam said, "I mean thaw those little guys out and go for it again, I'll be with you. I'll do whatever it is you need, be Auntie Pammy. And if you don't, I'll be here for that too. Whatever that is."

"Are you wearing a wire?" Nora asked.

Pam threw her head back and laughed. The wind blew her hair from her forehead. "God, I have missed you."

The two women hurried down the steps and hailed a cab.

That night, Nora begged for clarity. She railed at David for leaving her, for not being there to protect her. Panic rose as she imaged her child growing in another woman, being delivered into the arms of Barbara Steele or her daughter, Carolyn. She caught only moments of sleep, and even that was peppered with dreams of a figure in a gray cape swooping in and lifting a swaddled infant who lay cradled into the curl of her cello.

When she awoke she dug through the folder of bills and found the address for CryMark Labs. She dressed and left the house.

Nora Kanter Steele sits in Bryant Park winding the tiny plastic ice cubes around her fingers. A group of deaf children huddle in a semicircle nearby as a storyteller dressed as Little Bo Peep sweeps her hands and fingers in the air, signing stories.

When Bo Peep finishes, the children clap and make muffled sounds, then scatter, chasing each other around the park, oddly quiet. Nora is practiced at avoiding children, yet she doesn't move from her chair. Instead, she closes her eyes and lifts her face to the sun. The warmth and the crisp air infuse her like the exchange of oxygen turns dark blood bright. When she opens her eyes a small girl is standing before her, head cocked, staring into Nora's face. She furiously moves her fingers then pounds her little fist into the other palm.

"I'm sorry." Nora smiles at the little girl. "I don't sign. I don't know what you want?"

Quickly, Bo Peep comes over and kneels down next to the child. The two sign back and forth. A broad smile fills the storyteller's face.

"She wants to know if you are Snow White."

Nora smiles at the little girl who looks at her adoringly. She shakes her head and says, "No, I'm just a lady."

"I think it's your hair and your pale skin," Bo Peep says as she signs back to the little girl. "Here."

She shows Nora an old illustration in the book she'd been reading. In the image, a pre-Disney, womanly Snow White sleeps under glass. She has cascades of dark curls and a crimson shawl, like the red scarf Nora is wearing, draped around her shoulders.

"What's she saying now?" Nora asks, as the little girl is furiously signing.

A somewhat embarrassed Bo Peep answers, "She wants to know if she can kiss you awake."

Slowly, Nora closes her eyes, leans forward, and offers the child her cheek. When the little wet lips land, Nora yawns and stretches out her arms and opens her eyes. She looks down at the little girl and smiles. The child looks at Bo Peep, turns red, spins, and runs back to the other children.

Nora walks back to Thirty-Eighth Street and takes the elevator to the eleventh floor. Not bothering to hide her disapproval, the woman behind the glass looks at her. Nora hands over the key chain and the woman pushes the clipboard through the glass. Nora pushes it back and turns.

"What are your instructions, Mrs. Steele?" The woman's chill could have frosted the glass.

Nora spins back to the woman. "A little sensitivity would be a nice start."

"But what about . . ."

"My baby buds? Just keep 'em on ice." At the door Nora turns to the woman. "That key chain," she says, "it's not clever."

An hour later Nora and Pamela stand in lower Manhattan looking through a chain-link fence as bulldozers and men in hard hats move dirt around a giant hole. Tourists stick camera lenses through the diamond shapes and click. She and Pam have come together, like two arachnophobes testing themselves in front of a giant spider's web.

"Are you OK?" Nora asks.

"It's so big." Pam exhales. "I'm fine. You?"

"I'll feel it later."

The anxiety of the morning has finally dissolved. In its place is something Nora hasn't known in years: possibility. She reaches for her friend's hand.

"Tell me about Charleston," she says. "Is it a place where one could teach, raise a child, have a life?"

"It's beautiful," Pamela says. "The College of Charleston is a great school, wonderful music department. Beautiful old homes along the Battery, none taller than a church steeple." They pull their eyes away from the construction vehicles and smile at each other.

Somewhere in this vast hole a molecule exists that holds a trace of David along with the cells of thousands. Nora bends and pinches a crumb of dirt between her fingers. Might a tiny bit of David pass through her skin into a corpuscle and make its way through the rivers of vessels to her heart? She stands and rolls her thumb and finger together until the dust disappears into the circles of her fingertips.

A Split in the Seam

Amelia sat on top of a tall bureau watching the almost middle-aged couple make love in the bed across the room. Her long legs, crossed at the knee, dangled off the edge of the dresser. In the moonlight she looked down and admired her pedicure. "Cactus Bloom" the bottle in her hand read. She'd found it in a dresser drawer after her daughter fell asleep, before the husband awoke her and began stroking her neck and breasts.

"Is this some kind of Walkman?" Thad was in the doorway, his daughter's iPod in hand.

"He reminds me of you." Amelia smiled at the bed as her son-in-law moaned.

"Jesus, Amelia!" Thad closed his eyes and turned his back. "This is a little much don't you think?"

"Why?" Amelia looked down and brushed a line of Cactus Bloom onto a fingernail. "I mean it would have been before. But now . . ." She looked back at the bed. "It's sweet."

"Remember, we're just stopping by. This isn't a visit."

"I know." She didn't look up; she moved on to the other hand, spreading the polish evenly on each nail.

"So, what is this thing? How the hell does it work?" Thad stood outside the bedroom door and continued to look at the slim, white gadget in his hand.

"It's called an iPod." Amelia smiled at her husband's large fingers tangled in thin, white wires. She moved to his side. "Put the little buds inside your ears."

Thad slipped a tiny speaker into one ear, then repeated the process in the other.

"Here." Amelia blew on a nail, then pressed play.

"Mother of Christ!" Thad hollered into the room. "Now that's sitting right in the goddamn horn section. This Wynton Marsalis guy is something else." He winked at his wife, who had resumed her spot on the bureau, and walked down the hallway.

After her daughter and son-in-law had fallen back asleep, Amelia floated to the floor and sat on the dresser stool.

"Still not bad for fifty-five," she said into the mirror as she coated her lashes with her daughter's mascara. She applied some Elizabeth Arden, blotted her lips, and smiled at her reflection.

"They have no refrigerator." Thad was back.

"Of course they do. They're in drawers these days—those big drawers in the island—the thing in the middle of the kitchen. Pull them open, you'll see."

Thad walked away as Amelia pulled a pink satin gown out of her daughter's closet. She waltzed around the room holding it up by the hanger, then stopped when she got back to the closet.

"Lovely," she said with a sexy growl. "Stilettos are back." She slipped her foot into one of her daughter's shoes. "This new one sure does keep her well dressed." She winked at the bed.

"Cocktail?" Thad stood with a beer in one hand, something clear and bubbly in the other."

"Is that a gin and tonic?"

"Yup."

"We've never done that. Can we?" Amelia slipped off the shoe and took the glass.

"I don't see why not. Feels the same. Tastes good."

Thad gave his wife's ass a pat and followed her down the hall. They sat on the living room sofa in the dark. Amelia picked up a framed photo from the table.

"I forget how handsome you were with hair."

In the picture the two of them smiled, holding a toothless baby who was thrusting a toy airplane at the camera.

"He was a handful, wasn't he?" Thad took the picture, then put it back on the table.

"He is a very handsome young man today," Amelia said. "Looks a lot like his grandfather."

"I like this one." Thad picked up another frame.

It was an old photo of Amelia, pregnant and beaming, standing in the surf with a toddler holding one hand, another circling her thigh. Her free hand cupped her belly, low on the right.

"That was the day I went into labor with her. Remember?"

"I remember you hitting me, saying it was all my fault. But you said that after Tim and Karen too."

"I swore I'd never have sex again after each baby."

"Good thing you stunk at keeping your word."

Amelia tossed a pillow at her husband.

"What's that?" Thad said, pointing to a large black rectangle above the fireplace.

"The television, silly."

"Son of a bitch." Thad rose, put his beer on the coffee table, and looked behind the TV.

"No tube." He looked at the room behind him. "No projection either."

"Honey, everything's digital these days. The signal either comes from satellites or cables buried in the ground."

"How do you know all this?"

"I visit more often."

Thad found the remote and turned on the television. The brilliant screen lit the room. Within seconds he found ESPN. His shoulders dropped back into the sofa cushion.

"Can you believe Phil Jackson is coaching the Lakers?" He shook his head.

"You look like you've died and gone to heaven," Amelia said.

Thad looked over at his wife, smiled, and winked.

Early the next morning, Tess Delaney slipped on a tank top and pajama bottoms and hurried down the hall, out the door, and onto the curb where her husband, Peter, was getting into his car.

"You forgot something," she said.

"What?" Peter looked at his suitcase and the suit jacket draped over his arm.

"This." Tess lifted her tank top, revealing her torso and breasts, amazingly round and firm for forty-five. Peter quickly grabbed her and pulled her toward him.

"You're going to get us both arrested," he said, nuzzling her neck.

"You need to wake me in the middle of the night more often." Tess flicked his earlobe with her tongue.

Peter Delaney cupped his wife's ass and gave her one more kiss before he slid in the front seat of his car.

"Did you pack Jack's sweatshirt?" she asked.

"Yes."

"Give him a kiss for me."

"I'll give him a hug. Get back in the house. I'll call you after work, before I hit the road."

When he disappeared around the corner, Tess went back in the house, poured herself a cup of coffee, and turned on the little TV that sat on the kitchen counter. Joe Scarborough and Mika Brzezinski were interviewing Chuck Todd, who stood on the North Lawn of the White House. Tess pulled up a stool and propped her feet on the counter's edge. A member of the White House groundskeeping crew kept walking behind Chuck Todd. Each time he began to answer a question the gardener ripped the leaf blower and drowned out the reporter's answer. In the studio Scarborough and Mika had begun to laugh.

"Somebody should check that guy's credentials, don't you think, Chuck?" Scarborough said. "Ten bucks says he's a Fox contributor."

Chuck Todd adjusted his earpiece.

"I'm sorry, Joe. I didn't get that." He had begun to laugh himself.

A second later, a torrent of leaves and debris blew into the camera. Chuck Todd was spitting particles and wiping pieces from his hair and lapels. Tess began to laugh along with everyone on the television. As she threw her head back, she caught something out of the corner of her eye.

"Whaaa? What the fuck!"

Her scream was so loud and shrill it scared even her. But she kept it up. She jumped off the stool, spilled her coffee down her tank top and onto the floor.

"Jesus fucking Christ!" she screamed at the top of her lungs. "What the fuck? What the fuck?"

"Thad! Thad!" Amelia yelled into the hallway. "You better get in here. I think we've transitioned!"

"What the hell is this?" Tess backed up to the sink. "Who are you? What's going on here?"

"It's OK, sweetie. It's me. Everything's fine." Amelia was walking toward her daughter, noting fear in those beautiful eyes.

"Everything is *not* fine!" Tess moved and put the kitchen island between them. "You are dead. So this is not *fine*."

"Now, now, honey, 'dead' is such a final term. We don't use that word."

"Is this some kind of Disney thing? Are you mechanical?"

"Oh, no. It's me, see? Here, you can pinch me if you like." She moved forward again, but Tess held up a hand, then made a cross with her fingers.

"Oh, honey, that doesn't work. You've been watching too much Harry Potter."

"God, you sound just like her."

"I am her. I mean me. I'm me."

Suddenly, Tess brought her hands to her mouth, her eyes like donuts. The gasp filled the room as she looked beyond Amelia to the doorway to the dining room.

"What's going on?" Thad was in the doorway, took one look at his daughter, and dropped his shoulders. "She can see you?"

"I can *see* both of you!" Tess yelled.

"Jesus, Amelia, what'd you do?" Thad said.

"I don't know." Amelia looked at him and shook her head. "I was just standing here watching her laugh. I was so happy she was laughing, you know, like she used to. Then I remembered her at the airport."

Amelia turned to her daughter. "Remember, honey? Remember how sad you were? Pregnant, married to that asshole. You kept holding my arm, saying, 'Please stay a few more days, Mom, please.' I thought that would be how I'd always remember you. Then I saw you with Peter last night, and here this morning, and I got this feeling . . . so happy, so . . . like my tank was full."

"What do you mean you saw me with Peter last night?"

Amelia reddened.

"Oooo, gross. You are a pervert. This is some kind of weird ass shit."

Tess looked from her mother to her father and back again. She turned and walked out the back door, bent down, and put her hands on her knees like she did after a long run. Amelia and Thad heard a long, low groan.

"Is she doing that hangdog thing? The yoga?" Thad looked past Amelia, trying to see his daughter. "She always did that. Remember?"

"Downward facing dog," Amelia said. "No. I think she's just trying to catch her breath."

After a few minutes Tess walked back in.

"Still here." She looked from one to the other. "This is just fucking perfect. I finally get my life back, finally marry a man I adore, and now I'm having visual and auditory hallucinations. I'm fucking crazy. Schizophrenic, right? Thanks a lot, God." Tess shot her middle finger to the ceiling. "Once again, your timing is impeccable."

"Honey, you're not crazy." Amelia moved forward but stopped when Tess threw up a hand and moved to the other side of the island. "This is just some kind of leak though, sweetheart. Like a seam in a curtain that kind of . . . splits sometimes."

"Oh, there are curtains? Exactly how does that work, Mom? You're on one side, we're on the other? That's what happens when you die? You just slip behind a screen?"

Thad watched his daughter raking her fingers through her hair, bobbing her head at her mother, fists clenching, opening, then closing again. It was a familiar scene. To him, an old scene, with new words.

"No, Tessie, there are no walls," Amelia said. "Per se."

"Good. 'Cause I thought you just went to heaven and hung out with dead movie stars. Got to chat with Kennedy, Marilyn Monroe." Tess looked at the ceiling. "Oh Christ. Why am I seeing things? Why am I talking to dead people?"

Slowly, Thad moved toward his daughter. He could smell the spilt coffee on her shirt, her breath. She put up her hand. Thad stopped. Slowly, she lifted her palm and touched his shirt. It was the plaid thing he was wearing the day he turned before going down the Jetway. He had given her his usual thumbs up then, raised the thumb to his ear, his little finger to his lips. "Call you when we land," he mouthed. Now in her kitchen, she eyed the buttons on his shirt, then finally allowed her head to fall onto his collar, allowed his beefy arm to pull her tiny frame into him.

"Daddy," she said. "What is going on? Why are you here?"

"I'm not sure, kiddo. But here I appear to be."

An hour later Tess had showered and was lying on the bed with her mother.

"Does this happen to other people?" she asked.

"What other people?"

"Other dead people. Oh, excuse me, does that hurt your feelings to call you a dead person. Not politically correct in the afterlife? Do other life-challenged people visit *their* families?"

"I've heard about it only in the abstract. It's not like we sit around chatting about what we do."

"And what do you do? I mean how do your spend your days?"

"Well, you know your father and I didn't get a chance to retire, never really traveled all that much. So we go places."

"You mean like London, Paris?"

"Well, yes, but we prefer more out-of-the-way places. Just last week we were with the nicest family in this tiny village in the Maldives. Oh, honey, it is so beautiful there."

"How did you meet them?"

"Meet who?"

"The family, Mother. The family in the Maldives."

"Oh, we never met them. They didn't know we were there."

"So you just show up at someone's home, move through walls, and spy on people?"

Amelia laughed. "You know, I would never move through a wall. There's no need for tricks."

"I got Jack's bicycle tuned up." Thad came in, wiping grease from his hands. "Hell of a bike. But that helmet. Jesus. Thing looks like the top of a bug's head."

"Thanks, Dad."

"It's nice they get along so well," Amelia said.

"Who?" Tess looked at her mother.

"Jack and Peter. So nice they do things together, you know biking, basketball. Not all stepfathers get along with their kids."

"Do you read minds too?" Tess turned around and faced her mother. "I was just thinking how nice it is I don't have to take the bike in to get it tuned up because Peter and Jack are biking in Marin next weekend. You knew that, didn't you? And you know Peter's going up to watch him play Sacramento this weekend."

"I don't know if I knew," Amelia said.

"I knew," Thad said. "That Jack could go pro if he plays his cards right, best point guard in the PAC-10."

"That's why you're here now, isn't it?" Tess got off the bed. "Nobody's home. Husband driving up to see my son at college. No chance my anybody will come in and catch me talking to a couple of ghouls." Tess moved into the bathroom.

"Honey." Amelia was instantly sitting cross-legged on the bathroom vanity. "We're not crazy about 'ghouls' either." Amelia shook her head. "It's not a term that evokes a positive sentiment."

Tess spun her head. "Wow, I wish I could do that, just pop here, pop there. I would have caught my ex in the sack with that bimbo years before I finally did. And look at how limber you are. You could never cross your legs."

"I must say," Amelia picked up an eyeliner and looked at herself in the mirror, "it does amazing things for the joints."

The two women applied their makeup.

"Hey, how come I can see you in the mirror. You're not supposed to be visible in mirrors, are you?"

"No, silly, that's vampires. We're corporeal spirits. Vampires aren't real." Amelia blotted her lipstick on a tissue.

"Why me?" Tess asked. "Why don't you go visit Karen or Tim? They were perfect children and now they're perfect adults. Four point five children between them. Fabulous homes. I mean, come on, who doesn't want to go to Palo Alto or to the Upper East Side of Manhattan? Why don't you go scare the shit out of them?"

"They never call." Amelia had moved back into the bedroom and was smoothing out the bedspread, fluffing pillows.

"What did you say?" Tess came back into the bedroom.

"She's teasing," Thad said, adjusting the remote control drapes.

"No, she's not." Tess took the pillow out of her mother's hand. "What do you mean they never call? I didn't call." Tess looked pleadingly at her mother and sat on the bed. "I didn't call. Did I?"

Amelia looked at Thad, who had put his hands in his pockets and stared at his shoes.

"Did I call you, Mom? Is this like when the phone would ring and I just knew it was you . . . like when Tony and I started having problems? We'd have a fight and five minutes later you'd call?"

"Maybe." Amelia lined up the perfume bottles on Tess's dresser.

"It took me years to stop grabbing for the phone to tell you something wonderful . . . or horrible," Tess said. "Years to stop running up to strangers on the street who looked like you."

Thad had left the room. Neither woman noticed.

"Perhaps it's misleading to say that you called," Amelia said.

"Oh, I called." Tess had dropped her voice almost to a whisper. "I called you for years. After the crash. After I lost the baby. Through the divorce."

Her freshly applied mascara began to run, so did her nose. "I stood in that airport holding you, while Dad went to get his fucking newspaper and chewing gum. I remember telling you it would be good for the two of you to spend a few days apart, that Dad would be fine without you. I was scared, and all you could say was 'Be strong, honey,' and some crap about how we teach people how to treat us and how I needed to let Tony know that it was completely unacceptable to bully me. I told you I'd been spotting. You told me I was too thin. I begged you to stay a few more days, just a few more days." Tess stood, her entire face ran with tears, mascara, snot, and words. "He hit me and I was pregnant. I told you, but you didn't believe me."

"I did believe you! I also believed you needed to tell him to leave, or leave him yourself. I . . . your father and I believed we shouldn't meddle, that you should handle your own issues." Amelia pulled up the dresser stool so that their knees touched. She took a tissue and wiped her daughter's face. "You were so taken with his image, his work. It was like you were a devotee of his bullshit. Tony Besseli wrote a best-selling novel. He didn't write the goddamn Bible."

"He kept saying you had a drinking problem. Did you know that?" Tess said.

"Who? Tony said I had a drinking problem?"

"Yes. You'd have a glass of wine and take a nap. Remember? You seemed to be napping the whole time you were here that last time. 'Sipping and sleeping.' That's what he said. 'You're mother's turning into a drunk. I hope it doesn't run in the family.'"

"I can see how he thought that," Amelia said. "We'd bought a case of that Pino in Napa. Remember? It was lovely."

"I remember hoping you were good and drunk when the plane went down. I prayed that. Were you?"

"No."

Tess searched her mother's eyes, exploring the whites, the blue, the black pupils. She traced a wiry, red vessel that disappeared under an upper lid.

"It was quick." Amelia lied while brushing a strand of hair from her daughter's face. "A breath of hot burning air, then a beautiful blue sky."

"You were sitting together, right?" Tess asked.

"Oh yes." Amelia let out a chuckle. "Your father often says his last alive memory is of the perfume on my neck."

Amelia looked at Tess's eyes pinched closed, felt the shudder that moved through her daughter's middle. There was a long, thin scab that never quite closed the way it had with her other children. It could be loosened at one end, pulled and unzipped easily, revealing a wound that never seemed to heal from the inside out.

"I came home after I dropped you off at LAX and took a nap." Tess opened her eyes and pulled her legs up onto the bed and curled into a pillow. "Tony came in and woke me hours later. I don't know how long I slept. He was asking me what your flight number was and whether it was nonstop or if you had a layover. I didn't know what the hell he was going on about. Then the phone rang and it was Karen. I remember running into the den and looking at the television, that damn phone in my hand. Smoldering pieces of metal, some announcer saying your flight number, saying 'LA to Detroit,' saying 'apparently no survivors' . . . 'search for the black box will begin at daybreak.' I don't remember anything else . . . not until I woke up in the hospital staring at a bag of blood that was plugged into the crease of my elbow. A nurse patting my arm, saying I'd lost the baby. But you know all this, don't you?" Tess looked at her mother.

"I knew about the baby, but, no, I didn't know Karen called you. But of course she would. She's such a news junkie. Has the television on all the time."

Tess reached out and grabbed her mother's wrists. "'I can't do this without you.' That's what I kept saying the whole time I was in the hospital." Her eyes had filled her face, the tiny muscles around them flexed. "'I can't do this without them.'"

"But you did. And look what you did," Amelia said. "You survived a brutal miscarriage, finally left that bastard, and made a wonderful life for you and your son." Amelia climbed up onto the bed and slid next to Tess. "I know if I hadn't gotten on that plane, you would've only lost one parent. I know. I was selfish." She pulled her arm around her baby. "I wanted to get home to . . . Oh Christ. Anything could have waited." Amelia felt her daughter's head come to rest on her shoulder. She knew her eyes had softened.

Tess took her mother's tissue, wiped her face, and blew her nose. "I took it harder than Tim and Karen? Right?"

Amelia nodded. "They had their families. Good marriages, you know, settled in their lives. You were living in a powder keg—with a husband who liked to play with matches."

"The problem was I was addicted to fire." Tess snorted a laugh. "Getting out of that marriage? God, it was like peeling off skin. I don't know how I did it without you."

"But you did."

"Is this why you're here? To give me a pep talk, goose the old self-esteem?"

"No."

Tess looked at her watch. "Jesus, I have to get going."

She moved back into the bathroom and washed her face again, put on some mascara and lipstick, then went to the closet.

"Were you trying on my shoes?" She pulled her black pumps out of the closet and smiled at her mother. "Will you be here when I get back? I won't be long. Just going into the city for the ole tit squish. You know, a mammo, my first. You ever have one?"

Amelia nodded. "It was terribly uncomfortable as I recall."

Amelia walked with her daughter to the front door. Tess stopped at a big mirror in the front hall and pulled her hair up into a clip in the back. The bottle of Cactus Bloom nail polish sat on the table. Tess picked up her mother's hand, looked at the pretty red nails, and rolled her eyes. She put the polish in her sweater pocket.

"You are so beautiful," Amelia said. "So slim."

"I look just like you. Everybody says so."

"Oh no. I had tons of gray at your age."

"I color mine."

"I never had your presence, your grace."

"Mom, we are practically clones. Look."

Tess stood next to her mother and the two of them looked at their reflections. They were remarkably the same, the blue eyes, dark, thick wavy hair, large front teeth. Amelia, just slightly thicker in the middle with wisps of gray, was just ten years older than her daughter. Both of them thought about that. Neither mentioned it.

"I don't care if I'm crazy, Mom." Tess opened the door. "I'm just glad you're here."

"Me too."

Amelia listened for the garage door opener to grind shut, then walked around the back of the house. Thad sat in a chair by a little pond with water trickling over rocks.

"Jesus," he said. "That was a tough one. I thought these visits were supposed to get easier."

"Nobody ever said that."

"Well, this one was a bitch. Harder than the last time . . . on you, I mean."

"Oh, I don't know," Amelia said. "The anger is good. Don't you think?"

"I always hated it when you two fought. You and Karen never fought like that."

"Karen just shut me out. I hated that. I'd much rather have them hate your guts for a few years, get over it, and then snuggle back in."

"Tim was the easiest. That's for sure. Just had to knock him in the head now and then, take his car keys." Thad closed his eyes and put his hands on his stomach.

"I remember the first time we came, when she had just lost the baby," Amelia said. "There was no fear, no anger; she just crumpled onto the sofa, held me, and sobbed her heart out like I'd just brought over a casserole and flowers. I think she thought it was a dream, or maybe she was still on medication."

"I just remember the asshole had left town the day after she came home from the hospital—went to sign books in New York or Baltimore."

"Philadelphia," Amelia said. "I was afraid you were going to show up in his hotel room and beat the hell out of him."

"I could have just scared him to death or made him think he was crazy."

"He was crazy."

"No, he was just a melodramatic asshole who could never see anything except in terms of how it impacted him. You'd have thought *he'd* lost the fucking baby, all that drama in front of the doctor. Then he goes in the room and gives Tess a hard time for not taking better care of herself. Forget that she'd just buried her parents, and he'd actually popped her across the chops for paying more attention to Jack than to him."

"The time we came and she'd just moved into her own place, remember that?" Amelia moved to a chaise lounge and put her feet up.

"She ripped me a new one that time," Thad said. "I was selfish, possessive of you. Called me a big baby. Said I'd gone from my mother's tit to yours. Said I couldn't live a day without you. That I had no idea who I was all by myself." Thad opened his eyes, got up, and walked over to the pond. He squatted down and looked at the electrical box that controlled the fountain. "She was right." He looked back at Amelia. "I'm not easy with my own company. And I never wanted to be without you. I'm a chicken. Most men are, you know."

"Come, sit with me." Amelia patted the chaise next to her. "This reminds me of when we used to watch the sunsets at the lake."

Thad moved next to his wife. She reached over and took his hand.

"I was the chicken," she said. "I got on that plane because I didn't want to be without you."

"You got on that plane because you had an appointment the next day." Thad pulled her hand to his lips.

The back door suddenly opened and shut. Amelia and Thad looked up. Tess was standing on the flagstone path.

"You can't be back already," Amelia said.

"I didn't leave. I got halfway down the driveway and I figured this out. You're here because something's wrong with me. Right? I have cancer, don't I? I'm going drive into town, get my mammogram, and in a day or so the radiologist is going to call me and tell me there's a mass on one of my breasts. I'm right, aren't I?" Tess looked at her mother, who was biting her lower lip, then to her father. "Shouldn't at least one of you be dressed as the fucking reaper? Black cape, scythe?"

"Tess, you should go to the doctor. Stop this. Go, get your exam." Thad sat up.

"Tell me, please. Am I sick?"

Thad leaned back into the chaise and put his hands behind his head.

"I don't know." He crossed his feet at the ankles and closed his eyes.

"Then why the hell are you here?"

"I don't know that either."

"Mom?" Tess moved to the patio and dropped her purse and car keys on a chair.

"Maybe we got our signals crossed." Amelia waved her hands in the air, smiled at her daughter, then turned to Thad. "I mean it seems as though everything is fine. Doesn't it? She seems so happy." Amelia turned back to Tess. "Peter treats you like the treasure you are. Jack is doing great. Maybe I just thought you called this time."

"Ahem," Thad coughed and gave Amelia a hard look.

"I mean it was probably just a glitch in the system." Amelia looked at her red nails.

"This time?" Tess moved to her mother's chaise and sat at the foot. "You've been here before?" She locked her eyes on her mother's lowered lids until they lifted. "How does this work, exactly? Do you sense my desperation and just show up? Do I send out some kind of signal? Some scent that filters up through the stratosphere?" Tess shook her mother's knee. "What, what?"

Amelia tucked her lips between her teeth and bit.

"How often do you come?" Tess shifted her gaze to her father.

"Not very," he said. "She comes more often than I do. I watch Jack play ball. She never goes."

"I do so. I saw him play just last week."

"You stayed for one quarter."

"Hey!" Tess yelled. "Can we get back to the goddamn point here?"

"Exactly what point is it that you want to get to?" Thad looked at his daughter. "What is it you want to know? You want to know about being dead? It's pretty goddamn boring for the most part. That's why I go and hang out in the Piston's locker room now and then. I sat on a stool behind Van Morrison when he played in Chicago last month. That was the highlight of my week, until the piano player pulled out the stool. It's why we stopped by here, just to hang out for a while. To see how you're doing. You think because people die they stop caring about their kids, about what they loved, music, sports?" Thad closed his eyes against the low-angled sun.

"Oh Jesus Christ." Tess threw up her hands. "You know, just because you're dead doesn't mean you aren't still full of shit, Dad. I could tell when you were tossing me a pile when I was three. You are no longer the master of diversion, or diffusion, or whatever it is you try to do." Tess turned back to her mother. "Back in the house you said Karen and Tim never call, which means I do. Well, if I call, then maybe I can uncall or figure out how not to call. That is, if this isn't just some crazy hallucination and I'm in the throws of a psychotic break."

"You're not," Thad said.

"How do you know? As far as I know, I'm the only person on the planet who is having a heart-to-heart with her dead parents right now."

"Well, that's as far as you know." Thad kept his eyes closed. "How do you know it doesn't happen all the time?"

"I think it would be the topic of a lot of self-help books if it did. You don't think Oprah would have a field day with this?"

"I don't doubt it would cause a hell of a stir if people remembered. But they don't. You don't."

Tess got off her mother's chaise and sat in the grass next to her father.

"So you *have* been here before."

"Not as often as you might think." He opened a single lid.

"When?"

"After you came home from the hospital." Thad sat up, planted his feet on the grass. "And we sat in back of the courtroom when you got full custody from your first husband, who we prefer to call 'the asshole.'"

"Don't forget the time we came when she moved into that awful apartment. When she was painting Jack's room and the roaches ran up the wall." Amelia sat on the edge of her chaise.

"You saw that? Oh my god," Tess said.

"I actually enjoyed that one," Thad said. "You're the only person I know who shot roaches with a .32 instead of a can of Raid. That's my girl." Thad laughed and walked back over to the pond.

"All my finest hours." Tess picked at a blade of grass. "So were you around when I slapped Jack for crying for his dad, then sat on the bathroom floor with a bottle of vodka in one hand and a fistful of Ambien in the other?"

"Just for the bathroom part," Amelia said.

"Did you stop me?"

"No." Thad turned to his daughter. "You stopped you."

"Did I freak out those times when I saw you? Like I did in the kitchen?"

"Not so much. You were in so much pain . . . and frankly . . ." Amelia stuttered.

"So fucked up most of the time I didn't think it was weird that I was talking to dead people?"

Amelia and Thad said nothing.

"Oh God. I am such a mess." Tess flopped onto her back into the grass.

"You *were* a mess." Amelia slid down onto the grass. "You're fine now. Strong and happy and fine. And we didn't only visit when you were in trouble. Remember the night Peter took you to Chicago? It was snowing outside and 'Under the Boardwalk' came on the radio in the cab."

"You were there?"

"In the front seat, just me, not your dad."

"And Peter made the cabbie stop and open all the windows so we could hear the music. He pulled me outside and we danced in the middle of Michigan Avenue and the cabbie got out and danced too. The three of us dancing in the slush, snow falling in our eyes."

"Four of us. The cabbie was a wonderful dancer . . . better than your father." Amelia winked at Tess.

"But it's different when you both come. Why are you here?" Tess sat back up. "If all the other times—save the dancing in the street time—I was in a sewer, why are you here now? What's going to happen to me?"

"We don't know any more about the future than you do." Thad put his hands in his pockets. "We only know the past and the present."

"Go get your test. Just get it done," Amelia said. "We'll be here when you get back."

"I've already missed my appointment. It's no big deal."

"It is a big deal. Just tell them you got held up. They'll squeeze you in . . . so to speak." Amelia giggled.

Tess didn't laugh at her mother's joke. "Why do you care so much about my mammogram? I do have cancer, don't I?"

"I told you," Thad said, "we don't know the future. Just do what your mother says. Go."

"Okay, okay. Jesus." Tess stood and brushed off the back of her skirt. "Do you nag Karen like this?"

"She's a doctor," Amelia said. "She has one every year. She's fine."

Tess picked up her purse and car keys. "So, when I get back, will I go through the whole freaking out thing again?"

"No," Thad said. "There's a little grace period."

Tess walked toward the back door.

Amelia listened to the click of Tess's shoes on the pavement, then lay back on her chaise and allowed the sun to warm her face. Images of being on Nantucket with the kids when they were toddlers spread out before her like an old home movie. Those summers awakened nuggets of her womanhood determined when she herself was conceived—undeniable DNA that would make her savagely protective. She was young, and beautiful, her toddlers fat, and perfect. Baby Tess slept in a woven basket under the umbrella. She was so still in her infant sleep that Amelia would often pinch her foot to make sure that crib death, as it was known then, hadn't stolen her. As soon as she would squirm in her little oval basket, Amelia would go back to her book, every line or two steeling peeks at Karen and Tim in the surf with their father. The desire to protect them was so fierce and primal she could no more turn it off than will the milk in her breasts to stop flowing.

"Thad, remember the last house we took on Nantucket?" She looked up to see Tess standing above her. Eyes closed, she was shaking her head slowly. "Jesus, Tess, you're worse than us. You keep coming back."

"It was you." Tess looked at her mother. "You were sick. Weren't you?" She dropped her things on the grass in front of her mother. "You weren't drinking too much. You just couldn't hold your liquor. You were on some kind of medication, weren't you?"

Amelia looked up, frozen.

"Why didn't you just tell me?"

"We're not supposed to interfere," Thad said.

Tess laughed. "Oh, really. Wouldn't practically pushing me out the door just now qualify as interfering? Showing up here every time I have a crisis."

"You scheduled the appointment," Amelia said.

"Oh, Mom. Why didn't you tell me when you were here that last time?"

"Hearing you mother had breast cancer and had to get back home for chemo wasn't exactly what you needed to hear when you were at the end of your own rope . . . when you were pregnant, your husband was acting like an asshole, and you were feeling like crap," Amelia said.

"We were going to tell you." Thad sat on the grass by the chaise. "As soon as we got the next series of tests back. Your mother wanted to wait until she had something concrete to tell both you and your sister."

"Oh, Mom." Tess said again. She climbed onto the chaise and allowed her mother to wrap her wings around her. "How long had you known? I can't believe I didn't sense something. I was so wrapped up in my own shit."

"You were supposed to be wrapped up in your own shit."

"But you were sick!"

The tears that seemed to flow so easily with Tess quietly slipped down her cheeks onto her mother's blouse. Thad watched his girls, their pretty forms, curled into each other. It was something he had secretly envied of women, their effortless ability to hold and comfort each other. But death had its benefits. In a silent moment, born out of what, he never understood, he grew large, opened his chest, and pulled them both into his arms, cradling them like a new father holding twins. They slept while he oozed whatever it was that poured out of his middle into them. He let them slip back onto the chaise and sat on the grass beside them, leaning his head back on Amelia's knee.

"Can I please hold onto a little of this? This moment? I promise not to tell a soul," Tess said.

Amelia chuckled. "Oh, honey, you hold it. Believe me, you carry it in every cell. You wear it in the set of your shoulders and in the lift of your chin, in the way you love your Peter and how you mother Jack."

Amelia basked in the joy of holding her daughter. She tucked a shining curl behind her ear.

"Jesus, you make me sound perfect, like Karen." Tess said.

"When you have daughters you can't help but compare them. And I guess you're right, Karen always did seem like the perfect one, but . . ."

"But you're the one we admire," Thad said.

"So, you didn't come this time because I called." Tess rubbed the skin on her mother's arm.

"Even dead people have needs," Amelia said.

"You're not going to come again are you?"

"I doubt it." Thad picked up a pebble and tossed it into the pond. "Not like this."

Tess curled into her mother and draped her hand over her father's shoulder.

Perhaps it was the Pacific air, the warm sun, and the comfort of the chaise cushion along with the rhythmic breathing of her mother next to her that filled her with sublime tranquility. She drifted off, and only later, what was surely a marine layer wafted in from the coast, soaking her clothes, penetrating the layers of skin, muscles, and bones, breathing into her lungs, traveling along the miles of vessels into the tiniest corpuscles. When she awoke she was laying flat on her back, the afternoon sun burning into her eyes. Her cell phone was ringing in her purse.

"Mrs. Delaney?" the voice said. "This is Carol at Dr. Collins's office. You missed your appointment. Did you forget?"

"Oh God, I'm sorry. The time just . . ."

"It's okay. We have a cancellation. Can you be here at three?"

"Absolutely. I'll be there. I'm so sorry . . ."

Tess sprang off the chaise and went into the house. In the living room she stopped and picked up an empty beer bottle and a glass on the coffee table and noticed a picture frame lying facedown on the sofa. She picked up the photo of her mother at the beach with her brother and sister as toddlers. She traced a finger over her mother's big belly and smiled back at the beaming Amelia, whose eyes squinted into the sun. She took the edge of her sweater and wiped a finger-print from the glass, dusted the frame, and placed it next to the one of both of her parents holding Jack as a baby. She felt something in her pocket and pulled out the bottle of nail polish. Tess checked her watch, then sat, applied two coats of Cactus Bloom to her nails, let them dry, grabbed her car keys, and left the house.

Avalanche

Olivia stood with Jonathan in front of the open ski lockers. The smell of wool and polar fleece filled her head as she looked at the assortment of gloves and goggles, hats and scarves collected over the years. Hers, the kids, Ben's. Skis in one locker. Stuff in the other. Peter said he wanted his dad's down vest. "It fits me now, Mom. Don't let Jonathan take it. Just cause he gave it to Dad doesn't mean he gets to have it." She pulled the fluffy vest out of the locker and put it on the bench behind her.

Her own ski boots had been pushed to the back of the shelf, and here on the front edge of the locker were a pair of boots she didn't recognize. Brand new boots. Gray suede. A woman's boots. She pulled them out and looked at Jonathan.

"Yours?"

He chuckled.

"Wow." She lifted one and rubbed her thumb over the calf. "Shearling. Gorgeous," she said.

"Nice," Jonathan said.

He grabbed his jacket from the other locker and the running shoes he'd worn down to the basement more than a month ago. Olivia picked up the other boot. She reached inside and pulled out a watch and a makeup bag.

"Whose things are these, Jonathan? You dating somebody we don't know about?"

"Yeah, right." Then offhandedly he remarked, "Maybe they're Tilly's."

"Like I would buy boots like these for my sixteen-year-old. Hell, I wouldn't even buy them for myself."

She put the boots back and grabbed Ben's vest, a leather glove fell out of the pocket along with a piece of pink paper. The paper was a receipt from the Boot Black, a swanky shop in the village. Four hundred sixty-eight dollars, on Ben's credit card, for boots: Michael Kors, après-ski, size seven.

"Who is she, Jonathan? What the fuck is going on here?"

Every pore in Olivia's body opened. Her face burned. Then she was shivering. What felt like bugs crawled up her torso and spread out onto her neck and arms.

"They're not yours? Seriously? Maybe he bought them for you."

"I'm a size nine."

"Shit," Jonathan said and snapped his fingers. "Some chick skied with us for a while that morning. I'll bet they're hers."

"What chick?"

"I don't know. I didn't think they knew each other." He scratched his jaw. "I just thought they got to talking on an earlier run."

"Who?"

"I don't know. She rode up in the gondola with us, then skied part of the morning."

Jonathan pulled a fleece over his head. Olivia slammed a locker, almost hitting his head.

"Honest, Liv, honest to God, she was just some kid."

"How old?"

"I don't know." He zipped his jacket, checked the pockets.

"How old, you coward?" Olivia punched him on the arm, tears starting.

He rubbed his arm. "Late twenties, maybe younger." Jonathan looked at his friend. "Jesus, Olivia, I think I'd know if my best friend was fooling around."

"I'm sure you would. And I'm sure you'd keep it under that dandy little vest of yours until your dying day." She poked him hard in the chest.

A couple came into the locker room with wet skis. Olivia ignored them.

"What did she look like?"

"I don't know. Blonde, five six, seven, thin, alright looking, not beautiful, but pretty enough."

"Pretty enough to be a little something on the side, I'll bet!"

"I don't think so, Liv. She skied with us for most of the morning then took off before—before it happened. I never saw her again."

"What was her name?"

He shook his head slowly then closed his eyes. "Chris, Christine, Crystal, something like that."

Olivia left the locker wide open and walked toward the door.

"Don't do this to me. Please, please don't do this," she spoke to the ceiling.

Outside the day was blinding, beautiful. Tethered toddlers off to ski school crossed in front of her. She bent forward to stifle the need for a good, keening wail. When she looked up, the entire mountain was alive. Bright-colored bugs on a white giant's belly, crisscrossing down and down. The din of holiday voices was so brutal she brought her hands to her ears. *Breathe, Olivia, breathe.* Her eyes landed on her goofy pink boots. She'd showed them off the day she got them. Short slip-on things with a running-shoe bottom.

"Perfect," Ben had said. "Did they only have pink?"

"No, they had black, gray, beige, *and* pink." She threw one at him and he caught it high above his head.

"Like I said, I'm so glad they had them in pink." His gravel baritone shifted an octave. "You look mahveloush in pink."

Three weeks before she and Jonathan went through the lockers, Olivia faced a long line of mourners who snaked their way around the elegant credenzas festooned with Christmas greenery at Grace Brothers Funeral Home. Ben's partners wore expensive dark suits, somber ties, and kind smiles below knitted brows. Perfect second wives, all from the same doll factory, inched behind them. They wore frozen brows and diamonds the size of small fruit. It never ceased to amaze, or amuse, Olivia how many arm-candy wives were named after ornamental plants. *Heather* and *Holly* were frequent repeaters.

The partners hugged her heartily; the wives kissed her cheek, careful not to muss their lipstick.

"They're so boney," Tilly had said at the office outing to Wrigley Field last year. She was pointing to the group gathered in the skybox drinking wine, sporting pink baseball caps with the Cubs logo stitched in silver thread. "They're not like real moms, not like you." It was the closest thing to an affirmation of Olivia's mothering that Tilly had offered since entering the surly years.

On a normal day, all Olivia had to do was get out of bed and her daughter would snap. She knew the sweetness currently coming from her daughter was a temporary reprieve, an odd thing to savor. Death makes everyone kind. The morning of the wake Tilly had woken next to her—on Ben's side of the bed.

"You OK, Mom?"

"No."

"Me neither."

They each held up a hand, one praying with the other, an old game to see how Tilly was growing. Olivia remembered when the tiny fingers barely touched her life line. This morning the long slim fingers reached the tips of Olivia's.

"Caught ya." Tilly jumped out of bed and walked into her parents' bathroom. "Should I wear the dress I wore to Grandma's birthday? The navy blue?"

"That'll be fine, honey."

Olivia listened to her daughter pee and the toilet flush, oddly comforted by the sounds. Soon, she had known, she would be hugged and kissed by strangers and people she hadn't seen in years.

As the last partner's wife moved past her, Olivia pulled at her dress. The zipper dug into her side. She stared at a blue-haired woman she'd never met, or couldn't remember. The woman was pressing her hands, tearfully saying something about having been his first secretary. Olivia passed her on to Mary, who would introduce her to Paul, who would pass her on down the line of family that had been holding her up like a good bra since Friday.

Friday.

Jonathan had called on Friday and blown her world to smithereens. It lay twisted now like a trailer park after a tornado. Debris all around, pieces of her in this room and in that. Her perfectly messy, happy world gone in a single phone call. Just moments before the phone rang she'd fought with Tilly and Peter as they were leaving for a Christmas party. She'd yelled out the door as they stood waiting for the elevator. "Listen to me, the both of you. When your father gets home we're going to sit down and have a long talk about your language, *and* your attitude—" The elevator had swallowed them before she could get out another word.

Before anyone had arrived at Grace Brothers Funeral Home, Olivia stood alone and looked, then knelt beside Ben. His head was on a satin pillow. He'd be the first to laugh. There was the hint of stubble on his chin. She touched it then drew her hand back. So cold. So not Ben. White squint lines fanned out from each eye. The rest of his face, so tan. His hands rested on his stomach in the way he would sometimes nap while watching golf. If anybody dared to say that we should all take comfort knowing Ben died doing what he loved most in the world, she would scream. She could just hear some fat ass client who'd been dropped out of a helicopter with Ben on the backside of a mountain years ago acting like they were tight as boots. *That was Ben, always looking for the freshest powder.* She dreaded tomorrow, all the eulogies and tributes. God, she wanted this to be over so she could curl into a corner and wail.

Olivia stood and ran her hand along the wood of the casket. She pulled again at her dress. She kept meaning to lose weight between babies, but she loved her own cooking and Ben was never one to mind. He loved her bigger tits and ass and never once complained that she'd grown a belly. She wasn't fat, just not the tall drink of water she'd once been. Now she was a whole lot of woman.

The line of mourners stretched on. Peter came up behind her, so like his father it actually hurt to look at him—a senior now, shaving, that same rectangle for a face, black marbles for eyes.

"Jonathan said bottoms up."

She took the Starbucks, a grande, spiked with enough Bailey's to put her in a stupor for a week. The twins, Dylan and Charlotte had fallen asleep on a couch behind her. Charlotte's panty hose, her first pair, were twisted and bagging around her skinny ankles.

It had been going on since four. It was after nine now. There were times when it took over an hour for mourners to snake through the line to offer condolences, to kneel, look at the body, and bless themselves. Over an hour to see the posters the kids had made and the framed photographs they'd taken off of every surface in the house. The ski pictures, the Disney World shots, the one of Ben holding the twins in the delivery room wearing the Cat in the Hat's hat. Tilly's favorite, the one of Ben kissing a sheep, shot when he'd been a ranch hand in Australia after college. And Olivia's treasure, a black-and-white eight-by-ten taken during their wedding dance, her head thrown back, Ben's mouth on her throat.

These first days were balm on an open sore—the anxiety lifted by the holding. She kept having misfires. *Wait 'til I tell Ben Mrs. Steinmetz was here.* Then the synapse would shoot its serotonin across the space and the punch would land. But even this, she knew wasn't grief. The brain, she imagined, was slow to absorb tragedy. We revel quickly in joy. But grief, she was discovering, takes its time before it crushes. She understood that wakes and funerals stave it off until the body can take the real stuff. And ones like this, all Irish and Catholic, are reams of bubble wrap, so when the glass ball you've become is hurled up against a wall, you don't shatter. You slide down onto the floor protected by Xanax, plastic, and air.

For weeks she went back to bed after the kids left for school. Sometimes she slept; sometimes she stared at the ceiling for hours. Then along came Mary—around ten or eleven every day—and on a particular Thursday Mary dragged her out of bed and into the bathroom.

"You stink, Olivia."

"Well you suck," Olivia said back.

Mary laughed and slapped her sister on the ass.

"Get in there." She guided Olivia by the back of the shoulders into the shower.

Olivia looked at her sister through the steaming glass. She didn't pick up the shampoo or the soap; she just stood and let the shower soak her. *If Paul had died, would I pull Mary out of bed? Would I drag her into the shower? Would I be there every single day?* She watched her younger sister pluck her eyebrows in the magnifying mirror.

Mary turned to the shower. "Hey! Zombie! Lather up."

Olivia slowly turned and lifted her hand and extended her middle finger at her sister, a term of endearment neither had abandoned since leaving girlhood—and now a sign to Mary that her sister would, in time, heal.

After Olivia was in a pair of jeans and a sweater, they put their makeup on together then moved to the kitchen for coffee.

"I need to go to the cabin," Olivia said. "But I don't want the kids to come."

"Why not?" Mary had begun to scrape the morning's dishes.

"They'll want to ski."

She looked out the kitchen window at the terrace. Snow swirled, caught in the updraft between buildings. It was beginning to collect on the teak chairs, naked now without their cushions.

"Jonathan is going to meet me. He still has to get his stuff. If you stay here, I promise I'll take Kate and Tommy so you and Paul can get away next month."

"Deal." Mary patted her sister's hand with the dish towel.

As girls they rarely spent a night apart until Olivia went off to college. Even now, Mary lived five blocks away in a brownstone. Their husbands liked each other and their kids were so close Olivia never knew exactly whose T-shirts she was folding. Olivia was the redhead; Mary, the blonde. No mistaking they were sisters. Both had big eyes with slightly puffy lids. "You and your sister always look like you just woke up," Ben once said. The truth was they were just plain sexy. It's why their father was so strict and their boyfriends so addled, and why their mother made sure they were on the pill before they were out of high school.

"When are you going to leave?" Mary asked.

"Next weekend. I'll book a Friday flight. Jonathan will come in Saturday morning."

"Are you sure you're ready for this?" Mary asked.

"I'm thinking of selling it." Olivia poured herself another cup. She walked into the living room, put her coffee on a table, and reached for an ornament high on the tree.

"Give it some time, Liv. Don't rush." Mary slid the box with tissue over toward the tree. She took the fragile glass ball from her sister, wrapped it, and placed it in an old Marshall Field's dress box. "You know what they say. You should wait a year before you make major changes. Wait. Please."

When the tree was bare, they slid a white plastic bag up and over it, then dragged it into the back hall to the service stairs. They walked it down to the alley.

Olivia looked at the thing, lying on its side. "Good riddance to the Christmas that wasn't," she said.

"I second that." Mary put her arm around her sister's waist.

Ever since the accident, Olivia had tried to see how long she could hold her breath. Sometimes she'd put her head under the covers and see what it felt like to breath in her own air, to do it until she got scared. The last time she got dizzy and saw bright spots before she finally ripped off the comforter and sucked in deep gulps.

"There was an avalanche." Jonathan's voice had been weak, faltering over the phone that Friday. Thirty-six hours before she had dropped her husband off at O'Hare for a quick ski trip. Jonathan was on his cell and he cut out now and then. *Avalanche.* The first thing that popped into her mind was a *National Geographic* cover showing a rolling mountain of snow caught in flight, then song lyrics: "Riding Shotgun Down the Avalanche" by Shawn Colvin. *Why were Mary and Paul walking into the kitchen?* The gears slipped into place. Jonathan had called them first. She never even heard him break down, never heard "He's dead, Liv. Jesus fucking Christ, he's dead." She knew. She heard only "avalanche," not "He wasn't even covered by that much snow, but he didn't move, Liv, he just didn't move." She was holding the phone at her chest, staring pleadingly at Mary who moved across the kitchen quickly, arms open. Paul took the phone and began to talk. "No, I'll fly out tomorrow afternoon," he said. "You come on home. I'll bring it back." The *it* was her husband's body. Still her husband and now a body too.

In those first hours it wasn't a word yet. Dead. Not real in any way. The pinching and shaking and saying "This isn't a dream" did nothing. The walking up and down the back hallway then out onto the terrace was robotic. She hadn't smoked in eighteen years, yet she inhaled the cigarette Paul gave her like a barmaid and downed the vodka he poured, never feeling the burn. No tears came, just bugs crawling up and down her arms and an inability to sit, to be still at all. Her breathing was an irregular series of short gasps then long deep inhalations, with her hands spread on the counter, feet apart as she'd positioned herself in the early stages of labor. She screamed once and the sound of it made her laugh. Mary and Paul busied themselves in the kitchen: Paul made drinks; Mary mixed dough, greased cookie sheets. Olivia sprinted into the living room and found her cell phone. Hungrily, she scrolled through missed calls. There were two from Ben. She held her breath. The first call was at ten in the morning; the other, at noon. "Hey, Liv, give me a call" was the only message. She played it over three times, made Mary and Paul listen. She was certain he wanted to tell her something. "No," Mary said, "he was just checking in." Olivia got dizzy from the shallow breaths, the vodka. It was only at eleven thirty when the door opened and Peter and Tilly came in, arguing, that her breath moved back into her chest. The twins were at sleepovers. She'd tell them tomorrow. But that Friday night, Tilly and Peter stood in the kitchen doorway, and somehow she managed to say there had been an avalanche.

Olivia and Ben had talked the night before. He'd called to let her know he was at the cabin. He said Jonathan would be there in the morning, that they'd ski the back bowls and maybe drive up to Bachelor Gulch the next day. They'd chatted about the usual, Tilly's attitude, Peter's basketball game. He'd mentioned that he was meeting some kid out there who'd just graduated from law school and was job hunting. "Get Carlos up there to fix that furnace door," he'd said. Maybe that's why he'd called the next day, to remind her to call Carlos. But he would have just said it . . . "Don't forget to call Carlos." She thought those were his last words to her. Maybe "Night, babe," but she couldn't remember.

Arriving at the cabin at Juniper Lodge was another sucker punch. Towels lay where Ben had left them on the bathroom floor. His clothes tossed about, socks, shoes, jeans. Olivia fell onto the bed and brought a white cotton T-shirt to her face. Still a hint of him, his deodorant, his neck. She breathed it in. Then she grabbed the socks, the shoes, a sweatshirt, sucking all the Ben smells left in the world deep into her lungs. His cotton, his leather. Deep yoga breaths that pushed out her belly and lifted her chest with the last bits of Ben.

He'd bought the place before they met. It sat amid a grouping of small to medium timber houses that shared a common lodge, a pool, and ski storage. It was just big enough. A large room, with a kitchen, big table, and a sectional sofa their whole family could flop onto, was flanked by a master bedroom on one side and a bunkroom on the other. The vintage snowshoes over the fireplace were hokey, but there wasn't a chance in hell she'd get him to take them down. "I've actually walked in those things, goddamn it!" he said not long after they started dating. "The year I bought this place I walked all the way into the village for beer when there was snow up to my ass."

This was her first time back to the cabin since hiking with the kids last fall. They usually spent the week between Christmas and New Years here. Mary and Paul would rent the cabin next door. Sometimes Jonathan would come, with or without a pretty young friend. But this year Christmas hadn't happened and neither had the week after.

Twenty years ago they'd walk back in into the place and it'd smelled like sex. They spent days in bed, making love, eating pizza. They had even made love on the gondola one long whiteout ride up the mountain. It was fifteen minutes up, and by the time they arrived, she was zipping up her bibs, red cheeked, wobbly. They were married within a year. She wore a strapless, white silk thing, so tight around the bodice and butt you'd swear she was poured into it. But she was tall and thin and gorgeous and Ben was dazzled. Five years out of law school, he was on his way up at McKinley Brooks—not a big Chicago firm, but a fine one. And Olivia was teaching. But not for long. The kids came quickly. Peter was fourteen months when Tilly was born, and the twins just three years later. After Tilly, she quit work. They combined two units in a vintage building overlooking Belmont Harbor and spread out into every inch of it. Life was good. They fought now and then, but fast and furious, then made up in the afternoon when the kids were napping, or late at night on the living room rug.

Jonathan arrived around ten the next morning.

"You have to eat, Olivia," he said, watching her poke at her break-fast. "You look great, but you need to eat, for Christ's sake."

"Yeah, laugh's on me. I finally lose fifteen pounds and my husband can't see how hot I look. Sucks, huh?"

In the beginning, Olivia had joked that she had married two men: Ben and his best friend, Jonathan. Together, they made a great hus-band. One by one, as the children came along, attachments formed that uncles couldn't touch. And when Jonathan took a lover, they were genuinely happy for him and grieved along with him when things didn't work out, gleefully making room on the sofa for popcorn-and-movie night with the kids.

Once, when they were camping, not long after Peter was born, Jonathan was starting a fire and glanced over at the back of the open minivan where Olivia was changing the baby's diaper. Her back was to him as she cooed at her baby, bent forward to blow kisses on his tummy. He watched her short dress rise with each whoop and giggle, her creamy thighs open just a little, the crotch of her white pant-ies peeking then disappearing behind the curtain of her sundress. Jonathan lowered his eyes when Ben brought them both beers, then lowered them again when Olivia was breast-feeding as they sat around the fire in low camp chairs—a swollen breast and dark nipple escaped the blanket draped over her shoulder. He spent the entire weekend hiding random erections. After that he'd find himself staring at her freckled shoulder where the baby's mouth had been or at the wet spot on her blouse. It wasn't that Olivia and Ben didn't notice. They had, but they had mistaken Jonathan's darting glances and quiet moments for a longing for love and family. Even Ben knew that every woman had to measure up to Olivia in some way. He was flattered, never jealous. Jonathan's women were pretty and smart, but they didn't stay around long enough for anyone to find out if they were anything else.

"She's dead you know."

Olivia and Jonathan were in a bar at the base of the mountain. They'd brought the boots upstairs, along with Ben's coat and Jonathan's things, then walked down into the village.

"Jesus, Olivia, she's not dead. How do you figure a thing like that?"

"The boots, the makeup, the watch. She'd get them."

"Ben had the key."

"You said she skied off right before you two did—how long?"

"I don't know, a few minutes, maybe more."

"Did she make any plans to meet you at the bottom?"

"I don't know. They could have made plans to meet at the locker later—in the afternoon maybe. I don't know."

"They could have made plans to meet back at her place later in the afternoon too, Jonathan, but I bet she'd want her watch and her brand-new four-hundred-dollar boots on when she fucked him!"

"You've got to stop this, Olivia!" He leaned across the table and grabbed her arms. "This is not like you."

"This is not like my life, Jonathan, in case you haven't noticed."

He sat back and folded his arms. Their worlds had changed. They both knew they would adjust in time. Someday something would begin to fill the void. But now the emptiness was a black cavern they all wandered within. Which way is up? Is there a way out? Is it right to want to get out?

"Let's be real here," Jonathan said. "You have no proof she was anything other than somebody Ben lent some money to—a story he would have told you as soon as he called that night. 'Hey, I gave some chick some money for a pair of boots today. You better be worried . . . she was a looker.' Can't you hear him?" His impression of Ben's pseudostud was perfect. She smiled in spite of herself.

"After she left, didn't you ask Ben who she was?"

"Yeah, I did," he said, remembering. "All he said was, 'I'll tell you over lunch.' Then he skied over to the boundary fence. We looked for ski patrol, ducked under, and shot down the back." Jonathan rubbed his chin. They never made it to lunch.

"You didn't buy your lift tickets together did you?" she asked suddenly.

"No."

Olivia pulled out her phone. She called Mary and asked her to get the ski jacket that came home with Ben's things. Olivia asked her to read the number from the bar code on the ski pass attached to the zipper pull.

It didn't take much digging for the manager of the lift ticket office to dig up Ben's receipt. There were two tickets purchased. She contacted the credit card company next for a list of transactions the day before and the day of the accident. Along with the boots and groceries at City Market, skis and boots had been rented at Christy Sports. Ben had his own skis.

Olivia and Jonathan stood in front of the wooden counter at Christy's Sports. Rows of skis and poles stood like spears. A kid with blonde dreadlocks collected under a Nordic hat rummaged through a stack of yellow papers.

"Bingo," the kid said and walked to the counter. "Whoa," he said looking closer at the form. "I totally remember this chick. She was with this old dude. He like bought her all kinds of shit. Gloves, hat, those totally ripping Burton pants." He pointed to a rack of women's ski pants. "She was really quiet, he was like grabbing all kinds of shit, saying 'Hey, you need goggles, right? You need this, right?' Guy was loaded."

Olivia ripped the paper out of the kid's hands. The name on the form was Cynthia Murphy, five seven, one eighteen. *Thin. Of course she's thin*. The skis and boots were high performance. The only phone number listed was Ben's.

Save one skier with a broken arm and a few minor injuries, ski patrol brought no one off the mountain that day but Ben. The local police reported no one missing and called Olivia later to say that no one by that name was reported missing in the five-mountain region or in the Denver area either. She sat on the couch in the cabin, the phone book and her cell phone on her lap. She called every lodge and rental agent on the mountain saying she was Cynthia Murphy and needed a copy of her receipt for the night of the eighteenth. There was no booking.

"This woman is a fucking ghost!" Olivia glared at Jonathan. "You swear she didn't stay here, you swear?"

"Swear. I told you ten times. My flight got in an hour late. By the time I rented the car and drove up here, it was almost two in the morning. Your bedroom door was wide open—unlikely if he had a visitor. I didn't hear him get up. He woke me at nine, called my cell. I met him at the gondola a half hour later." Jonathan's smooth edge was growing sharp.

"And she was there."

"Yes, Olivia, she was there."

She checked the Chicago police next, maybe it was a long-term thing, maybe she lived right in the neighborhood and they saw each other every day. Nothing. Olivia's heart sunk deep. He had such huge appetites. She had too, once. But he had opportunities. She had children. *Damn him, God damn him!*

Later, Olivia was in the bedroom on the phone with the kids. Jonathan grabbed a beer and stood at the big window that looked out on Wolfpacker, a long black-diamond run with an afternoon shadow thrown on the bottom half. Just a few skiers this late in the day sailed down the run then disappeared into a turn he couldn't see.

He and Ben did it all the time, skied out of bounds in powder so light it felt like cloud flying. For Jonathan, it had begun with more trepidation than thrill. But each time out he could feel the balance shifting into the bliss zone. Ben wasn't reckless, but he didn't show an ounce of fear. Eluding the ski patrol took a little effort, but they were good at it after all these years. The day of the accident, after a run that took a half an hour or more, they'd cut over on a little ridge that dumped them right into the middle of Elephant's Tusk, a wide blue run, legal territory. That's where they had said good-bye to the girl.

"Just one more," Ben said. "Then we'll grab a bite to eat."

They were half a football field apart, alone on the mountain, a cloudless sky above, endless white beneath them. Ben was ahead and over to Jonathan's left. When he first felt the stinging bite of blowing snow, Jonathan thought it was coming off the trail of his skis; the wind had shifted and was blowing down on them. Then everything was white. Soft plunks—a thousand little snowballs hit him in the back.

"Ben. Whoa, whoa. Ben!"

Jonathan flew up but regained control just in time to hit a tree with his right shoulder. A swoosh, like a wave hitting a beach or air moving through a tunnel rushed into his ears. He breathed in a cold, fine mist, coughed. He was losing control again. The bark of the next tree grazed his jaw and he grabbed hold, spun around the tree and stopped. He pushed his goggles up onto his head and waited until the whiteness cleared. It didn't for a while. When it did, he looked up then down the mountain.

"Ben, Ben! Where'd you go, man?"

He was on the high edge of the bowl, looking at what should have been down, but now it was only slightly spooned out.

"Ben!" He yelled even louder this time.

His skis and boots were under deep snow. He jammed a pole into the snow behind each leg, pressed, and clicked out of his skis. He bent, dug them out, then stuck them into the drift. He was banging the snow off his boots on the tree trunk when he saw it, or heard it, coming again. He was far enough up on the rim of the bowl to actually watch. Stunned, scared, he clung to the tree like a petrified boy to his father's leg. Less like a wave, a layer of mountain the size and muscle of an aircraft carrier slid, kicking up clouds only at the edges, filling the bowl, ending angles. A terror filled his chest as he looked up the mountain, trying to see the end of it. Then it was as though the aircraft carrier parked itself. Crystals floated, sugaring the reshaped mountain. Thirty-foot evergreens became shrubbery poking out from a fresh snowfall. Later, they would tell him it was a moderate slab avalanche, a hell of a lot worse than a sluff, but they'd seen worse. *Slab* and *sluff,* new terms for something so delicate as snow.

Where he'd seen Ben last was sloped up far to the left, but he couldn't be sure. Maybe Ben was long gone. Maybe he'd ridden the thing all the way down—if one could do that. By now he was probably at the ridge sneaking into Jupiter. Ben was a better skier than Jonathan. Surely he was fine, had beaten the thing. Jonathan was afraid to call out again, not sure if the last surge had been caused by his yelling for Ben in the first place. He stood and surveyed, breathed slow and deep to calm his racing heart. When he decided to venture out, he was tentative. *Does it act like quicksand?* He managed to click into his skis and skied about fifty yards, hugging the tree line on his right. He stopped and surveyed every few feet. The world was blue and white with only the thin line of trees on his side. The other side, Ben's side, met with the sky. He put his goggles back on and looked again. How could something as ephemeral as snow seemingly shift tectonic plates and alter the world? Then, something caught his eye. Way down, not on the left but right in the middle of the aircraft carrier, something poked out of the snow. Even more hesitantly he skied onto the middle of the mountainside, then down. He was afraid to breathe, but he skied fast. It was the tip of a pole, Ben's pole. He clicked out of his skis and began to dig.

After he and Olivia had gone into their separate rooms, Jonathan tried again to reconstruct the day with Cynthia Murphy. She was pretty, a square face, brown eyes, and a dimple deep in her cheek. He couldn't remember which one. She had a thick sun-streaked ponytail pulled up almost to the top of her head with a wide, red fleece headband covering her ears. Cynthia Murphy was direct, and when she laughed, her eyes disappeared into crinkled lids. The more he thought about her, the more he realized that she had made the morning pleasant. She'd had a slight accent. British, he thought, maybe South African, but she seemed very American. He knew Ben didn't know her well, and though he'd never tell Olivia this, Jonathan had seen Ben studying Cynthia Murphy as she talked and moved down the mountain with them. On the lift Ben had asked her how old she was when she learned to ski. Fourteen, she'd said. Her mother had taught her, she said, in France.

At three in the morning, Olivia slipped on her pink boots and a heavy ski sweater. The light under Jonathan's room, the bunkroom, had been dark for hours. She closed the front door quietly behind her, took the elevator down, and walked over the footbridge that took her into the village. She walked by the Peppercorn lift, its gondolas hanging like boxes twenty feet above her in the black night. A light snow was falling, dry as soap powder. She moved past the big Sno-Cats, idle now after grooming the mountain for the next day. She trudged straight up the face of Peppercorn, slipping now and then on the combed surface. She moved to the right side of the mountain and created a series of switchbacks until she met a group of trees about a hundred yards up. She walked in, then went even further into a clearing. Soft powder was past her knees, but she didn't feel the cold through her jeans or the snow that was packing into her short boots.

Finally, she found the spot: a grove of Aspens stopped at a slope that eventually fell into Peppercorn's wide face. She'd hiked this trail in summer and knew what skiers didn't. What appeared to be a white meadow was in fact a deep gulley. It would often fill with drifting powder, feet of it; then the meadow was just as likely to blow away the next day. Tonight, there was no dip between the trees. A long deep pocket of snow that didn't crest for thirty, forty yards down the mountain lay like a wide white blanket. Immediately before it dropped into Peppercorn it hung like a wave between two rows of aspens, something a snowboarder would love if it wouldn't vanish beneath him—too soft, too new.

She walked up another thirty feet and turned to face the village twinkling through the trees. She knelt down, inhaled deeply then dove face first into the fresh snow that had been falling since before dinner. She swam. Wide breaststrokes took her deeper into the drift. The mountain became a soft pool of powder that swallowed her whole. She felt the weight of it on her neck and head, now on her back, but still not the cold. And then she breathed—easily at first, aspirating a few crystals, but there was air enough. She corkscrewed her body into the drift like an otter then slid on her belly deeper into the drift. She dug the toes of her boots into the tunnel and stopped. She managed to bring her arms up and carved a pocket the size of a basketball and breathed quietly for what seemed like minutes. Then she breathed the air around her mitten, the smell of wool from her sleeve. She took snow into her mouth, made it liquid, and swallowed. She breathed in more crystals and air, choked a bit, and coughed. *Did he smother or drown?* She hadn't read the medical examiner's report. Couldn't.

In the next inhalation, the air was warm and the smell of the mints she chewed after dinner was all around her. In an instant she was gasping. The angle of the mountain was steep. She pushed forward, but she wasn't moving as fast as she had been. She tried to kneel up; but the snow above was too heavy now, and the snow below caved away, taking her down even deeper. She panicked and began to swim wildly, crawling, clawing, thrashing, not sure of up from down, but craving air. And life. *Fuck. Fuck. Fuck.* She saw faces, then babies swimming in her belly. Spots dancing, white, pink. Suddenly she felt icy hard snow beneath her. She was sliding fast, arms pinned to her sides; snow was in her mouth, up her nose. She was tunneling, hurling downward. She'd been sucked into an Alice hole, a blind, human luge that could slam into a tree trunk. Dead in an instant. In a flash her arms were flailing wildly. In the air. She was sliding on her back, and then spinning, fast, like a disk down the mountain. But breathing, finally breathing stinging, cold air. She stopped, spread-eagle, not ten inches from the tractor foot of a big Sno-Cat, its grooming brushes wide as a house. Snow fell into her eyes.

Where Ben was rugby dense and tall, Jonathan, who'd been around since law school, could have modeled suits. He was soft-spoken with a sadness Olivia could never quite understand. He dated beautiful, smart, likeable women but kept them at arm's length. Yet, with all his quiet dignity, he held his own with the locker-room insults that went on among the armies of men who littered their den on the weekends during ball games.

"You play it like any other contact sport," she had chided them once while taking an armful of empty beer bottles into the kitchen.

"What?" Ben said.

"Busting each other's balls," she answered

"It's what we do to keep from doing what we really want to," Jonathan said.

"Oh, and what is that?"

"Paint each other's nails," Ben said.

"While watching *Steel Magnolias*." Jonathan gave Ben a kiss on the cheek.

Olivia came back into the cabin and went straight to the bathroom and turned on the steam shower. She was freezing, crying and freezing. She peeled off her clothes and left them on the floor. Everything was soaked or frozen stiff; the pink boots were caked with snow. She shook for a solid five minutes as the steam hissed and rose around her. Her arms and legs tingled and stung as the blood pushed its way into surface capillaries and revived her skin. Shivers and sobs jerked her body in convulsive rhythms. When she was thawed, she sat on the little teak stool and washed her hair and ran soap over her body. Tears and water ran down her face, her breasts, her belly, now flat as a girl's. She shaved her legs for the first time in weeks, then under her arms. She stood, lifted a leg, and made the triangle between her legs barely visible—the way Ben had liked it.

After, she huddled in her terry robe on the floor by the heat vent and allowed the black pain to sear through her torso and up into her throat.

"This is grief," she said to the tile. "It has its own life span and will work its way through me like a worm. It will leave me either better or worse. This is grief. No bubble wrap, no Xanax."

Olivia put on panties and a camisole and walked into the room where Jonathan lay sleeping. She could see his form, long in a bottom bunk, one arm arcing over his head. She lifted the covers and slid in.

"Wha . . . Olivia?" Groggy, he rose up on an elbow.

"Shh, shush," she said. "It's alright, shh."

He let her curl into him, her back to his chest. In minutes he heard her steady, rhythmic breathing, and in time he too fell back asleep. But later in the night they both awoke. She turned to him in the tiny bed and put a finger on his lips. Jonathan dug his fingers into Olivia's hair, still damp, and spoke her name. She was grateful he didn't remind her of Ben.

She awoke alone and pulled the blanket around her and walked into the living room. He'd made coffee and stood in a pair of sweatpants looking out at the mountain.

"I'm telling you, Olivia," Jonathan turned and faced her, "he didn't sleep with her. I'm sure of it."

By the end of March, Lincoln Park was showing signs of life, however tentative. The occasional tree sprouted a bud and runners returned to the jogging path. Olivia had never tired of the view out of her sixth-floor window. She often sat on the arm of the sofa and stared over the treetops at Lake Michigan, some days blue as the Caribbean, others steely gray and sulking. But lately as she stared, she started imagining the phone ringing and a voice from ski patrol telling her that the snow had melted and that they had found a body . . . a woman, blonde, perfectly preserved. She even saw herself standing over a long slab in a morgue staring into the beautiful face of a total stranger. Once, she traced her finger over the cold cheek that hovered right outside her window; it hung like a hologram over the lake.

She had stopped going back to bed after the kids left for school. She became one of the joggers and slowly, slowly began to resume old routines and create new patterns.

She and Jonathan would smile at each other when he came to take Peter to a Bulls game or when they saw each other at a dinner party. Often he would wrap an arm around her, and now and then she'd let her head drop onto his shoulder. But then she'd pat his hand and pull away.

The counselors at the high school reported that the kids were "adjusting." They gave her warning signs to look for: slipping grades, pushing friends away, not sleeping or eating. The usual signs of depression. Only Tilly lashed out. She was to spend the night with a girl she'd just met at school. Olivia discovered quite a few kids were to spend the night and that the parents were in Florida.

"Well, you're simply not going," she said after she confronted her daughter.

"You're like from another culture, Mom, another era. This is not the Stone Age. Anyway, Katie's sister is going to be there—she's like a junior in college."

"Now, that's certainly a comfort. You're not going."

Tilly's eyes welled up with tears. "Sometimes I wish it had been you instead of Dad. I hate you."

Without thinking, Olivia slapped her daughter so hard her hand stung. She and Ben never hit their kids. Tilly spun into her room and slammed the door.

"I hate you. This is child abuse." The door opened a second later. "I think you should send us to live with Aunt Mary. You're obviously unbalanced."

At midnight, she opened Tilly's door and crept over to the bed. She crawled under the covers.

"I'm sorry," she whispered into her daughter's hair.

"When will it stop hurting?" Tilly allowed her mother to spoon into her back and wrap an arm around her.

"I don't know," Olivia said. "I think it's like a long-term flu. It has to run its course."

"Will you sing my song, Mom? The one Dad sang to me?"

"You sure? You think my singing sucks."

Olivia's raspy voice sang slowly to the room.

> *Once a jolly swagman camped by a billabong*
> *Under the shade of a coolibah tree,*
> *And he sang as he watched and waited 'til his billy boiled*
> *"You'll come a-Waltzing Matilda, with me."*

Tilly rolled onto her back and sang in the dark with her mother.

> *Waltzing Matilda, Waltzing Matilda*
> *"You'll come a-Waltzing Matilda, with me"*

And he sang as he watched and waited 'til his billy boiled,
"You'll come a-Waltzing Matilda, with me."

Two nights later Olivia went through the stack of papers that had come from Grace Brothers Funeral Home and the hospital in Vail. There were copies of paid bills, death certificates, the obituary clippings, and the autopsy report. It was something she hadn't even thought of, didn't know they had even done one. She read down the headings, until she got to cause of death. Not asphyxiation, no water in the lungs. A cervical fracture. It was the first thing she'd thanked God for in months.

In late March Ben's cell phone was discovered by a man who had been snowshoeing on the back side of Elephant's Tusk. Ben always slipped his phone into a ziplock bag when he skied. Ski patrol juiced it up and called the office. Ben's secretary sent it over by messenger as soon as it arrived. Olivia was waiting in the lobby. She held it to her breast like a prayer book then took it upstairs. She plugged it into a charger, pressed the on button, and watched it light up with the picture of her and the kids filling the screen. She immediately went to the call log. He'd called her cell that morning, but he hadn't left a message. There was the call made to Jonathan down the list and a call made out to the office later in the morning, and at the top, the most recent calls were from the same number in a 415 area code, San Francisco. There were four of them. The first was at 4:30 the day he died; then another, two weeks later; a third, a month later; and one, just last week. Olivia's hands shook, blood rushed in her ears. She hit voice mail.

A strange female voice spoke haltingly, awkwardly, in an accent.

"It's Cynthia. I'm here at the locker. Didn't we say four? Well, no worries. I'll get my stuff in April. Won't really need the boots until I get back from Perth anyway. I've got another watch and plenty of makeup. Tell Jonathan hello. Bye now."

The next voice mail was full of enthusiasm.

"Ben, I got a job. Harold Baines, here in San Francisco. And I'm sending you money for the boots. Mum says I have to pay you for them. Lift tickets are one thing, but, she says, footwear is quite another. She says hello. After she got over the shock, I think she was actually glad I did it. But I think she's a bit afraid of what you think of her. Anyway, I've sent a check to your office. Call me back on my cell. Uh, hope everything went well when you told Olivia. Bye now."

The last voice mail was tentative, serious.

"Ah, Ben. Cynthia here. Are we still on for April? If not I'll just stop by and get my things if that's alright. I've booked my flight, you know, like you said. If you're worried about me meeting the kids, that's fine. I'm just barely getting used to the fact that I have a father, let alone brothers and sisters. But please ring me back. Bye now." She left her office number and her e-mail address.

Cynthia Murphy had called a fourth time, but she didn't leave a voice mail.

Olivia held the phone in both hands. She listened three, maybe four more times. *Cynthia Murphy, Cynthia Murphy.*

"Carol Murphy!" She shouted it, and her hands flew up to her face; the phone slipped to the floor. *Oh my God.* Carol Murphy was an old girlfriend of Ben's from the year he'd lived in Australia. Olivia recalled memories of lying in bed in the early years, telling each other the stories of their lives and lovers, the pain and bruises. Carol Murphy had been the one who broke Ben's heart.

"She'd moved here when I started law school, then dumped my ass and vanished," he'd said. He'd called her parents in Perth. They said she was traveling in India. They would tell her to call him when they heard from her. She never did.

Later, Jonathan listened to Cynthia Murphy's voice as he and Olivia sat on the sofa. Their wine glasses stood barely touching on the coffee table. The kids were in their rooms doing homework.

"I certainly didn't see this coming," Jonathan said. "Wonder how long he knew?"

Olivia shook her head. It wasn't something he would have kept from her. He would know it would be okay. It would be crazy but okay.

"I think he'd just found out." Olivia sipped her wine.

"How?"

"The kid," she said. "He said he was meeting some kid who was job hunting. I assumed it was somebody's son, a partner's or some client's kid. He told me about it when we talked right after he got to the lodge. I forgot all about it."

"He was supposed to meet this kid where, when?" Jonathan asked.

"There on the mountain, I guess. I don't know when. But this was obviously the kid."

Jonathan sat back on the sofa and shook his head. "He was going to tell me over lunch. I'd asked about her, remember? I told you. He said he'd tell me over lunch."

Olivia wanted to break Cynthia Murphy's neck. She wanted to break her mother's neck. *How could you have a kid and never tell the father? Was Ben an asshole to her? It didn't sound like it. He'd been broken-hearted, he said. Was it some feminist, I-can-do-it-myself thing? Was she totally fucked up, on drugs?*

Olivia sat twirling the stem of the wine glass.

"What do I do, Jonathan?"

She remembered Charlotte standing flat against the wall, eyes and mouth wide, no tears, no scream, when she told her about Ben. Her sweet Dylan dove into her lap and sobbed. Tilly had curled into a ball on the sofa; Peter held her by the shoulders, like a man when she knew he wasn't.

"I can't do this again." Olivia's nose ran before the tears started. "I can't fucking do this again."

But she did. They called Cynthia Murphy just before six—eight Chicago time. She practiced what she would say for half an hour. How do you tell someone who had just met her father for the first time that he was dead—died minutes after you said good-bye?

There were long, awkward silences, then both talking at once, and what seemed to Olivia like the sound of a bottom lip quivering. Olivia waited while the girl cried. She struggled for composure herself and managed it.

"I thought it had gone all bad, you know, when he told you." Cynthia Murphy's tearful voice shook from across the continent. "I thought . . . Oh God, I thought all kinds of things. I was sure I'd really blown it."

Over the conversation, pieces fell into place. An old friend, Patty Boyle from Madison, had called Ben and asked him to meet with this kid who'd just graduated from law school. Patty had kept in touch with Carol and knew her daughter. When Cynthia ended up at Stanford, she'd called Patty. But it wasn't until after Cynthia had graduated that Patty agreed to intervene. She actually *was* looking for a job. Ben said it would have to be the following week; he was going skiing. Patty called back and said, "How 'bout this for luck, she's staying with friends in Beaver Creek. How 'bout if she drives down to meet you?"

Cynthia had called his cell at about seven, she said. She was right in the village at Slappin' Sam's. It surprised her that he came right away.

"I assumed he wanted get it over with and have the next day free to ski."

Getting it over with was fine with Cynthia. Butterflies, she said, were flying her around the room. He was much bigger than she thought he'd be. He shook her hand and sat, and she was immediately at ease.

"Right off I told him my name, then told him I was Carol's daughter, said I was twenty-six, just out of Stanford law. He asked if I had dual citizenship. I told him yeah. He crossed his leg over his knee, tapped a straw from the table on his boot. He ordered us beers then he started singing 'Waltzing Matilda,' quite badly I must say. I laughed and sang along, even more badly. Then it was him who asked me. So easy, really. He looked at me for a quite a while, then shook his head and closed his eyes.

"'Are you here for a job or are you here to meet your dad?'

"'More the latter,' I told him. 'Though I am job hunting.'

"And we both laughed. I was so glad he laughed. He said I was the spitting image of Tilly, whipped out his cell and scrolled through a huge lot of pictures of her and the rest of you. He took one of me. Even I saw the resemblance. He kept saying, 'Jesus Christ. Wait 'til I tell Olivia. She won't believe this one!' Then he did the strangest thing. He said . . ." Olivia heard her choke back a sob. "He said he wanted to buy me something. I thought it was so odd. 'I should buy you something,' he said. 'To celebrate.' So we went shopping. I got boots, expensive boots. We walked for hours and talked. It was one in the morning when he walked me to my rental. He said for me to come back the next day and ski with him. His friend was coming and we'd get to know each other a bit. And so I did. We had a splendid day. It was beautiful; we didn't talk much, just skied, chatted it up a bit on the lifts. I set off around noon. I had to meet my friends for lunch. I talked of nothing else. Oh God." She stopped and blew her nose. "I can't believe this. I just can't believe it. I'm so sorry, for your loss. I'm so sorry." Then there were sniffs and gulps.

When she hung up, Olivia scrolled through Ben's phone. There were two photos of Cynthia Murphy. The one taken in the bar was dark, but her eyes twinkled and her dimple dug into her cheek exactly where Tilly's did. The other photo was taken on top of the mountain. She was athletic looking, red jacket and headband, thick blonde pony-tail. Her goggles were pushed up on her head. Her eyes were slits as she squinted, but her smile was broad. A laughing smile. Ben's smile.

It was Mary who said they should meet. Insisted on it. "You have to know her a bit before the kids meet her. This has to come through you."

A week later, on April 3, Olivia stood in the lobby of Juniper Lodge, nervous, picking balls off her sweater then nibbling at her cuticles. Finally, a Mountain Express shuttle pulled up under the timber canopy and stopped. A couple got out, pulling long ski bags from the back. Then a lovely young woman, with sun-streaked hair spilling down her back, sprang from the van. *Oh God, she did look like him.* The square face, dark eyes. She moved like Tilly, catlike. She took her bag from the driver and gave him a tip. Then she faced the door and moved right through it. She looked directly into Olivia's eyes, smiled, and shot out her hand. But Olivia pulled her into her, breathing shampoo and sun. The girl dropped her bags and circled her arms around Olivia. When they moved apart, Olivia put her hand on Cynthia Murphy's cheek, warm and rosy.

"I have coffee at the cabin." She took the girl's bag. "And after that we'll ski. I haven't skied all year."

Liar, Liar

'll be honest with you. I'm a liar. I've told black ones, white ones, and ones that don't even register on God's inventory of lies. I even perjured myself once if you count the time the North Carolina state patrolman pulled me over for speeding. I quick-like opened my blouse just enough to show him a little something, then told him I was rushing to meet my husband at the hospital when I knew damn well Charlie was sitting in a skybox at the Hornets game.

Sometimes I have a good reason to lie. If I need you to find me a size eight and a half narrow at the store across town, I might tell you that your lipstick is perfect for your complexion when in fact nobody in her right mind has worn that shade of coral since Angie Dickenson. So I won't hurt your feelings, I might say *delicious* to the tiny hot dogs you call hors d'oeuvres before I cough them into a napkin. But mostly lies just tumble out of my mouth like water dripping out a faucet. Could be I just need a good plumber.

The other day I began with a pink lie. Willa came in the kitchen, and for the first time in almost two years, she asked my opinion.

"Skirt too short?"

"Absolutely not. It's perfect. Now, come give me some love."

She allowed me to hug her. God it feels good to hold your baby, doesn't it? Willowy Willa. I'd hoped to remain taller than at least one of my children. I thought it would help during the teenage years. But the marks on the wall by the refrigerator tell me I lost the battle last July when Willa reached five nine and a quarter. I sucked at discipline anyway. I could have been six one with a bark like a pit bull. Didn't matter. I have no bite in me. Maybe that's why I lie.

I smelled her shampooed hair and a dot of Clearasil on an erupting pimple on an otherwise perfect face.

"Remember, he's an asshole," I said.

"I know," she mumbled into my robe. "I just wish the asshole wasn't in my 8:05 French class."

"You get any sleep?"

"Some."

We continued rocking back and forth.

A horn honked and I was hugging air. Only the slightest hint of Pantene Pro-V was left on my cheek.

The skirt was so short she could have made a pole dancer blush. It stopped where the asshole's low-slung khakis usually started. I pondered any possible symmetry, then just prayed she'd make it through the day without a detention. I could have told her the truth, but then I wouldn't have gotten my hug, and just maybe it'll drive the asshole a little bit crazy, and he'll feel bad about breaking my baby's heart.

My husband doesn't know I'm a liar. He thinks he is good looking. He never checks the credit card statements. He believes that my manicures, pedicures, massages, and facials have medicinal purposes, and that they ultimately enhance his sex life. And who's to say they don't?

He isn't my first husband nor is he the father of my children. That would be Jeffrey. On my fifth wedding anniversary, I got a call at work from the preschool where the two older kids went. Samuel and Sarah were both covered with chicken pox sores. I picked them up, then went by the day care center to pick up Willa. We walked in the house and you guessed it. Jeffrey was having an *afternoon delight* with a shapely little thing in our king-size bed, where I had planned to plunk all three kids in front of the TV while I called the doctor.

"What was daddy doing with that lady?" the kids asked as Jeffrey and the shapely little thing scrambled into clothes and hopped down the hall and out of the house.

"She was just helping daddy make up the bed," I lied as I started packing his bag. I put off calling the doctor for calling a lawyer.

Jeffrey wrote a child support check for six months. A year later he moved to San Francisco. Then he moved to Portland. Then he moved to Seattle. Then he moved off the edge of the earth. Then I met Charlie Wilson.

Charlie was a self-made man who had just ended a relationship with a pretty Charlotte debutante. He could never quite understand why she threatened to throw herself into Lake Norman every time they had a fight. New to the area from Wilmington, Charlie didn't quite know the lay of the land, nor of the lake. Finally he called her bluff, and she jumped from her daddy's veranda, clutching the bottle of pills she didn't quite have the guts to swallow. She broke her ankle and sat in three feet of water until her daddy fished her out and drove her to the hospital.

Charlie is about as solid as a rock, and he looks like one too. I know that doesn't sound good, but at the time, it was exactly what I needed. To his credit he hasn't changed a bit in fifteen years, just a little grayer. He's tall, about six three, and could stand to lose about twenty pounds. His face is shapeless; actually, it kind of melts into his neck, which angles out into broad shoulders. But Charlie has a twinkle in his eye and a smile that begs you to smile back. His world is a place you want to watch just to see what's going to happen next. He's the smartest engineer in the Southeast, they tell me at cocktail parties. When they do, Charlie just gets quiet. He never shines his own light. Doesn't need to.

Within six months Charlie told my lawyer to stop looking for Jeffrey and his checks. He wanted to marry me and tuck my babies under his wing. And he did. He bought us a big house on Beverly Drive, which is lined with water oaks so tall they don't so much form a canopy as a cathedral nave to drive under. At first we rattled around in it, but in time we spread into every inch of this lovely old thing, like filling out a pair of blue jeans you had bought a size too big then forgot to watch what you ate.

At first I lied to Charlie. I know, big surprise. I told him I loved him. Told him I couldn't live without him. Truth was I was just worn out. I'd been working full-time at the bank and raising three babies alone for almost three years. Samuel was seven, Sarah was five, and Willa was going on three. And here was a good man who loved me and adored my children. I'd learned my lesson. Jeffrey might have been good looking and smooth talking and able to talk me out of my panties in a New York minute. And if he'd walked into Myers Park Presbyterian Church the day I married Charlie, my face would've likely gone red. But I wanted something else. Charlie made me laugh and he made us safe. All Jeffrey'd done was get me pregnant and leave me with a mortgage.

"You know I had my tubes tied," I lied after Charlie and I had had sex on our wedding night.

"I thought I saw a diaphragm in your medicine cabinet."

"That's the case for my mouthguard," I lied again. "Before I met you I used to grind my teeth at night." Then I let out a sigh. "But you have really calmed me down."

The truth was I would have had another baby if Charlie had pressed the point, but I'd worked my ass off to get it back into shape after Willa, and for the first time in six years, I wasn't collecting formula and baby shit under my fingernails.

"I could maybe have it reversed," I said about as sweet as I could possibly muster.

"Absolutely not!" He pulled me into his bearlike chest and kissed my hair. "We're about as lucky as we can get with the ones we got, and if Jeffrey Jello doesn't surface within the next year, I'd like to adopt the little rug rats if it's alright with you."

It was.

The minute we got back from Barbados, I disposed of the *mouthguard case* and made an appointment with my gynecologist. I became sterile while Charlie was on a business trip. It was the first time in my life I felt I had actually broken a commandment. I knew I was taking something away from Charlie Wilson, but my own logic told me I was giving him something even more precious than any silly debutante could. He was getting three perfect children and a woman who not only had never stepped out onto the ledge of the seriously neurotic but one who knew the shoreline of Lake Norman like the back of her hand.

A year after the wedding, I came in the den in the middle of the night when everybody had colds and croup. I found them all asleep, all three children straddling a part of Charlie, an arm, a leg, a stomach. I knew that minute I loved him, not just because he knew how to daddy my babies but because a current had begun to flow between us. It lit a lamp in me that has never gone out. I carried the kids one by one to their rooms that night, and came back and lifted my nightgown for my husband.

Did I mention that as well as being a liar I am uncommonly vain? Maybe all women are, but I think I take the cake! Most women can't seem to pass a store window without checking themselves out, under the pretense, mind you, that they're looking at the dress on display. They're usually looking for flaws. Not me. I simply want to take another look at how great my legs look in the new pumps I'm wearing, or how my boobs are bouncing under my sweater. I've kept my chestnut hair shoulder length since college, and when the occasional gray one rises up in dissent, Ellen at Tressed to Kill does her magic and the aberrant strand settles back down like a brainwashed lemming. But lately I have been assaulted with a cruel reality. I've skipped three periods in the past year, and you and I both know I'm not pregnant. I'm fifty, okay, fifty-two, with two children in college and one about to graduate high school, and my neck and eyelids, not to mention the lines around my mouth, and my nasolabial folds—a term I read in *Vogue* last month— are beginning to bother me to no end. Aging has come on me like a semi barreling down the interstate. I thought I was checking my rear-view mirror, but all of a sudden it's riding up my ass, yanking its damn air brake, blowing that horn to beat the band.

"What would you think about me getting a face-lift?" I floated the concept while Charlie was partially attentive.

"You do, and I'll buy the old one back," he said, not even turning his head from the John Daley putt he had two hundred dollars on.

"But look at these wrinkles, Charlie, and my neck. God, I look like a turkey." I pulled the skin up toward my ears.

"Jesus H. Christ!" he bellowed.

Even I turned to the TV. Big, loveable John Daley, with his 84 Lumber logo on his shirt, looked up to God and shook his head. The camera panned to Tiger Woods who barely smiled and hiked his putter up over his shoulder like a baseball bat. Seemed like even Tiger felt bad for John Daley.

"Louise, you look like you're thirty-five." Charlie got up and grabbed a beer out of the refrigerator. "Everybody says so. You let a doctor go anywhere near your face with a knife and I'll send you to Butner."

It's funny how people still do that, threaten to send you to state mental hospitals. In Georgia, they'll send you to Milledgeville, but in North Carolina, the mere mention of Butner gets the even slightly feebleminded shaking in their boots.

"They're closing that awful place." I picked up his empty from the coffee table and walked to the kitchen.

"I'm sure there's somewhere that'll have you if you go and do a fool thing like get a face-lift." He took a long draw.

"OK, forget I brought it up." I tossed the empty. "I'll learn to live with my turkey neck and crow's-feet."

He came over and pulled me to him, then took my face into his hands.

"Now that I think about it you do seem to be taking on some peculiar characteristics of the bird family, Weeza." He studied my face.

"Like what?" I was crushed.

"Like sex. Birds don't actually have sex, do they?" He laughed and nuzzled my neck.

"Oh, get out of here, you have more sex in a week than most men get in a year. Why last night . . ."

"Now, Weeza." He nibbled my ear. "Let's don't live in the past."

A second later Sam was tapping on the window. He was home from Chapel Hill for the weekend. Charlie slapped my rear and walked out the French doors onto the patio where Sam was bouncing a basketball. Charlie stole it middribble and scooped it into the basket.

Of course I'd already scheduled my face-lift for the second week in October. I'd done it months ago. If Charlie had been neutral to the idea, it simply would have made things easier. His reaction was sweet, actually, and not at all off-putting. He'd be in Scotland playing golf with his buddies for three weeks. By the time he got back, the lovely Dr. Irgens assured me, I would be healed. My crow's-feet would be erased by lasers, my neck would be hiked up behind my ears, my lips would be plumped, and my eyelids would lose an extra fold. Charlie, who never really looked at things all that closely anyway, would accept that I just had an especially good facial.

Dr. Irgens, a native Norwegian who left her Park Avenue practice for a more agreeable climate (and clientele, she had confided), had set up shop in the Buckhead area of Atlanta and was affiliated with Piedmont Hospital. I would have my procedure on a Thursday, spend that night in the hospital, then be spirited to a nearby hotel where I would spend the following week. I could drive down from Charlotte and back and no one would be the wiser.

Willa was going to spend the first weekend with Sarah at Winthrop, then stay with her best friend for the rest of the week. She believed I was visiting my mother in Asheville, something that initially threw her off as my mother and I have never been close. Mama invested in lengthy tours of Europe and Asia after I left for college. She was rarely in the country, and as a matter of fact, I had no idea whether she was home now or gallivanting through the Rhineland. Other than all of them having my cell phone number, I was on my own.

When the time came, I kissed Charlie at the airport, dashed back home, and got my bag. On the way down I-85, I imagined myself looking like the twenty-five-year-old me. The truth was, at twenty-five there weren't too many months I wasn't pregnant, but I was beautiful. Everybody said so, even the mirror. I wouldn't lie about a thing like that.

I made it to the hospital in plenty of time to fill out my pre-op forms and get my blood drawn.

"Emergency contact?" The intake clerk asked.

"Excuse me?"

"We have to have a phone number, just in case of an emergency. You will be under general anesthesia."

I gave them Charlie's cell phone number hoping to high heaven that if they had to call him it would just go to voice mail. If I ended up a drooler, I'd die of shame anyway.

Within an hour, I was gowned and hair-netted, and the lovely Dr. Irgens was drawing on my face with a magic marker.

"Ven yur husband zees you next he vil say you look more booteeful dan effer, and so vell rested!"

The next thing I knew I was waking to a drugged fog. My head throbbed and my jaw was locked into place by what felt like a vise-grip. I couldn't see beyond the shadows floating in front of me. A sugar-sweet male voice asked how I was feeling.

"Thitty." I managed with my thick tongue.

"On a thcale of one to ten, one being none, ten being ethcruciating, where ith your pain?"

"Theven."

"Do you have nauthea?"

"Yeth."

It went on like that for hours; my pusher and I were bound by our mutual speech impediments and by my increasing love for Dilaudid. However, the narcotic or maybe the anesthesia had rendered me unable to pee in a bedpan. Finally, they moved me out of recovery into my own room, and I was able to wheel my IV pole into a bathroom and sit. The relief was wonderful, but as I stood, the shock of the thing in the mirror was mind-numbing. The fact that they even allowed mirrors in post–plastic surgery suites showed insensitivity, if not downright poor judgment. There I, or, please God, some freak of nature, stood looking like a lightbulb protruding from the neck of a hospital gown, and we all know what haute couture those are. The gauze and ace bandages fashioning the lightbulb provided two slits for eyes and a third for nostrils and mouth. I blinked and two bloodshot orbs blinked back. I pursed my own lips, and these other lips, swollen and malformed, snarled back, looking like Angelina Jolie's would look if they could give Jennifer Anniston the finger. *Vi'll jus add a leetil Reestilin around the outer contours of ze lips to fill zem out. Like you looked ven you vere a girl.*

"Mrs. Wilson," said a lovely red-haired nurse. "Let me help you back to bed."

Oh my God, what have I done? I thought. *I didn't even look all that bad. Charlie thought I was beautiful. I was beautiful. Here I am with lips that look like somebody's butt and God knows what's underneath here!* All I could do was thank God for the drugs they squirted into my IV whenever I said a number high enough to get a reaction.

"How is your pain?" the pretty nurse asked without a lisp.

"Theven," I mumbled through the gauze. "Theven."

Sometime in the middle of the night, I thought I heard my cell phone, but I was helpless to answer. At first I imagined it was Willa telling me the asshole wanted to make up with her. Then it was Charlie asking Dr. Irgens how he could buy my old face back. I was immobilized by the opiate, and my ears were somewhere beneath the yards of gauze that made up the lightbulb. I couldn't have heard them anyway.

But when I awoke the next morning a miracle had occurred. I felt remarkably better. Dr. Irgens came in with her resident and clipped away the bandages.

"Oh, dahling, you vill feel much more comfortable now. Za pressure dressings are hideous. Are zey not?"

I reached up and felt my matted, blood-caked hair, my numb neck and cheeks. I could see her beautiful silk suit through her open lab coat. Her highlighted hair glistened under the fluorescent lights. Perfect bleached teeth smiled at me in her gorgeous forty-something face. I was immediately reassured.

"Thank you." I was able to speak normally again. My pain was reduced to three.

In an hour I was in my hotel room watching *Oprah.* I had showered, even been allowed to shampoo! A bottle of Vicodin sat like a queen on my bedside table. I looked like a boxer who had taken bilateral punches to the head and neck. But the lightbulb was gone, replaced by an ice pack neck sling. One hour on, one hour off.

My cell phone rang in my pocketbook again. Just voice mail. I got up and looked at the calls I had missed. Only one number and not a Charlotte area code. The call was from Asheville and not from my mother. I didn't have a clue. I hit voice mail, but the message was vague.

"Louise, this is Blanche Weatherly. My townhouse is in the same complex as your mother's. Could you give me a call as soon as you get this message? I have some information about your mother that I need to discuss with you."

She left her number and that was it. How peculiar. I'd never heard of Blanche Weatherly, but of course that was no surprise. I had called Mama in June to invite her down for a barbeque to celebrate all the children being home. She called back from some place in Canada. I called again in August. She was on her way to Peru. I hit redial.

"Hello." A woman answered.

"Blanche?"

"Yes."

"Blanche, this is Louise Wilson."

"Oh, thank God."

"What's wrong?"

"Oh, Louise, I'm so sorry to tell you, so very sorry, but your mother has had an accident. I'm afraid she has died, Louise. Your mother has gone to her glory."

The rest of me went numb along with my neck and face. The information didn't filter in slowly. It gushed in, all cocks open. My mother, a widow, was dead, and I was an only child. Here I was holed up in a hotel in Atlanta, high on Vicodin, looking like the losing end of a bad night with even worse company. I had a funeral in front of me. I was just wishing it were mine.

I know what you're thinking. But the fact that I hadn't been close to my mother doesn't mean I had no grief. I had grief aplenty. The number of years I spent on the couch of a certain psychologist in Dilworth could tell you that I had done a good bit of grieving, and though it hadn't cured me of lying, it had turned me into the huggingest, kissingest, most doting mother and wife I could be. That being said, I still sat propped up on the pillows of the Heavenly Bed at the Buckhead Westin, immobile, staring at Oprah, who I could swear looked a hell of a lot younger than she did the last time I caught her show in the waiting room at my dentist's office. Not just thinner, mind you, but younger. I snapped back to reality. What the hell was I going to do?

I called room service and ordered coffee and hit redial again.

"What kind of accident, Blanche?"

"Car wreck, darlin', comin' down 441. Your mama loved the Smokey Mountain Parkway this time of year. But the deer do too. She hit a buck the size of a tractor. Even the air bag couldn't save her."

"Thank you, Blanche. I'll be there on Monday. We'll plan a Wednesday funeral."

Within two days, I'd weaned myself off the Vicodin and somehow drove myself to Asheville on Monday. All the pancake makeup and chiffon scarves at Dillard's would have been useless anyway, so I drove north, without camo, and made it to my mother's by noon. I had a key and let myself in. An hour later Blanche Weatherly did too.

"You must be Louise."

She moved toward the sofa, her hand outstretched. A second later both hands flew up to her face.

"My Lord, darlin', what happened to you?"

Blanche was about five foot nothing, gray and plump. She looked to be about my mother's age, late seventies. Her mouth hung wide, a large circle with teeth.

"I had a little fender bender myself, Blanche."

I got off the couch and put my Jackie O's back on. I moved toward her and took her hand. She let me shake it, continuing to look shell-shocked, eyes the size of cake plates.

"The truth is," I went on, "I was overserved at a party on Friday night and my husband's out of town. When he gets back he's going to be very angry with my host, who happens to be his best friend. Between you and me, I wish I could just lie and say I ran off to have a face-lift or something."

She finally closed her mouth and moved to the kitchen and put the kettle on.

My first call was to Willa. She was the easiest. The second was to Sam. The conversations were identical, so in the interest of time, I will record them here as one.

"I'm calling from your grandmother's, baby, there's been a wreck."

"Mama, are you alright?"

"I'm fine, sugar, but I have some bad news."

"What's happened? Mama, you sound awful?"

"I'm afraid your grandmother is gone. She's dead."

"Mama, are you OK?"

"I'm fine, baby, I just have some bruising." It slipped out of my throat as easily as ice cream slides down.

"Oh my God. The air bag, right? Was she driving?"

"Yes, honey, she was."

"Oh, thank God you're OK, Mama."

The call to Sarah was similar until the end. Sarah is in training to be me. Not the liar me, the mother me. You know, oldest daughter.

"You just take care of yourself, Mama, we'll be up on Wednesday. I'll call Daddy."

"No, no, no! You hold on, young lady. Don't you call your daddy. Why, he hardly even knew my mother. I'm not going to have him come all the way back from his golf trip for this thing. Why, it's only a memorial service and tea cakes here at the house. I'm not even sure y'all need to drive all the way up here."

"Mama!" she said with such indignation that I almost dropped the phone. "You are our mother and she was *your* mother and we will be there Wednesday morning at nine sharp, shoes shined!"

God had blessed me with these wonderful children. One day he would smite me silly for lying through my teeth to them.

Blanche and I agreed that if anyone asked about my appearance, she would say that I just didn't want to discuss *the accident*. The irony was that this was *her* idea. I considered that lying might be contagious.

I met with the funeral director, selected a headstone, called a caterer, and ordered flowers. By Tuesday morning, I had spoken to scores of my mother's friends, people she had garnered on her travels over the years. I discovered that she and Blanche had been bus partners on many a trip through Europe, South America, and Asia. For a gal who grew up on the wrong side of a mountain, my mother had come a long way.

The day before the funeral I looked at a picture of my mother and me that sat on her mantle. It was taken the day of my high school graduation. She had her usual faraway look. We had just lunched at the Grove Park Inn, the lovely stone hotel that overlooks the Blue Ridge.

"You are so beautiful, Louise, and so smart," she had said as she toasted me. "I never worry about you. You are going to be fine. Just fine." And then she stared off into the middle distance.

I never knew my father. The story went that he had owned the better part of a valley and a ragtag diner. Not long after I was born, he died. A year or so later golf courses started popping up in North Carolina like toadstools. My mother got some good advice and sold off the land to a developer from Florida. They say she went from backward mountain girl to city woman in a just a few years. She went to night school and read everything she could get her hands on. I remember none of this. I only remember growing up in Asheville, a middle-class girl with a mother who always seemed to have one foot out the door.

As soon as she packed me off to Queens College in Charlotte, she moved the other foot out too. In the beginning I got postcards, but after I married Jeffrey, I only got Christmas cards, and now and then my kids would get a card for their birthdays. On the couch at Dr. Shelton's I cried and used a pillow to hit. But the best healing I got was by loving my own babies and by being loved by Charlie. I knew that somewhere in my mother's world was something worse than a hollow loneliness. There was a pain so deep, so dark that she could never show it to anyone, certainly not to me. To the world we were the attractive widow and her pretty daughter who lived in the stone cottage on Mountain View Road. People thought she had a shy dignity. I knew she was depressed.

I don't want you to think she never showed me affection. She didn't fawn over me like I do my kids. But when I cried over lost kittens or lost loves, she would come in my room and curl up with me, and on Sunday mornings we always read the funny papers in her bedroom and drank milky coffee. But she would drift away. As a little girl, I would actually snap my fingers in front of her face, and she would startle back. But by the time I was a teenager, I had learned to let her be. I had found girlfriends with big families and had weaseled my way into them like a runt puppy happy with the last tit. They took me in because I was beautiful, and smart, and nobody ever had to worry about me.

Wednesday morning arrived loud and bright, with crows cackling in a sky so blue it hurt your eyes. The mountains put on a show too, like dancers lifting bright-colored petticoats. Lipstick maples and trees every orange and yellow God ever thought of spread out across Asheville and the hills beyond. It was a better day for a wedding than a funeral, but we would make do. The only colors that rivaled the mountains were found on my face and neck. The blacks and blues around my eyes were giving way to greens and yellows. My swollen neck looked like I had survived a hangman's noose. When my children arrived, I immediately put up a hand and begged them not to fuss. Charlie arrived just as the limo was pulling up to Mama's townhouse. He held me gently, afraid to give me his usual bear hug.

"Everything's gonna be fine, baby. Whatever you need."

I had found a lovely black chiffon scarf to camouflage a good bit of cheek and jowl. Along with my big Jackie O's and an expensive black turtleneck dress, I simply looked like a woman who was overly dramatic showing off at her mother's funeral.

The service was uneventful and lovely. At the gravesite, the minister said a few kind things about a woman he didn't know and gave me a rose to place on my mother's coffin. We all walked to the limousine, Charlie holding one of my hands, Willa the other. I could hear Sarah crying softly behind me. Sam came up and put his arm around her. I didn't deserve them.

When we got back to Mama's, the casseroles began to march in with blue-haired ladies in tow. Within an hour, the food I had had catered was pushed aside. Deviled eggs, cheese straws, and ham biscuits were edging off of every horizontal surface my mother had owned.

The large living room opened out through French doors to an expansive green lawn. Indoors and outdoors were filled with elderly men and women who offered, first, condolences, then their wine glasses to the waiters I had hired. Sam brought a Nora Jones CD from his car and put it on the stereo. There was an easy buzz that I doubted this room had ever known. It felt like our house.

No one was going to ask me about my bruises. Who would dare? I took my sunglasses off and discarded my scarf. I relaxed into a big chair and took a sip of chardonnay that almost emptied the glass. Just as I threw my feet up onto the matching ottoman, I saw him, and almost threw it all up. Across the room, looking no different than he did eighteen years ago when he tripped down my hallway with the *shapely little thing*, stood Jeffrey Jello. Bruises or not, he recognized me immediately and made a beeline for my chair.

"Louise!" Smooth as ever, he slid onto the ottoman and took my hand in his. "My God! I heard you were with her. Are you OK?"

Charlie had been sitting on the big rolled arm of the chair talking to someone on my left. He cocked his head.

"Jeffrey, this is my husband, Charlie Wilson."

The two men shook hands. And then like baby penguins sensing a long overdue parent, one by one our children filed in. *Awkward* needed redefining. But of course Charlie rose to the occasion.

"Jeffrey, this is Sam, Sarah, and Willa."

He had to have known they'd be here, but he looked up at them like they had sprung from the ether.

"Kids this is your dad," Charlie said. "How 'bout I show y'all some privacy so you can have a little kumbaya."

Charlie ushered the four of them out into the yard. I sat there like I'd just taken a volleyball to the chest. *I deserve this*, I thought. *I've been so bad I deserve everything I get.* When Charlie came back in, he brought the bottle of chardonnay with him.

"You taking any pain medication? Prescription, I mean?"

"No."

He filled my glass to the rim and kissed the top of my head.

"Sarah needs Kleenex."

"In my pocketbook."

Twenty minutes later, Jeffrey and the kids emerged from the yard. The girls were red eyed. Sam looked bored. They kissed Charlie and me, then went back into the garden. Unbelievably,

Jeffrey reclaimed his spot on the ottoman, and Charlie retook the arm of the chair.

"I am so humbled," Jeffrey said. "The girls are gorgeous. Sam's a goddamn stud! And smart? Well, you can bet they don't get that from me. No siree, Bob."

You couldn't have shut him up with a .44 magnum.

"You're a hell of a guy, Charlie." He moved up on the ottoman. "Shit, they even call you Dad, and why the hell not? I left their asses high and dry, didn't I, Louise?"

Even a liar like me can spot phony soul bearing. The more I listened, the more I thought Jeffrey and Bill Clinton might be in the same twelve-step group.

"You two were meant to be parents." He went on. "I sucked at it, didn't I, Louise? But you? Came to you like breathin' air, didn't it, darlin'?" He patted my knee. "I was a total fuck up." He looked at Charlie. "Hell, I can't believe you two didn't have kids of your own. You never met a more beautiful pregnant woman in all your life, man. And with her—hell, two good pushes and bingo bongo baby! I mean it, bud, y'all should have had a houseful."

Charlie sat with a polite smile plastered on his face, and I prayed it meant he'd suffered a temporary hearing loss.

"Jeffrey," I finally blurted. "Let me walk you to the door."

I was glad I didn't let Dr. Irgens talk me into Botox, because right then I needed my brows to knit deep dark furrows. We left Charlie sitting with the volleyball in his chest.

"All these years we tried to find you and you show up today. What the hell were you thinking, Jeffrey? You want to be part of their lives, or you want to just show up every fifteen years and say hey."

"I think it meant something to them, Louise, and I think it meant something to you too."

"I think it means you make me sick. Don't you ever, ever take hold of my hand again. And don't call me darlin' either. You hear me?"

By the time I got back inside the mourners were starting to file out. I told Blanche Weatherly not to pick up one more wine glass, that the caterers would take care of everything. She tearfully thanked me, and Sam walked her home. The girls were content to look through my old high school yearbooks. I went onto the screen porch and faced Charlie, who still sat with the hole in his chest fresh from the bomb that Jeffrey Jello had dropped.

"Do you want to talk about this now?" I asked.

"Which this are you referring to?"

"How many thises are there?"

"Well I don't know. How many you got?"

"Charlie, you're scaring me." I stuck out my already protruding bottom lip. "The fact that I had my tubes tied behind Jeffrey's back may have made me a conniving wife," I lied. "But he was a scoundrel and I didn't want to have another baby with him."

"Looeeze!" he bellowed and took me by my shoulders.

"I couldn't care less when you had your goddamn tubes tied. I have never once in all the years we've been married wished for anything more than what I have. I've never needed to see my own flesh and blood to be a daddy. I have my children. What I'd like to talk about is this. *This* is about to drive me crazy!"

And he produced a bill from the Buckhead Westin. The bill that was in my purse. The purse he'd gotten Sarah's Kleenex from.

"I'd like to know what you were doing staying at a hotel in Atlanta for three nights? A damn nice hotel, costing me, what is it, nine hundred and thirty dollars, while I was way the hell over in Scotland? Now what am I suppose to think about that, Louise?"

He plopped into a chair. I looked at the bill and my knees buckled me into the little wicker thing opposite him. I was speechless. My craft failed me. I had no defense whatsoever.

"You having an affair, Weeza? Zat what all this face-lift crap's about? That's what they always say, you know. Women start working out, start losing weight, buying new clothes, talking about getting their hair done up. Boob jobs. They say it happens around your age too, you know. They say women start getting insecure, start feeling like they're not loved, not important. Kids going off, empty nest, change of life. You think I don't read the magazines at the dentist?"

He dwarfed the pretty wicker chair he sat in, his elbows planted on his knees, the bill dangled between them.

It was so in me to lie. So easy, so downright normal, like reading off a phone number or telling you what time it is. The rest of you breathe. I bear false witness. I allowed myself a second or two to think before I threw my face into my hands and admitted to the affair. It was just a meaningless thing of course, a midlife crisis, an acting out that would never happen again. Hell, men do it all the time. They sleep on the sofa for a week, buy jewelry, and are eventually forgiven. Another thirty seconds and I would have convinced myself I'd had sex with another man. Then I looked hard at Charlie. I'd never in my life seen him this way. He was fighting back tears and had a hard line drawn for a mouth that was quivering at the corners.

"I'm not having an affair, Charlie."

"Then what were you doing there?"

"I had a face-lift."

"Jesus, Louise, I'm no fool, they don't do face-lifts in hotels."

"No, silly. That's where you recover. I had the surgery at the hospital across the street."

"Then why the hell'd you even ask me if you were gonna do it anyway? I can't believe you did this. I'm not even sure I do believe you."

"Well, I can produce the surgeon's name and you can call and verify the whole thing." I was suddenly righteous.

"And the wreck? How could you do this? I was worried sick the whole flight over here."

"Now, Charlie, I never actually said I was in a wreck."

"For Christ's sake, Louise! You sure as hell let everybody think you were."

"Well, I was in a pickle."

"That's your response! You were in a pickle! That's fucking beautiful, Louise. That takes the goddamn cake."

"Please don't tell the kids, Charlie. I just couldn't bear it. I'm sorry I lied."

"I'm not going to tell 'em. You tell 'em!" He grabbed his suit coat and walked to the door.

"All the years we been married, Louise, and you never once lied to me." He slammed the door and was gone.

Did I mention what a good liar I am? The force of a volleyball knocked the breath clean out of me.

They left the next day and I stayed on for a while to sort through my mother's things. What I cried over most was finding a bottle of Zoloft. I met with the lawyers and began probate. In time, the green bruises faded to ochre and were easily concealed with a little Estée Lauder. A doctor I found in Asheville removed all the stitches that hadn't dissolved on their own, and my lips began to look normal again. As a matter of fact, my face took on a familiar youthful look. It made me feel even worse to see its innocence.

I called him every day, but Charlie was always on another line or out of the office. The kids sounded fine. Willa was busy with school. The asshole was history. She had moved on to college applications.

"Dad thinks I should apply to Duke."

"Puke in a bucket!"

"That's what I said."

"But you could surely get in, baby."

"Think so?"

"Know so."

"When you comin' home, Mama?"

"Tomorrow. I'm finished up here for the time being. I'll have to come back in a few weeks, though. Will you come with me?"

"Sure," she said absently.

"Willa?"

"Yeah."

"This is hard."

"You OK, Mama?"

"No. I miss you. Miss your daddy."

"Dad's been weird."

"How?"

"Mopey. You know how he is. You're not here and he acts like he's missing a leg. Won't eat. God, I think he's lost about ten pounds. Watches TV 'til like three in the morning. I'm glad you're coming home. Hey, Mama?"

"Yeah."

"Could you go to Harris Teeter on the way home? There's like nothing to eat in this house."

"Go to sleep, Willa. I'll see you tomorrow."

Early the next morning I had to meet the marble man at the cemetery. I had ordered a headstone for both my parents—we never had a proper one for my father. I watched while the crane moved the rose marble monument into place and wondered how much of my need to lie had to do with the two ghosts that hovered here. I was sure that vowing to lie no more was of little use, like an alcoholic promising not to drink. And I was sure there were no twelve-step groups for people like me. After it was in place and the sod was snug around it, I stood back and looked at the marker: John "Jack" Tree and Mary Alice Tree, their dates of birth and death flanked by etched magnolia blossoms.

For the first time since it all happened I cried. Not soft daughter-who-lost-her-mother tears, but sit-down-in-the-dirt-choking-up-snot, wailing-so-much-that-they-might-send-you-to-Butner tears. I thanked God that only the dead could hear me, and I swore right then and there that the fanny-lift I'd read about in *Vogue* last month could send some other woman into divorce court, not me.

For the first time in three weeks, my bruises were healed enough for me to pull my hair into a ponytail. I pulled on a pair of jeans and a T-shirt, packed my bag, and locked my mother's house. Before I hit the road, I stopped off to return the dress I had bought for the funeral. It had ripped along the zipper, and I refused to spend six hundred dollars on a dress, Armani or not, that couldn't handle a single wearing.

"We have another one in your size," the sales woman offered.

"Just credit my card," I said. "The more I think about it, that dress is a little severe for a woman who's only forty, don't you think?"

The Penitent

The woman folded back the perfectly pressed sheet and, with a wrinkled hand, smoothed it over the old man's chest. Like an altar cloth, she thought, embroidered white-on-white linen. His thick hair, snow on the white pillow.

He was a tall man. Thin now, but still his large frame filled the bed. His face was a rectangle, sunken, but beautiful bones kept the architecture of his cheeks high, his jaw strong. When they opened, his eyes took in the room around him and then her face. She refused to imagine the not-seeing of death that would steal the way he examined whatever lay before him: the sun setting over a castle ruin, a meal, the eyes of a dead boy he had tried to save.

"Should I make tea?" she asked.

"Say my name, Catherine." His voice didn't reveal his age. It was deep and clear and still reached into her middle, the way it had more than fifty years ago. "Say it."

She took a deep breath and sat on the wooden chair by the bed. He wore a jersey T-shirt with *Red Sox* printed on the front. From the neck down, he could have been mistaken for a younger man. He reached for her hand and she let him take it.

"You haven't said it since you got here. Why?"

Gnarled fingers laced for a moment. He traced a vein with his thumb, past her wrist, almost to her elbow.

"Oh, the flowers," she said, rising. "I'll put them in a vase."

But he caught her wrist and pulled her back down. His strength surprised her.

"Say my name, Catherine. Like you used to."

She looked at him then closed her eyes.

"Paul." She whispered at first, then said it again so he could hear. "Paul."

Saying it brought the echoes bouncing off hills and empty rooms, growing softer, then finally gone. *Paul, paul, aul, ul.* And other sounds: a long thin whistle, then a bomb exploding, the squeal of ambulance breaks, Churchill's drone and Hitler's rants above radio static. Behind her eyes, images played of a time long before phones rang in pockets: guns, and soldiers, and little morphine ampoules all marching in lock-step after the name *Paul.*

———

Catherine didn't love Geoffrey when she married him. She hadn't come to love him, like he said she would. She was good to him, if duti-ful is good. And kind. He'd fallen in love with her when his father was recovering from a surgery at a hospital in London.

"You were so beautiful," he said on their wedding night. "Even in that miserable gray uniform, stiff as wood, you were lovely. You had a long dark curl that kept escaping your veil. Remember? You kept stuff-ing it under while you took Father's pulse. I fell in love with you then. Couldn't wait to get you out of that awful place. You were not meant to nurse . . . except perhaps our children."

Geoffrey gave Catherine a wicked look and pulled her to bed.

Catherine smiled at her new husband. She didn't mind his touch, but it didn't thrill her. Though she had little experience in matters of love, or lovemaking, she knew that obligation and comfort were a poor substitute for passion.

When he left for the war, rather handsome in his uniform and new boots, she smiled and waved at the ship.

"You're so brave, darling." Geoffrey's mother reached for her hand and squeezed. But Catherine's smile was no camouflage for relief.

A year later, when he came home from North Africa in a chair, with half his face drooping, her indifference shifted. She recoiled. He knew her on most days, and on the days he didn't, his mother wept. Over the next two years his parents and a small staff hung on to slight improvements: an asymmetrical smile, wiping his own chin, lifting a spoon. She hoped for nothing. Large shovels of dirt buried them both. Often she had to remind herself to breathe.

"I'm going Belgium. To the Front," she told them at supper one night, after they'd helped Geoffrey to bed. "To work."

From across the table, Geoffrey's father reached for her hand.

"Brave girl," he said. "But you'll do nothing of the sort."

Then he returned his attention to his boiled egg.

"But I am," she told them. "I've signed on with the Royal Army. I leave in a fortnight."

"Dear girl, you haven't been a nurse in years." Geoffrey's mother threw a dismissive hand. "You worked in a tidy hospital in Chelsea, not on a battlefield. It's sweet of you, of course, but no." She stirred her tea and reached for a biscuit. "How about the bandage roll and the tea line at the station. You can even wear your uniform. And everyone will call you 'sister.'" She dropped her voice and leaned forward. "We simply cannot lose you both. Now, stop this nonsense."

But you are losing us both, Catherine thought. *Surely I am dead already.*

When she left, she took her guilt along with her, a gray little man forever wagging his finger, throwing up images of Geoffrey's drooling lip. As she crossed the Channel, she watched the black water from the bow of the ship and dismissed the sting of the cold wind that ripped through her cape and stockings. An hour into the crossing, she took off her wedding ring and let it slip into the sea. *I am a coward,* she thought. *The worst kind of coward, for I let them think I'm noble.* She didn't notice that her breathing was easy and rhythmic.

Catherine arrived at a casualty clearing station in October. By Christmas, the remains of her uniforms were more blood and mud than wool. She discovered trousers, synched at the waist. Her stockings had become tourniquets; her cape, a blanket for some poor boy from the Midlands. She replaced it with a jacket taken from a soldier from Bromley. He died with his head in her lap—not of wounds, but of pneumonia.

They moved the mobile unit four times over the next ten months: north, then west, back south, then north again. Then, finally, word reached the station, now settled in an old abbey, that they were to set up shop. There were tents in the courtyard and canvas flaps hung over stone archways. An Allied surgical team was coming. There would be Yanks and Canadians. "They'll have morphine," said Sister Jean, a Queen's Nurse from Scotland. "The Americans have everything."

But after a month, the morphine was rare as silk and rationed like sugar. The only thing they had a lot of was a particular doctor, a lieutenant who all the nurses said looked like Gregory Peck. They called him *Paul* when they smoked cigarettes together, *Doctor* when they handed him a scalpel, and *Lieutenant* when the Major was around. He was everywhere: bringing in the wounded, in the operating tent, on the abbey grounds giving triage orders. She found him once injecting the contents of a morphine vial he'd hoarded into a dying soldier's arm and what seemed like seconds later yelling at a young boy to get up off a cot so a soldier who was really sick could use it. When he listened, he studied a face like a deaf man. And on the rare occasions when he smiled, his black eyes disappeared under squinted lids. Fresh out of a surgical residency, they said, but he was older, or perhaps so tired he looked older.

"He doesn't look like a doctor, does he?" Sister Jean said as they watched him triage the incoming wounded from an upper window. "They say he did something else before this. I think a pilot. Looks like he should be flying planes."

"Looks like an illusionist," Catherine said as the incoming siren blew. "Surely there are three of him."

The two women hurried down the steps. *He moves so calmly*, she thought as she watched him direct stretchers. *But he does more in an hour than the Major does in a day.*

"Where I come from, nuns are sisters," he said an hour later, not looking up. "Nurses are just . . . nurse."

His left hand was buried deep in a boy's belly. A hemostat circled his thumb and forefinger. The unconscious boy stirred.

"Catherine, then."

"Could you grab me a bowl . . . Catherine?" His broad American sounded like the movies.

She handed him a kidney-shaped pan. The shrapnel he pulled from the boy's gut plinked against the enamel edges.

"Can you close this?"

Rising, he kept his eyes focused on the boy and handed her the sulfonamide and sutures. He turned his back and moved on to the next one, not waiting for an answer. A dark, wet spine spread out like wings on his back. *A force comes off him,* she thought, *like the scent of steel and steam rising from a locomotive. A force of sorts, but often oddly quiet.*

When night bombings shook the old abbey, they all moved into cellars and trenches. In the mornings, hunched in earthen corners, they had tea and canned milk and smoked as if cigarettes were food.

"Where's home?" she asked one night when things were finally still.

"Montana. It's out West."

"Doctor Cowboy, then."

"Humph," he said, with a trace of a smile. "I'll bet you've been on more horses than I have, nice English girl like you."

A month later it began to rain, for days. Nothing dried, not even if hung by a fire. But it had been quiet. She had bathed and washed her hair and now stood on a stone terrace blotting her curls with a towel when she saw the major's jeep come up the main road. It was full. Four, maybe five men bounced up and down as it managed the rutted road and fanned wet mud into the air. She could hear them laughing above the rain, or were they singing? She stood smiling at the jeep, enjoying the scent of the shampoo Sister Jean portioned out like liquid gold. She was just pinning her hair up into a knot when she was suddenly rocked back on her heels. There was a flash. The gray sky went blinding white. An explosion followed what felt like fists pounding her chest while it sucked all the sound out of the world. Men flew from the jeep into the sky, with arms and legs thrown in directions they were never meant to go, like dolls twisted by evil little boys. In seconds there were no men, just smoke that billowed where the jeep had been. Heart pounding, she ran inside, down the stone stairs and out into the court-yard. Others ran behind her toward the gate. There was no sound now, no screams, just the steady, droning rain and their footsteps on the stones. Then she saw him, rising out of the smoke yelling.

"No! Go back. Go back." Paul was carrying the Major, both of them bleeding, uniforms torn and blackened. She didn't go back. She moved through the abbey gate.

"There are mines, goddamn it. Get the hell back!"

She watched the Major's head, flung backward over the crook of Paul's elbow. It rolled and bounced with each step. When she reached them, she lifted the man's head and helped bring him into the abbey. The smell of smoldering wet wool was in her nostrils.

The Major was treated and given enough laudanum to get him through the night. While they stood by his bed, a soldier knocked at the open door.

"I need a cause of death, Doc. For the others."

"Put Hitler's subterranean little secrets on your form." Catherine's bitter voice bounced off the walls. "They'll be mangling lives long after this war is over." She tucked the blanket under the Major's feet. "You'll see." She turned and looked at the soldier who looked to Paul for help. "After all the treaties are signed, children will go out to play and never come home."

"Corporal," Paul handed the clipboard back to the soldier, "that'll be all."

"Sorry," she said after the door closed. "The combat wounded is one thing—it's horrid of course, but it's fair in a perverse way."

"Fair?" He laughed. "There is no fair. There's just who can kill the most the fastest."

He took off his jacket, gathered some supplies, kicked a chair over to the window, and sat.

"Mind stitching me up?"

He took off his hat, revealing a long arched gash just below his hairline. Without the hat's pressure, it began to bleed again.

"Right."

She washed her hands in the basin, moved to the window, and pushed his dark hair away from his forehead. He leaned his head back on the windowsill and closed his eyes. When she dabbed antiseptic, he barely flinched, and didn't move at all when she dripped Novocain directly into the oozing wound. She dabbed around the deep gash and soon the bleeding stopped.

"It's rather like the Thames, your gash."

"The river?" He opened his eyes.

"As it looks on a map winding through London."

She squinted as she worked, pinching the skin together with one set of fingers, moving the needle through with the other. The rain had stopped. It grew uncomfortably hot in the room. The breeze through the long narrow windows barely stirred the curtains. She stitched, tying one off, snipping the black sutures, and beginning another. The Major snored loudly from across the room and they chuckled.

She knew his eyes were on her breasts and felt them move to her face. She bit her lip as she worked. A slightly crooked tooth overlapped another. "The perfect flaw," he would tell her later. "It makes you like no one else." His eyes settled back on her breasts. She imagined his head falling between them, his blood seeping into her smock. She all but felt her hands cradling his head, digging her fingers into his hair. Just as she banished the thought and imagined him as another boy with an open head, he reached for her elbow and slowly traced a line up to her hand, the one without the needle.

"Don't," she whispered. "I'm just stitching in the Albert Bridge."

She snipped the suture and dabbed at the line on his head. She cut a square of gauze, tore off a bit of adhesive, and lightly pressed the bandage onto his forehead.

"There. All done."

Before he had time to take her elbow again, she moved her hand from his forehead to his jaw then bent to his face and kissed him. The ensuing explosion, this time inside her, ran like a current through every vessel and nerve ending in her body. He rose, pulling her up with him, and crushed her to his chest. She felt his fingers on the bones of her back, then climbing up to her neck, raking through her hair, then cupping her face as he pulled away. He ran his tongue across her crooked tooth then kissed her eyelids. She'd never known a kiss to move from erotic to tender so fast. Never felt a pulse beat like a drum so loud it was impossible to tell whether it was hers or his. It was a moment she wanted to swallow, to hold inside, to keep where she could call it up at will.

"My name sounds like something I've never heard coming out of your throat," he said. "Say it again."

"Paul," she said, then leaned her head into his chest, smelling the smoke and his body through his shirt.

"I'll stay here tonight." He kissed her lightly, then disengaged. "Come get me if you need me."

"What if I need you now?" Catherine knew her face was flushed. Sweat ran down her back.

"Oh, here, I forgot." He grabbed for his jacket and pulled a package from the inside pocket. Stuffed into a sock and wrapped with a rag were at least a dozen ampoules of morphine. He dug again and pulled out another one. Then he grabbed the Major's coat and dislodged two more.

"My God, you are an angel." She took them as if they were jewels in velvet sacks.

Paul moved the chair over to the Major's bed, put his muddy boots up at the foot, leaned back, and closed his eyes.

"By the way," he said. "Your hair smells nice."

Across the hall, Catherine opened the door to the long ward. To the moans and labored breathing, she dangled a sock.

"Teatime, boys." She lifted a syringe from a metal table. "A delightful blend this evening, with a remarkably soothing effect. Who will be first?"

By springtime, they were lovers, escaping into the night trenches when there were no bombs, only the sounds of zippers and snaps and them, falling onto their knees, then halting gasps, muffled cries.

"You're beautiful," he said one night. They lay naked on a rough woolen blanket under a sky strewn with stars.

"You're mad. I'm too tall, awkward."

"Elegant." He traced circles on her shoulder. "But I am mad," he agreed.

"The truth is, you're the only sane thing in this entire place."

She sat up and began to dress. He undid each button that she fastened, then slid his hand up to her throat and kept his thumb at the pulse of her neck as he kissed her. The wild rhythms of their hearts moved into synch. It was something they toyed with when they made love, coming to know the beats, the harmonies, the percussions of their bodies.

"How long can you stay?" he asked.

"How long have you got?" She tossed the shirt to the ground and reached for him again.

"The rest of my life," he said. "And maybe a year or two after that."

In an hour they were back in the thick of it, saving some, tagging others. These were days that never ended. Days when Paul was demanding and distant, then at night, tender and burning. Days, Catherine told only herself, that were the happiest of her life. At first they stole clandestine moments, but in time they were simply discrete. Theirs wasn't the only hospital affair. In war, convention lives elsewhere, along with God and the good china.

After Normandy, the soldiers were American too. They died the same as the Brits and the French, calling for mothers, wives, and lovers. She held their hands and wrote their letters, then tagged their toes and sent them home. Hundreds of times she saw Paul place his hand over a dead man's chest and close his own eyes for no more than a moment. Once she saw him bless himself. Strange, she never thought of Americans as needing religion. She thought only the Irish and the poor were Catholic. She didn't know one she didn't pity—so indebted to their priests who kept them ignorant, pregnant, and devoted to a fairy tale. For her, God was simply a mystery she hadn't the time to unravel. Still, when soldiers died, she would brush their hair away from their foreheads, especially the young ones, and she'd kiss two fingers and touch them to their lips. *Last rites* she called it.

And then it began that Paul would leave for weeks, sometimes months, to prep field hospitals and direct mobile surgical units as the Allies moved east. Each time he left it was a death, and when he returned, a resurrection. He arrived back one afternoon and found her passing scalpels to another surgeon.

Gowned and masked, he slipped behind her and he whispered into her hair, "I could undress you with my teeth." He slid the back of his fingers down her spine.

Catherine grabbed the edge of the table, lost focus, and bit her lip beneath her mask until she tasted blood. "Go," she begged.

One night he asked, "Were you in London during the bombing?"

"No, Kettering, in the Midlands. But I grew up in London, Sloane Square, just off the King's Road. Been to London?"

"Nope," he said. "Only to Billings, and Boston for medicine. Oh, and now Europe. I'm finally well traveled."

"We'll go," she said. "After this madness. I'll show you."

"I'd rather go to Kettering," he said. "I'm afraid there's not much left of London."

She wrote banal letters to Kettering, never knowing or minding if they got through. Then one day a letter got through to her. It was from Geoffrey, with handwriting clear and straight. "I'm walking," he wrote, "and strong. When are you coming home, Catherine? When?" Her gray companion swallowed her whole. She lay curled in a belly of reproach; the letter, in a ball crumpled in her hand.

"Incoming." Paul pulled back the flap of her tent. "Hurry."

She grabbed hold of his outstretched hand and the misery dissolved. Later, she would wallow in that guilt too. It was only right she do some kind of penance for all the joy she felt.

On the nights she hadn't already fallen asleep on the seat of a jeep or in the nurses' tent, she stole into the cot he had curtained off at the end of the long ward. But she always awoke alone.

One morning she saw him coming up over a hill at daybreak.

"Where were you?" she asked, annoyed.

"I've moved the morgue—graves registry—down, farther away." He pointed with his thumb over his shoulder.

"Paul! You're the one always telling us these hills are literally growing mines." She was angry. "Promise me you won't go back down there."

"I promise to be very careful. Come," he said. "We have work."

By the spring of '45, the world began to breathe again. Often an entire day would pass when no wounded arrived—time to nurse, to be kind. Paul would brood, then disappear for hours. Then one day he came back and put her in a jeep he'd borrowed from the Major.

"Where are we going?" she asked.

"Home."

He drove her to a tiny village where you could stand in the middle of the street, spread your arms, and touch the houses. The hotel had six rooms. Not one was taken.

"I want to marry you," he said, unbuttoning her blouse, kissing her hair. "But I have an entanglement." He was awkward. *Entanglement* didn't seem an American word.

"So, you are married." She took in what wasn't a shock, just a bitter disappointment and one of God's little jokes. On her.

"I'm not married." He kissed her ear and the spot behind it.

A sweetheart. Of course he'd have someone waiting for him. She was relieved and pushed the little gray man down and away.

"I have to talk to—" he began.

"No." She put two fingers to his lips. "I don't want to know. We both had lives before this. I don't mind, really I don't."

How could she possibly? She had to disentangle, too, from a man and a family that would hate her, if they didn't already.

"How long can we stay?" She moved toward him and put her arms around his neck.

"How long have you got?"

"The rest of my life," she answered. "And perhaps a year or two after that."

They bathed each other until the water went cold, then slept so long they awoke on their own. In the morning they looked at each other's bodies on clean white sheets and laughed at the joy of it.

"Do you want to get married in England?" he asked over breakfast.

"In Montana," she said. "I want to get married under a sky so blue it will hurt my eyes."

When they drove back to the abbey through the gate and into the courtyard a limping soldier came running toward them, each step joyfully off-kilter.

"It's over!" he yelled and jumped into the jeep. "It's over. We're all going home!"

Red canvas crosses undulated on the tents as nurses and soldiers danced beneath them. Music conquered the static, Glenn Miller, loud and brassy. It was May and the air smelled like peace.

Within a month, transports arrived and left daily. A new breed of soldiers was among them now, dismantling unexploded bombs and sweeping for mines. The wounded were going home. But even on the last days some died.

The Americans played baseball in a grassy area the minesweepers had cleared. Paul told everyone where to play and taught the Brits how to hold a bat and run the bases. He laughed at how the nurses threw like girls. They all laughed.

"So, this is what you did before the war," Sister Jane said as they lay sunning themselves after a game.

"Every chance I got," he said.

They were to meet in Boston in September. She would break her husband's heart a little more, then cross an ocean. They would make their way to Montana and marry on a mountain with green grass under a dry sky. There was a church, he said.

"Is it Catholic?" she asked.

"No. Episcopal, or Anglican as your tribe likes to put it."

For her return to England, she was to sail from Calais. She'd been packed for days, counting the hours. She had been so breezy and kind to the remaining soldiers she could hardly stand herself. The Major asked her twice if she was drunk.

"Yes," she answered both times. "Want some?"

The morning she was to travel to the coast, she looked in every possible place for Paul. He wasn't on the wards, nowhere, not even in the bombed-out chapel where once she had found him sleeping. Finally, she looked to the gravel road, to where he'd moved the graves registry. Until the minesweepers, the abbey had been a cloistered world.

No one dared to traipse about on paths or in fields. Even now, with the all-clear markers that dotted the landscape, she walked in the footprints of others, looking for the slightest rise or dip in the gravel.

The road, she discovered, curved around a grouping of poplar trees. Beyond them stood a long gray-green tent. Canvas stretchers looked like tombstones propped up along a stone wall. She was sweating when she stopped. The sun burned the back of her neck. Paul's shirt hung on a nail just outside the tent. *Why do you come here?* she thought. *They have no need of you now.* Angry, she pulled back the canvas flap. It took a second for her eyes to adjust to the dark. Rows of cots with neat aisles between them looked like church pews. Her reproach was on her tongue when she finally saw him. But instead of speaking, she gripped the canvas, transfixed, stunned.

Alone and all in black, Paul stood at the far end of the tent with a purple stole around his neck, curled in memory of wherever he kept it hidden. Unaware of her gaze, he dipped his thumb in a little brass pot. Oil. Holy oil. He made a cross on a dead man's forehead, then his lips, and his chest. He made a final cross with his whole hand.

"*In nomine Patris, et Filii, et Spiritūs Sancti.*" So soft and intimate he spoke his Latin. The same way he said he could drown in the hollow between her breasts.

Oh, God, she thought, *which is the blasphemy?*

Something broke in her middle and fell into shards around her feet. She'd asked him once if he were terribly religious. He'd surveyed the ward and said: "Only saints find God in a place like this." Then he turned and walked away from her.

She watched this other Paul, surrounded by the stench of death mixed with his sweet-smelling oil, so much taller and darker in the long black cassock, the tiniest bit of white at his neck. What kept her from rushing at him, screaming, tearing the stole from his neck was her little gray man pushing down the keening wail, finally getting his way.

"Amen," Paul said and pulled the sheet over the dead man's face.

Once a priest, always a priest, repeated gunfire in her head. *My penance,* she thought. She took a last look at her priest, then let the canvas drop. She walked back up the hill, not looking for the tracks of others. Did he take to God first and then to healing, or the other way around? Sister Jean said he had done something before this. This was not something one did. This was something one was. At the top of the hill she remembered to breathe.

The abbey of death had come to life, like a country carnival. Woody Herman blared over the loudspeaker. A transport was being loaded, the canvas rolled up on each side, just the skeleton of metal bars, allowing the smiling soldiers and nurses to wave good-bye. The music stopped. The speakers popped and scratched as the needle landed on another record. Vera Lynn's "A Nightingale Sang in Berkeley Square" slowed the pace but a little. Soldiers and nurses lined the wooden benches on either side of the lorry, giddy, smiling, cradling bundles on their laps. As the truck began to move, an American soldier holding a bottle of wine stood at the back and stretched out his hand.

"Come on, sweetheart, let me buy you a drink!" he said. He had a small bandage over an ear and dark, wet rings under his arms. "Come on, honey, jump on up. Let me take you to Georgia. You gonna love Savannah." He winked. "It's almost as pretty as you are."

Catherine walked behind the lorry and stared blankly at the drunken man.

Two Red Cross nurses that had come toward the end of the fighting were passing a bottle between them and singing along with Vera Lynn:

> *That certain night,*
> *the night we met,*
> *there was magic abroad in the air.*
> *There were angels dining at the Ritz,*
> *and a nightingale sang in Berkeley Square.*

One of the nurses took a long drink and laughed at the curly-haired soldier. "Sit down corporal," she said. "She's the Lieutenant's gal."

"I don't see no lieutenant." The boy reached up and held onto the bar above him as the truck bounced over the cobblestones. He smiled at Catherine. "You see any lieutenant?"

Catherine quickened her pace then began to trot to keep up with the transport as it moved under the tall abbey arch. She kept looking at the soldier and began to whisper the song along with the Red Cross nurses:

> *I may be right, I may be wrong,*
> *but I'm perfectly willing to swear*
> *that when he turned and smiled at me,*
> *a Nightingale sang in Berkeley Square.*

Catherine grabbed the soldier's hand. He pulled her up and into the back of the transport. She took the bottle from one of the nurses. The hearty wine, mixed with the salt of her tears, slid down her throat. She managed to sing as they bounced on the stones through the gate:

> *Our homeward step was just as light*
> *as the tap-dancing feet of Astaire,*
> *and like an echo far away*
> *a nightingale sang in Berkeley Square.*

As the truck turned down the entry she caught sight of the burned, now rusted, bits of jeep, as much a part of the present landscape as the rocks and trees. The Major stood at the final turn onto the main road, saluting each truck. When he saw her, he lifted a hesitant hand and waved. Her packed rucksack was left sitting on her cot, along with directions to a rooming house in Boston.

———

Of wounds, she came to know, time isn't so much a healer as a slow-acting opiate that, over the decades, eventually dulls the pain. For her, it happened around the time the letters that she sent back unopened stopped coming. And yet, on the days when the flags flew in remembrance, and whenever someone called the name *Paul*, the pain seeped back in, like blood wicking up through gauze.

When she was seventy, a letter came. It sat for a day on a table by the door. Then finally she opened it.

"Go." Her little gray companion, dead, she thought, these almost fifty years, rose up again and tugged at the hem of her heart. "Cross an ocean. Go."

She had come to know that sometimes guilt is a wise teacher.

And now as the afternoon shadows stretched long across the bed where her one-time lover lay, Catherine allowed the pain to flow along with the remembrance of joy and passion old women pretend to forget. She lifted the glass of water like a chalice for the old priest. She held the bottom firmly then wiped the drips with a clean white cloth.

"You were married." He didn't ask; he told.

"You knew?"

"The Major told me. Our paths crossed at conferences on wartime triage and the like."

"I had left him."

"I know that too."

The anger that had been so long dormant filled her middle and rose up into her throat. "And when you spoke in London four years ago. Was the Major there then? When you spoke about God on the battlefield, trends in military ethics?"

His eyes widened. "You were there?" He moved to sit up in bed.

"In the back. I watched you, heard very little. Watched how your collar cut into your neck. You kept tugging at it, like a man in white tie and tails dying to throw them off." She walked across the room and stood at the window. A bird pecked at a stone wall. "There were twenty-seven physician-priests in Europe during the war. Did you know that? Twenty-seven. All of them, save one, wore a collar."

"Did you love him, your husband?" He put his head back on the pillow.

"Don't ask me that." She didn't want him to know that over time she had come to love Geoffrey in a way that made her life good and whole. That he had been a good father, and when he died five years ago, her loneliness became a hole she had yet to fill.

"I had left, Catherine." He rose up again and leaned on an elbow. "I was a doctor."

"You were a Jesuit, Paul. I just intercepted you during your doubting phase." The bitter words were spit at the window.

"That's not fair. Why else would I have asked you to marry me? I was done with it."

"But you weren't. In the end you were not done. All the time you were with me you had your God. We had a flat tire when we left the abbey, about ten miles out, in a little village called Ermè." She turned and looked at the bed. "Does that sound familiar? There was an old woman in the square who brought us water while we waited. She wanted to know if the priest was coming. He was an American, this priest, and also a doctor, she said. He delivered a baby there once. She wanted to know if he was coming back to say Mass."

Like a storm, the anger peaked then broke. Tears pooled then slid down her wrinkled cheeks.

Paul let his head fall back onto the pillow. "They hadn't had a priest since the war started." He looked away and shook his head. "It seemed harmless, a kindness." He turned back to her and held out a hand. "I was in love with you, Catherine."

"It wouldn't have been enough that you left for me. If I couldn't hold you in the midst of a war, how could I hope to hold you through something as mundane as a marriage?"

He patted the bed. She took a step nearer.

"I never let go of your face. And I never had a picture. Not a single picture of you, but I could conjure your lips and eyes, your hair."

"I believed in heaven," she walked closer, "but not God. I'm not sure I ever did."

He chuckled and reached for her hand. She sat back in the chair.

"You went back too, Catherine," he said. "Perhaps we were both cowards."

"Yes, I think we were."

She put her other hand over his. Her linen dress had small splashes on the breast. She sat in silence until they dried, until her breathing was slow and steady in her chest.

He closed his eyes and after a long while he asked, "How long can you stay?" A smile crinkled his eyes.

"How long have you got?" She smiled in spite of herself. Her old, wrinkled self.

That afternoon he slept. She brushed his white hair away from his forehead and traced the scar shaped like a river with her finger. It had faded, of course. The tiny dots where the sutures had entered, allowing the bridges to cross, were barely visible after so many years. She folded the sheet over his chest and laid her head next to his.

"Paul," she said, moving her hand over the embroidery. "Paul."

A Whore for Thursdays

Frank Pella lay in room 2311 at New York Presbyterian Hospital. He asked his wife, Gina, to get him a priest.

"A priest? For Christ's sake, Frank." She patted her husband's hand and pulled a Kleenex from her purse.

"Come on, Gina, grant a guy his dying wish." Frank scooted up in the bed.

"Like I would be that lucky." Gina wiped away a drop of applesauce from her husband's chin.

"It could happen." He scratched at the tape above where the IV was inserted.

"Cut the drama, Frank." She tossed the tissue and reached to adjust her husband's pillow. "Drink your juice."

"I'm not thirsty."

"Doctor says you have to stay hydrated, baby. Now drink." Gina lifted the Styrofoam cup and held the straw up to her husband's lips.

"I'd get *you* a priest." Frank drank and swallowed.

"I wouldn't ask."

"Please, Gina, I'm serious here."

Gina cocked her head and looked hard at her husband. "Jesus, Frank, you are, aren't you?" She put the cup on the tray table. "Well forget about it. Remember every one of 'em should burn in hell? Remember saying that, like a million times?"

"Ma." Ellen Pella Anthony looked up from her reading. "He says he wants to see a priest, so get him a priest."

"You get him a priest." Gina glared at her daughter.

"Me? I don't know any priests."

"Well, neither do I, except that little bagpipe Father McCarthy who's doing time upstate for ruining the lives of precious children."

"Oh, Christ Almighty, Ma. Not every priest in New York abused children."

"But how can you tell the ones who did from the ones who didn't? I thought Father McCarthy was a nice man, coaching those boys, taking them camping."

"You know, you're right, Ma." Ellen turned to her father. "How 'bout I find you a rabbi, Dad. Think you can tell your sins to a rabbi? I bet I can find one of those who never diddled a little boy."

Frank and his daughter laughed.

They were so much alike, Frank and his girl, with those big brown eyes and the strong chin. They had dimples so deep you could dive in and never find your way out. And both of them had hair dark as crow feathers. They were tough as nails, except when they weren't. Gina recalled the two of them sitting on the couch crying at *Rudy, Steel Magnolias, Terms of Endearment.* Ellen was an actor now. She did parts off Broadway, a commercial now and then.

"Gina." Frank's voice was stronger today. "It couldn't hurt."

"Just tell me, Frank, what sins do you have to tell a priest? You have a dirty thought last week? Felt envy for your brother's fifty-inch television?"

"I got sins."

"You are a good man, Frank. A saint. Everybody says so. And anyway, you only had a little heart attack. Dr. Torelli says you're going to be fine. You just need to lose a little weight, eat a little more escarole, a little less braciole." Gina sat in the chair next to Frank's bed.

"Never mind." Frank threw his hand at his wife. "I'll get one of the nurses to get me one."

"The hell you will." Gina stood. "If anybody's going to put you in a confession box, it'll be me!"

"Good. I'm glad you're seeing reason." Frank closed his eyes.

"But why, Frank? Why all the sudden you got to see a priest?"

"I got sins." He opened his eyes and raised his palms.

"Well, if you got sins, you tell me first, not some goddamned priest who doesn't even know you."

Frank looked into his wife's eyes, the same eyes he looked into forty years ago on their wedding day. She was still pretty to him. Still trim. Shiny, silver streaks ran through a smart new haircut, and a matching set of wrinkles framed her pretty blue eyes. Suddenly his face contorted and he began to sob.

"I betrayed you, Gina. Every Thursday, except for Thanksgivings, I betrayed you. For thirty years. I betrayed you."

The doctors had said he might behave somewhat irrationally, be more emotional. *This must be it*, she thought. She sat on the bed next to him and put her hand to his cheek.

"Thursdays?" Gina wiped his cheeks with the edge of the sheet. "Thursdays you go to Brooklyn to do the books for Marty. You betray me with Marty Jacobi?" Gina looked over at her daughter, who had put down her script and moved to the foot of the bed, then back at her husband. "I don't think he's your type, Frank."

Gina's big, handsome Frank suddenly looked frail, vulnerable.

Ellen moved to the side of the bed and took her father's hand.

"Dad, don't," she said. "We'll get you a priest. Whatever you want. I'll ask Bobby. He'll know somebody."

The doctors told Gina to relax. It's normal, a resident said. Labile, they called it. Even short bursts of delusional thinking. It happens with heart patients, especially those who end up in ICU for a while. They become disoriented; with no windows, they mix up their days and nights.

On the way home from the hospital Gina made peace with the thought of a priest. Ellen's husband, Bobby, a voice coach at the Actor's Studio, used to teach at Fordham. The idea of a Jesuit hearing Frank's confession wasn't quite so bad. Jessies were skeptics, smart, and as full of doubt as she and Frank had been when they left the Church twenty-five years ago. A Jesuit she could stomach.

"Whatever," she said to Ellen later. "Just make sure Bobby finds him somebody nice, and you know, somebody who's not, you know."

"Don't worry, Ma, I'll make sure he's not a faggot. Just because we're in the theater doesn't mean we don't know any straight people."

"Oh, don't give me that look. You know what I mean. I just want somebody your father can relate to."

The whole thing had thrown her for a loop. Frank was the one man in the world who could make her feel safe. When she was with him, God and Satan could be at the door and neither one of them could as much as ring the bell. The day Frank slumped over at the dinner table was the first time she'd ever seen him sick. He kept grabbing his left arm and trying to spread his fingers. It was the fear on his face in the ambulance that shook Gina to the core. Her familiar interior was tossed about, like someone had flipped the carpets and tossed the furniture.

"I don't care what it takes," she said to her daughter. "I just want him home so I can get him strong and better. If it takes a priest, so be it."

But Frank didn't get strong. Frank got worse. After his death, Ellen and her three brothers, along with their spouses, hovered over Gina like bees around the queen. She shooed them away, taking on the funeral arrangements, writing the obituary, getting Frank's best suit pressed and his shoes shined.

"Ma, nobody's going to see his shoes," his oldest son said.

"I'll see them," Gina said. "I'll see them each time I imagine him stuck in a damn box in the ground."

After the funeral, Frank and Gina's home was full of people offering condolences and grandchildren running through the house like it was Thanksgiving. Platters of the same foods that had killed Frank Pella covered the dining room table and littered the kitchen.

"Ma, Mr. and Mrs. Jacobi are here." Ellen knocked on the bathroom door behind which Gina had sought a reprieve from the bone-crushing hugs.

"She's with him?" Gina asked. "The chair or the cane?"

"The chair."

Gina came out of the bathroom, blew her nose, and asked her daughter how she looked.

"You look beautiful, Ma."

Gina stopped and wiped a bit of mascara from under her daughter's eye before heading to the living room.

Gina didn't know Anna Jacobi well. She saw her once every five years or so at a holiday party. Anna'd had a stroke in her twenties while giving birth, losing the baby, and from then on, she lived her life with her face pinched and drawn to one side. One useless hand was contracted, pulled to her middle, and hung like a small bird's wing. With each step, she threw a hip forward and dragged her braced leg up to meet the other. While Gina felt sorry for Anna, watching her ambulation was exhausting. And listening to her slurred speech took more concentration than Gina had patience for. But she never failed to notice the small rose Anna had tattooed at the wrist just above her good hand, a talisman perhaps of a time when she ran wild, smoked pot, and slept with boys in the backs of Volkswagen buses. Her thick, wavy blonde hair, somewhat silvered now, was shoulder length, and if you only looked at her good side, you could mistake her for a younger woman who, with no makeup, was attractive in a frail sort of way.

Marty gave Gina a hearty hug and patted Ellen on the cheek when the two women came into the living room. He went on about what a wonderful fellow Frank had been, how he'd never find a more competent accountant, and how Thursdays would be empty now.

"You had a wonderful father, Ellie. Next to your mom, he always said you were the apple of his eye."

Gina walked them into the dining room and offered them something to eat and drink. Marty piled a plate full of ziti and sausage. Anna had a glass of ginger ale. She pulled a straw out of her purse and sipped.

"You know, before Frank died he was a little out of his head," Gina said. "He kept going on about how he'd betrayed me . . . every Thursday for thirty years, he said. The nurses called it ICU psychosis. What is it they say causes it, Ellie?" Gina looked at her daughter.

"The medication, sensory deprivation, sometimes lack of oxygen. Heart patients can act totally out of character, they said."

"I feel so bad," Gina said. "I was giving him such a hard time. He was asking for a priest. Can you believe it? Frank asking for a priest. Then he started crying, didn't he, El? So not like my Frank." Gina shook her head and choked back tears.

"Oh, Gina," Marty put a beefy arm around her. "Frank would never betray you. Why, you and the kids, you meant the world to him. And look at you, you're still a head turner."

Gina smiled. "There's other ways to betray a person, Marty."

"Well, he didn't do it when he was on the clock with me. I can tell you that." He chuckled and squeezed her even tighter. "He got there every Thursday at nine on the dot. Reconciled the books, did the taxes, you know, whatever the hell he did to make the numbers make sense, and walked back to the train around five thirty. Sometimes a taxi. I'd offer him a ride, but no, rain or snow, he liked to walk."

"That was Frank," Gina said. "He loved to walk, especially in the snow. Remember, Ellie? Remember how he would take you guys all the way up White Plains Road to the Blockbuster then all the way back. You'd be frozen little things, then sit by the fire, eat popcorn, and watch your movie."

Ellen smiled.

"And he'd draw snowflakes on our arms with a pen. No two are alike." She imitated her father.

"You were very kind to come all this way," Gina turned and looked down at the woman in the chair. "Thank you, Anna, it means a lot to me that you made the effort."

Gina walked with the Jacobis to their car. While Marty was putting the wheelchair in the trunk, Anna stood on her good leg holding onto the car door.

"Did a priest get there in time?" Anna worked the words out through her twisted mouth.

"Yeah," Gina said. "Early one morning. He was leaving as I got there. My son-in-law, Bobby, found him. Bobby's a voice coach. The guy was having trouble delivering his sermons. He was sweet, a red-headed boy. Father Flynn his name was. Said Frank was a noble soul, a real mensch, he said. I liked that, a priest using Yiddish." Gina tried to hold Anna's gaze as she spoke, but she had to look away when a bit of spittle dripped down the woman's chin. "I guess I'm glad. You know, even if he was out of his head, it's what he wanted."

"Ga-good." Anna balanced herself. She managed a smile and got into the car.

Marty Jacobi waved back as the car drove down Mulberry.

"Lying bastard," Gina said into the air. "Frank would never use the phrase 'apple of my eye.' Ever."

Before Gina turned to the house, a taxi pulled up to the curb. The driver got out and came up the walk.

"Mrs. Pella?" the driver said.

"Yes?"

"These are for you." He handed her a small bouquet of flowers and his business card. *Joe Tillman, Personal Taxi*, the card read. "Your husband did my taxes for years. Hell of a guy. Talked about you all the time. I just wanted to pay my respects. Sorry I didn't make the funeral."

"Thank you, Mr. Tillman."

"I want you to keep that card. You ever need a cab, to the city, the airport. You call me. No charge."

Gina smiled at the man and thanked him for coming. Frank was so loved, she realized, by people she didn't even know. The thought warmed her.

A few weeks after the funeral, Gina drove to Brooklyn on a Thursday, grabbed coffee at a food truck on Flatbush at Atlantic Avenue, pulled around the corner, and parked her car half a block away from Jacobi's Blinds and Draperies. She had brought a book along and settled in to wait. At eleven forty-five, Marty came out of the side door to his business and got in his car. Gina followed him to Lafayette Avenue, took a right, and stayed a couple of cars behind him until he parked in front of a nondescript brick building with a small sign on the door she could hardly read. After he walked inside, she pulled up in front of the building and read *Therapeutic Massage*, printed in silver stick-on letters you could get at the hardware store. She parked across the street and waited. An hour later, Marty left, hopped in his car, and drove away.

Gina put down her book, grabbed her purse, and walked across the street. She buzzed the door and waited, buzzed again and finally saw the peephole darken. A woman, wearing a kimono, who Gina imagined to be Japanese, opened the door and bowed.

"You have appointment?"

"No."

Gina looked around a small tidy waiting room with framed certificates from the Academy of Massage Therapy in Hackensack hanging on the rice-paper-covered wall. A waterfall trickled onto an arrangement of rocks in a corner. A beautiful bonsai tree sat on a table in front of a small window with a bamboo shade. The soft plinking of a string instrument came out of tiny speakers in the corners.

"Who recommend you?"

"Ah, Mary," Gina said, not knowing why the name popped into her head. She didn't know a Mary.

"Ah, Mary Glenn?"

"Yes, Mary Glenn. She says she really loves it here."

"You want Swedish or Shiatsu?"

"Ah, Swedish."

"OK. We have cancellation. We take you now."

In five minutes Gina lay naked under a sheet on a massage table. The room was not unlike the one at the Moontree Salon where she got her hair done and, a couple of times a year, got a facial and a massage. The low light, the meditative music, and the mellow scent of essential oils finally did their magic and she began to relax. *So Marty Jacobi gets a massage every Thursday. Good for him. Maybe he brought Frank along with him. Good for him too.* It would be just like Frank to think getting a massage was an indulgence he didn't deserve. Christ, getting his hair cut at a salon instead of a barber made him feel guilty. They washed his hair, rubbed his neck after lying back in the bowl. She smiled remembering Frank telling their neighbor about switching to Moontree. "Costs twice as much as Johnny's by the train," he said the first time he went. "But you leave there feeling like you just had sex."

Gina was lying on her stomach, her face in the cradle, when a tall blonde girl, with her hair up in a knot, walked in wearing a tank top and short sarong. The girl sat on a small rolling stool at the head of the table.

"Hello, Gina," she said in a thick Nordic accent. "My name is Kirsten. So, you are a friend of Mary's. So she told you about me, yah?"

"Well, not a close friend. But, yes, she said you had amazing hands," Gina said.

"How can I help you today? Do you have any areas that are especially sensitive?" The woman spoke very slowly and smiled sweetly.

"No, not really. Just do what you do for Mary, you know, your basic Swedish magic."

"Swedish Magic is my specialty."

Kirsten rolled her stool over to a little table and rubbed oil onto her hands. She stood and pulled the sheet down to Gina's hips. The girl's strong fingers moved along the muscles of her back, kneading her neck, shoulders—long strokes allowed her muscles to roll beneath the girl's fingers. *Good for Frank*, Gina thought again. *This was just what he needed.* He took so little time for himself. Other than her opulent cooking, he rarely indulged himself at all.

"You have beautiful skin for a woman your age," Kirsten said.

"Thank you."

Gina was basking in the moment, feeling relaxed for the first time in weeks. Then suddenly the girl's strokes moved down, under the sheet, onto Gina's rear. She caressed her upper thighs, allowing a light fingertip to trace between them. At first Gina was confused; then she saw the sarong hit the floor and felt the girl's breasts brushing over her back.

"What the hell . . ."

Gina flipped over and looked at the girl. Kirsten's beautiful tan body was looming over her; the long blonde hair, loosened now, curled around her breasts.

"What the hell are you doing?"

Gina sat up as the girl crawled toward her, reaching for a nipple that had escaped the sheet.

"What you said, baby. Swedish Magic."

The girl knelt up and bit a pouting lower lip. Her golden body, without a single tan line, wore only a small blonde patch of hair below a pelvis that she jutted forward.

"I just want a massage." Gina pulled the sheet up to her neck and wiggled free.

"Oh yah, I can play coy, baby. Swedish Magic is my specialty."

"No. No coy. No nothing! I *really* just came in for a massage."

"You said you were a friend of Mary's," the girl stammered and jumped off the table. "You said you wanted a Swedish. You said Swedish Magic!"

"And if I'd said I wanted Shiatsu?" Gina had pulled the sheet around her and slid off the table. She reached for her clothes.

"You'd have gotten Misaki. She's quite small. Does amazing things with her toes." The Nordic accent was gone.

"I don't need to know what she does with her toes." Gina pulled her panties up, dropped the sheet, turned her back, and fastened her bra. "I knew something wasn't right. Why didn't I see that this was a brothel?" Gina turned and lifted her dress from the hook on the wall.

"This is not a brothel." Kirsten stood erect; her lovely nipples pointed upward. "I do have a certificate in massage therapy. A perfectly legal certificate."

"Well, I have a degree in interior design. And you know what I do? I design interiors and somehow I manage to do it fully clothed."

Gina slipped her dress over her head and zipped it up the back. The girl was reaching for her sarong.

"Look, I won't report you." Gina turned. "You can do whatever you want for a living . . . or for pleasure, for that matter. Just tell me this . . ." Gina rummaged through her purse, found her wallet, and pulled out a picture of Frank. "Do you know this man? Did he come here on Thursdays?"

"Sorry, I only do women." Kirsten had slipped her tank top over her breasts and was tying the sarong around her waist.

"But you might have seen him here. Look, please." Gina thrust the photo of Frank's broad smiling face at the woman. "Maybe somebody else . . . did him."

"Are you a cop? You're vice, aren't you?" Kirsten put a hand on her hip. "You look like you could be a cop."

"You just said I had good skin."

"Look, lady, I mean Gina, nobody's going to tell you this guy was here. He could be here right now, and I promise you, nobody has ever seen this guy."

"Well, he's not here right now. I can promise you that," Gina barked at the girl as she put her earrings back on. "He's not here because he's dead. He was my husband and now he's dead."

She had begun to sob. She sat on the edge of the massage table and buried her head in her hands.

"Oh God. I'm so sorry." The girl pulled the stool out from under the massage table and rolled to face Gina. "You poor thing." She put her hands over Gina's. "Oh God," she said again. "I'm so sorry." After a minute she reached down and took the photo from Gina. "Good-looking guy. How long you married?"

"Forty years next month."

"You got kids?"

"Four, six grandkids." Gina sniffed.

"You're a lucky lady, Gina."

Kirsten rolled over to the little table and brought back a box of tissues. Gina blew her nose.

"I'm not lucky; I'm mad. I am so mad. He's dead and I miss him and I'm so fucking mad at him because he was seeing whores on Thursdays."

"Therapists," the girl corrected. "And maybe he was. A lot of guys do. Even guys who have really good marriages." She took a deep breath and blew it out in a sigh. "But I never saw your husband around here." She handed the picture back to Gina. "I'm not saying he never came; I'm just saying I never saw him."

When Gina got home she showered the remaining oil off her back and crawled into bed. *So, that's what he had to tell his priest. That he got a massage every Thursday and a happy ending.* She wondered whether he preferred Swedish or Shiatsu. Did he tell the priest that too? What did the sweet-faced boy think after he heard Frank's confession? *Oh God,*

Gina thought. *I have to make a place in my heart for the fact that Frank fooled around on me. That's a lot of furniture to move.*

Gina's interior self was a series of rooms. Her head was a neatly ordered home office furnished by Pottery Barn. Her belly, a large inviting kitchen with soups bubbling, pies and cakes baking. But, lately, her heart was a big messy bedroom—the bed never made, the boudoir chair turned on its side, clothes strewn about the floor and pouring out of dressers. All the books on death and dying lay face up, the pages flipping between denial and anger.

It never occurred to Gina that Frank would be unfaithful. She knew women who'd lost their husbands to younger women or to a midlife crisis that didn't shake off. The signs never appeared in her marriage. They fought and made up. She felt loved, adored even. And she loved her Frank. She missed him like the other half of her soul had been spirited away. The phantom pain nagged and would send her into a fury. The thought that he had died with a secret on his lips, shared only with a priest, haunted her night and day.

She hated the mornings most. She dreamed about something that involved Frank almost every night—some mundane thing, like looking out the kitchen window and watching him mow the grass, or hearing him curse at the television when the Knicks were getting killed. When she awoke and he wasn't there, it was like getting the call from the hospital all over again: "Mrs. Pella, I'm afraid I have some very bad news."

Two weeks later, as she was putting Frank's winter clothes in a box, she got a call from her friend Carol who had an extra ticket to an off-Broadway play called *Doubt*.

"It's not a comedy, Gina. But it's supposed to be quite good," Carol said.

Gina had heard about the play, a gripping drama in which a nun accuses a priest of pedophilia.

"Sure," she said. "It'll be good to get out of the house."

Although Gina had forgotten her glasses, she was able to read the playbill insert announcing that the role of Father Flynn would be played by Joseph Greenberg. She didn't care of course. She didn't know who was supposed to play Father Flynn in the first place. But within seconds of hearing the man's voice, the hair on the back of her neck rose like the fur along an angry cat's back. At intermission, she excused herself, walked out to the curb, and called her daughter.

"You hired an actor to hear your father's confession!" She spit the words into the phone.

"Whaa . . . What are you talking . . . I . . . What actor?"

"The actor who is playing Father Flynn in the play *Doubt*, a play I'm sure you and Bobby never dreamed I'd see."

"Joseph who?"

"Oh please, Ellen. The Joseph Greenberg who 'studied at the Actor's Studio under famed acting coach Bobby Anthony,'" Gina read directly from the playbill. "You know, the Bobby Anthony who happens to be your husband!" Gina let out a deep breath. "No wonder he called your father a mensch." She flipped the phone shut and threw it into her purse.

After the audience stood and applauded Jospeh Greenberg and the rest of the cast, Gina told Carol she'd grab a cab, said she needed to walk for a while. She buttoned her coat and walked around the block, then back to the side door of the theater and waited. In less than twenty minutes Father Flynn, minus his black garb and collar, came out the door.

"Father Flynn, we meet again." Gina moved toward the actor who had come out the door with a couple of other members of the cast. He looked puzzled but extended a hand.

"Did you want an autograph?" He patted his chest. "Sorry, I don't have a pen."

"Understudies give out autographs these days?"

"When you knock one out of the park like he did tonight, you bet." The woman who played the young nun put an arm around Joseph Greenberg and smiled at Gina.

"I'm not here about your performance tonight, Mr. Greenberg. I'm here about the role of a lifetime you played at Presbyterian Hospital a few weeks ago."

"I'm sorry, have we met?" Joseph Greenberg looked closer, studying Gina's face. After a moment he told the others he'd catch up with them.

"Look lady—"

"Mrs. Pella, Gina Pella. My husband was Frank, Bobby Anthony's father-in-law. The man whose confession you heard?"

Joseph's eyes widened, then closed in what Gina hoped was shame.

"It was a favor," he stammered. "I mean Bobby asked and I . . . shit. I thought it would be, you know, good."

"Good for who? Good for you, for your career? Bone up on your bless-you-my-child crapola? Any thought at all to my husband, to the fact that you were an imposter?" Gina brought her scarf up around her neck.

"Here," the actor said. "It's cold."

He pressed the buzzer at the stage door and an older man opened it. Joseph led Gina into the darkened theater and put his jacket on the stage steps. Ninety, maybe a hundred, seats sat empty, facing a stage no more than three feet off the ground.

"He thought you were wonderful, by the way." Gina sat on an aisle seat and loosened her scarf, unbuttoned her coat. "He said you were very warm, a good listener. Not at all judgmental and very modern with the absolution. How did you fake that, Father? You mumble some high school Latin?"

Joseph sat on a step across from her. His hands dangled over his knees.

"Look I needed the money, OK? I was short. Waiting tables and hoping the lead gets the flu doesn't pay too well. And you're right. I thought it was an opportunity to test my skills, so to speak. I figured if I could pull it off with your husband, I could pull it off here." He rapped his knuckles on the stage.

"I can't believe this. Aren't you ashamed, even a little? You should be."

"Why? You don't buy all that hocus-pocus, according to your daughter."

"That isn't the point. In the end, my husband did."

"I'm not so sure about that. I think he was just hedging his bets."

"Oh, you know him so well."

"Bobby and Ellen, they thought it was a way to calm your husband down. They said he was maybe depressed about the whole thing, the heart attack, being in the hospital for so long. Nobody thought he was going to die. I certainly didn't. Hell, he was actually in a great mood when I got there . . . cracking jokes, complaining about the draft picks. He said he was just playing all his cards, just in case there really was somebody up there. But then I realized he just wanted to talk. He seemed like a guy who wanted to get something off his chest."

"And what was that?"

"I can't tell you that."

"What do you mean you can't tell me?"

"Because, you know, the sanctity thing, the privacy of the box, you know, the confessional."

"And I thought Frank was delusional. You just said it was hocus-pocus and that Frank was probably just hedging his bets." Gina stood and glared down at the young man. "You're not a real priest, Mr. Understudy. It's make-believe here and it was make-believe there."

"But he thought it was the real thing."

"But it wasn't. If this is some kind of twisted integrity they teach you as part of the Stanislavski method, you've got it all wrong! Now tell me my husband's confession."

"I just can't do that, Mrs. Pella. I just can't."

"Well, how about I tell you." Gina sat back down and folded her arms across her chest. "Frank went to a massage parlor every Thursday with Marty Jacobi and got a blow job, or a hand job, or a full-blown fuck and he just couldn't live with himself anymore so he had to tell a priest, get a little absolution just in case St. Peter was actually checking names at the end of the white tunnel of light. Don't spare my feelings, Father Flynn. I already went to the place. I'm just looking for confirmation here."

Joseph Greenberg shook his head back and forth.

"I'm not going to tell you what your husband said, Mrs. Pella, but I can tell you this, he never mentioned anything even remotely like what you just said. Absolutely nothing." Joseph stood and picked up his jacket from the steps. "Look, I don't know squat about your husband, except what Ellen and Bobby told me, that he was an amazing, funny, loving father. I only spent an hour with the guy, but I know guys. He wasn't the type. He thought you were the most wonderful thing that ever happened to him. Said that after forty years he still found you sexy."

Gina got up and put her coat back on. She shook her head.

"I don't know what's worse, Mr. Greenberg: what you did or that you believe your own bullshit. The world has gone upside down, that's all I can say."

"Your husband was a good man," Joseph said as he followed Gina to the curb. He held up a hand and hailed a cab. "And if you ask me, what he thought was a sin was, in my book, a mitzvah."

He held the door for her. She got in and slammed it shut.

The following Thursday, she went back to Brooklyn. She waited for Marty to leave the massage parlor and walk to his car. When he got in, she opened the passenger door and slid into the seat.

"So tell me, Marty, you get a little Swedish or a little Shiatsu this afternoon?" Gina was growing so comfortable accosting the unsuspecting she didn't even flinch.

"Gina, my goodness." Marty's eyes grew wide. His smile was forced. "I'm just on my way to New Rochelle. Window treatments for the new Radisson. But this is such a pleasant surprise."

"I'll bet it is, Marty, but not as surprised as I was last week to find you visiting a storefront brothel."

"This?" Marty pointed at the building and laughed nervously. "No, no Gina, this is a perfectly respectable place. I've been having some back pain. My orthopedist recommended this place."

"I'll bet he did, Marty. Did he also recommend it to Frank? 'Cause back pain wasn't Frank's problem."

Marty Jacobi had finally grown into his age. Even when he was in his thirties he'd dressed and acted like a sixty-year-old. He always wore suits, dark in the winter, light in summer. He wore his pants too high at the waist and always had a hat. Men stopped wearing hats when Kennedy took office, but Marty Jacobi had them in every type—straw ones, fedoras, woolen caps, you name it. He wasn't a bad-looking guy, a little round in the middle, but what man over fifty-five wasn't these days? He wore what hair he had short. His glasses were the same rimless things he'd always worn.

"Oh, come on, Gina. You see what I deal with. You going to judge me because I get a little touch once a week?"

"I have no interest in judging you, Marty."

"Anna is a wonderful woman and God knows she tries, but it's not like we have any kind of sex life." He ran his hands around the steering wheel then put them in his lap. Marty lowered his eyes to his hands. "She can't, you know, have sex. The doctors say it could cause another stroke." He looked up. "I'm a patient man, Gina, but I'm not a monk. She understands. Maybe even knows."

"How modern," Gina said. "How sad."

While Marty drove to New Rochelle, Gina headed to Jacobi's Blinds and Draperies. Years ago she had been in the building looking at fabric samples for a client. She wasn't impressed with the inventory and never went back.

An elderly receptionist smiled and asked if she could help her.

"I'd like to speak to someone in accounting."

"Is this about your bill?" the woman asked.

"No, it's about my husband, Frank Pella."

"Oh, Mrs. Pella!" the woman moved from behind her desk. "I am so sorry for your loss. We thought the world of Frank. He and I worked together every Thursday morning for, God, almost thirty years. I'm Alice, the bookkeeper. I'm just covering for the receptionist while she's at lunch." The silver-haired woman stood holding Gina's hand, patting it with her other one. "Let me get you some coffee."

They walked down a hall into a small staff room and sat. Gina remembered Frank mentioning Alice through the years. He dealt with so many bookkeepers. Alice was one of the smart ones. Gina vaguely remembered shaking her hand at the funeral, but there had been so many people whom Frank had worked for over the years who came.

"So, Frank was just here in the mornings?" Gina asked

"Yes, until about twelve-thirty," Alice said. "A taxi would pick him up out front. He must have known the man because it was the same driver every Thursday. He'd bring him back at four-thirty in time for the bank drop. Then Frank would walk to the train."

Gina immediately remembered the cab driver who came to the house after the funeral.

"Where did the taxi take him?"

"Oh, he had other clients in the area, a few home businesses, I think."

The woman asked about the kids, the grandchildren, how Frank Jr. was doing taking over the business. Gina never knew there could be so many synonyms for the word fine: "he's getting along," "they're okay," "we're managing," "day by day," "not bad," "she's alright." Nobody really wanted to hear the truth. A woman sobbing and screaming "Goddamn you, God, why did you do this?" should be heard only in the privacy of her own bedroom. Gina knew that. She was no longer a Catholic, yet she was not ready to let go of God.

"Thank you, Alice," she said as she walked to the door. "It was nice to meet you. You know, it's strange meeting all these people who saw my husband every week and I never knew them. We're never really anybody's whole world, are we?"

"I don't think we're supposed to be," the older woman said. "But you made the sun shine for Frank. He talked about you all the time."

Gina went to her car. She reached in her purse and found the card the taxi driver had given her just over a month ago. She dialed Joe Tillman's number.

"I took him to Jacobi's house after he finished at the office," Tillman said. "He did the guy's personal finances, helped out with the household bills, 'cause, you know, the wife, she's disabled."

I keep turning up nothing, Gina thought as she drove to Marty and Anna Jacobi's house. She and Frank had been there once for a Christmas party. The drapery business had been good to Marty. The house, a lovely old brownstone in Brooklyn Heights, had an elevator, which was installed after Anna's stroke. An attractive young woman was leaving with a folding massage chair as Gina rang the bell.

"Is Anna home?" Gina asked.

"Yes. Is she expecting you?"

"No. I just thought I'd stop by and say hello."

"She usually sits in the whirlpool after her massage." The woman put her chair and bag down in the entry hall. "I'll run up and tell her you're here. What's your name?"

"Gina. Gina Pella."

"Oh, Mrs. Pella." The woman turned back, put her hand to her breast, then took Gina's hand. "God, do we miss Frank."

Gina suddenly felt a little faint. Did anybody in Brooklyn not miss Frank? She closed her eyes, then reached behind her and felt for a tufted bench that ran the length of the foyer.

"Oh God, I'm so sorry," the woman said. "So sorry. I can't imagine what you're going through. What can I get you?"

"Nothing. I'm fine, just a . . . a little confused. So, Frank came here every Thursday."

"Like clockwork. At twelve forty-five, he took Anna for a walk after her massage. He'd be coming as I'd be leaving, but we always talked for a few minutes while Anna got her coat on. Sometimes the three of us would have a little lunch."

"He took Anna for walks?"

"Oh yes. They walked all the way to the park and back. In the snow, he'd take her in the chair. Oh my, could he brighten her up. Once, when I was driving past the park, he was pushing her as fast as he could run. The snow was falling in flakes big as buttons. She had her head back and was laughing like a girl. He did her more good than the physical therapist and I ever could."

The little elevator door opened and Anna swung her bad leg forward, planted her four-pronged cane, and moved into the hall. While she lumbered across polished floors, her soft white sweater and black silk pants fluttered, revealing the silhouette of her leg brace and dormant traces of grace and femininity.

The massage therapist squeezed Gina's hand again before she left and handed her a card.

"If you ever need a massage, Mrs. Pella, I'd be honored. I do in-home, with the chair, table, I do full body . . . deep—"

"Thank you," Gina interrupted. "I'm not the massage type, but I'll keep you in mind."

A few minutes later, Gina and Anna sat alone in the living room with cups of tea on the coffee table. Anna smoothed the back of her hair, pressing it into her neck with her good hand; the pretty rose tattoo shortened and stretched with each stroke.

"Your hair looks nice," Gina said. "You just get it cut?"

"Yes. It's a little t-t-too sh-short this time." Anna's speech had improved over the years, but still she struggled.

"I never knew Frank came here. I don't know what to make of it."

Gina lifted her teacup with both hands and looked around the pretty room. Anna sat on a linen sofa with her lifeless hand resting on a pillow the color of persimmons. White silk drapes framed the window. Black tree branches moved up and down, back and forth. Gina's eyes darted from the Oriental rug to the marble fireplace. On the far wall a painting of a woman weaving by lamplight hung in a heavy black and gilt frame. A child and a small dog curled in the foreground. They slept, oblivious of the loom, amidst shuttles fat with rose-colored yarn. Gina's eyes moved back to Anna.

"Why did he see taking you for a walk and having lunch with you and your therapist as an act of betrayal?"

Anna shrugged and twisted her mouth to one side.

"I know he felt bad about—"

"He did not feel s-s-sorry for muh-me." Anna's clear blue eyes shot at Gina. Her garbled words were barbed.

"I didn't mean..."

"He was my friend." Anna put her cup on the table. It rocked in its saucer; tea sloshed. Gina reached for her napkin, but Anna stopped her with a hand. "Friends. We were f-friends."

"Of course you were. I don't doubt that."

"We t-talked." Anna took a deep breath, closed her eyes, and allowed her face to soften. When she opened them, she looked at the napkin in her hand.

"With Frank I could talk easy." The sentence was spoken slowly, beats between the words without stuttering.

"He wasn't like M-Marty. Didn't go with wh-wh-whores." In an instant her mouth twisted back into her cheek.

"You know about that?"

"Phh," Anna shook her head and threw her good hand at the air.

"But, couldn't Marty be protecting you? I mean if it is likely you could have another stroke—"

"He tell you that?" Anna snorted a nasty laugh, then pulled again on the hair at the back of her neck. She looked out the window, bit hard on her lips, and shook her head at the trees outside. A minute later she brought her napkin up to her mouth, wiped a drop from the corner of her lips.

"I'm fine, G-Gina." She bit the words and spit them out. "I'm as l-likely t-to have an-another s-stroke as I am t-to ha-have another b-baby."

Gina sat for a moment staring at the rose on Anna's arm. The room grew so silent Gina could hear her own breathing, then Anna's. The clock ticked on the mantle. It had begun to snow. Both women looked out the window as the flakes flipped and fell to the pavement then disappeared. After a moment Gina stood and walked over to the sofa. She stood above Anna, looking out the window.

"Frank always loved to walk," she said. "We took long hikes up in the Poconos every autumn. He loved things falling from the sky. Leaves, snow, even rain. There was something about the way nature danced to the ground, he said, that made him feel a part of it."

Anna looked up; tears had collected. Gina sat on the coffee table and faced her.

"Right after she was born, Frank had Ellen in his arms. I remember wincing as his rough stubble touched that perfect new skin, like a wire brush on a ripe peach. Then her little hand reached up and circled his finger. 'That's where God lives,' Frank said. 'Right here between her and me, and me loving you. That's all the God I need.'"

Gina gently reached up and took Anna's hand away from her neck. Anna's eyes closed as tears ran down her cheeks. She dropped her head forward and allowed Gina to pull her hair away. Just behind her left ear three small and beautifully drawn snowflakes the color of the sky at dusk were etched on Anna's neck.

Gina's stomach lurched, sweat dripped down her back, a hot flash burned through her dress. She let the hair fall back onto Anna's neck and looked back at the snow.

After a moment she asked: "You were never afraid Marty would see, wonder what they meant?"

"He would n-n-never get that close." Anna raked her good hand through her hair. "I got lucky. He finally repulses me as much as I d-do him. I h-have learned what Marty couldn't. P-p patience. Frank, he taught me that."

Anna stood and pulled herself up straight. *She's tall,* Gina suddenly noticed. Slender, and for a second, with the gauzy light coming through the window, she looked oddly beautiful, frail and defiant, hardly deserving charity.

Gina got up and moved across the room into the hall for her coat. She slipped it on and draped her scarf around her neck. She felt weak, wobbly like she did sometimes after she and Frank made love. She needed air, cold, sharp air.

"It was Frank who felt guilty. N-n-not me." Anna stood by the sofa. "I'm sorry that you know, Gina, but I'm not ashamed. I'm not. He was muh-ma-my friend."

"He was also your lover."

Gina moved back into the living room. Anna stood by the white sofa. The curtain of snow behind her, the silver-blonde hair, even the beautiful silken white sweater shrieked of halos and purity and long-suffering sainthood. Only the fruit-colored pillow that Anna squeezed with her good hand hinted at sin.

Gina pulled on her gloves. A tornado furiously blew around her middle, tossing pillows and bedsheets, wedding photos and bronze baby shoes around the room.

"I'm going to have to find a way to hate you," Gina said. "Because I will torture myself with images of my husband's hands on you. I will drive myself crazy wondering if he knew your body as well as he knew mine. And if you knew his. If you watched and worried about the mole on his left shoulder, about his blood pressure." Gina was looking at the woman, wishing she were wearing red with makeup high on her cheeks and lips. "He kept his clothes next to mine. He shaved in the mirror next to me every morning. He held my hand and yelled right along with me at each birth. I will learn to hate you, Anna. Because I cannot hate Frank."

Gina slammed the door behind her. *A mitzvah! Ha. This is a woman who has lived more than half her life with the world pitying her*, Gina thought as she walked to her car. *Even my own husband felt the need to take care of her. Well, I won't pity her. I won't allow myself to think that she deserved a little happiness even if she was married to a swine. She could have divorced him, could have lived a very nice life. What judge in his right mind wouldn't make sure that Anna Jacobi lived the rest of her life as well as she does now?* Gina turned, walked back to the house, and rang the bell. The door opened faster than she expected.

"Why didn't you divorce him, Anna? If he was such a pig, why didn't you just leave?"

With barely a slur Anna spoke: "Then I wouldn't have had Frank. If I were free, he'd have to choose. And he would never choose me."

Anna stood just inside the door with the wind blowing her clothes and hair. Gina wanted to strike her, slap her twisted mouth, smack the tears off her cheeks. But she turned and walked down the path as the snow fell and swirled around her.

A week later, Gina sat in the back of the Eighteenth Street Theater at three in the afternoon. An understudy again, Joseph Greenberg, defrocked of his Father Flynn collar, sat next to her. Rehearsal was over; the house lights went up. Now that they could speak freely, he turned to her.

"Okay, so now you know what I know. What do you want from me?"

"I want you to tell me how he saw it . . . how he allowed himself to do it, to cheat on me."

He shook his head.

"I know you think I'm an asshole. And maybe I did something really wrong. But I got to be honest with you, Mrs. Pella. I don't regret it. Your husband was really something. I'm a better man for the hour I spent with him.

"Okay, I get it," she said. "I guess you have your right to this peculiar Jewish-Catholic integrity shtick you've constructed the backstory for. You're a good actor. Really good. Is that what you want? I won't lie to you; I had moments during your performance when I bought you hook, line, and sinker. I completely forgot you played my husband for a sucker. Do this. Don't tell me what he said. Just give me your opinion. Tell me what you think."

Jeffery Greenberg sat forward in his seat and looked at the stage.

"I think your husband thought the two of you were so lucky, so perfect . . . even your flaws were charming." He turned and looked at her. "Your kids were great, smart, good looking. You both had successful businesses. You were a big messy family. The two of you, lucky to meet each other . . . On the subway, right? . . . Riding to and from the city for work. He saw so many things as strokes of luck. You could have taken a later train. But the train broke down that day and the two of you shared a cab." He looked back at the stage.

"He said that a lot." Gina twisted her wedding band on her finger. "He said, everybody's going on these days about how they got where they are because they worked hard, but nobody thinks about all the ironies, the little accidents of fate that put you here, or there. Some people think God's up there orchestrating the whole show. Some say we make our own luck. Frank hated that. You try the best you can with what you got, he always told the kids, then you take your punches and your glory when it comes. Don't ever put it on anybody else."

Joseph nodded as though they were talking about someone they'd both known for years.

"You were a brick," he said. "You made him laugh." He took in a deep breath and turned to look at her. "In the end, isn't that all that matters? I mean, what more do we really need?" He said it as though they were on the same plane.

"I need to erase the idea that I had another person in bed with us for forty years. That's what I need. God, you are so naïve." She choked back tears. "And the sex? What about the lovemaking?"

"I don't think it was what you think, not erotic or passionate. He got that with you. Honestly, he said so."

"It's the secret that haunts me," she said. "That I was married to this man, I mean really married. It's like discovering you have a split personality, like you go off and become someone else and don't even know it. Suddenly you find pictures of yourself dressed in clothes you don't even own, wearing makeup, and you never even put on mascara. How is it a person can do this? Take a part of his life and put it in a little box and only open it up on Thursdays?"

Joseph stood. He grabbed his coat from the seat next to him.

"I can't tell you, Mrs. Pella. I only know he loved you, loved his family."

"Well." She stood and shook her head at the carpet on the theater floor. "You know what they say, to commit a crime you have to have motive and opportunity. I get the opportunity." She looked up at Joseph Greenberg. "I just don't understand the motive. We were so . . . complete, me and Frank."

He helped her with her coat and watched her walk down the narrow theater steps, turn, and go out the lobby door. He sat back down and put his head into his hands. He breathed deeply and hoped that it was over.

"Your secret is safe with me, Frank," he said to the empty theater.

It wasn't what he'd bargained for either. "Sure, I'll hear your dad's confession. What could it hurt?" he'd said to Bobby and Ellen. He figured gambling maybe, fooling around here and there. But no. Frank had gone to the Jacobi's house to do the personal taxes in 1980. Anna had only been home a week from the hospital. A caregiver was trying to feed her some kind of glop. So he ran out and picked up a pint of ice cream. For months he fed Anna one spoonful at a time and wiped her chin with a napkin. He stretched her contracted fingers and showed her flash cards and laughed with her as she struggled back to speak. He took notes from the physical and speech therapists when they came to visit. And three years later he taught her to climb the stairs, helped her into the whirlpool, and later, traced his hand down the numb and unfeeling side of her body, then gently and carefully folded her into him. He didn't recoil at the twisted side of her face any more than he delighted in the curl of her lip and the dimple in the other cheek. He was the only one who let her cry about the baby and the knowing there would never be another.

"So what about my penance, Father?" Frank had asked. "What do you want, a string of Hail Marys, ten Our Fathers? What's a good sin get a guy these days? Don't tell me I have to tell Gina I cheated on her. I can't do that."

Joseph thought of Frank sitting up in a chair, the hospital gown unsnapped for the IV line. He'd removed the oxygen tips from his nose, and now and then, he reached over to drink water from a straw. "Have to stay hydrated." Salt and pepper hair and a strong jaw couldn't conceal the boy caught in a lie that still lived in the man's face. It was the face of a man who'd lived every second of his life and somehow found the balm to make somebody whose life had been cursed feel a little bit lucky.

"Don't ever tell her," Father Flynn answered. "That's your penance. Never, ever, ever tell her. And especially don't tell her why you did it."

"How could I? I don't even know why I did it."

"Yeah you do, Frank. Sure you do."

As Joseph walked up Eighteenth Street, it began to snow. He knew he wasn't necessarily a good person, but he had done a good thing. It was a start. What Gina said about motive and opportunity stuck. Even a fake priest and a want-to-be actor could figure out that motive can take its good sweet time to reveal itself. And it didn't matter whether Frank knew why or not. Sometimes we don't even know what we need, but we get it in the spreading of the balm.

Acknowledgments

I'd like to thank my brother Paul Cason for inspiring "The Army Jacket" and "What Solomon Saw." He continually adds to our family folklore by randomly releasing long-held secrets from the extensive archive nestled between his ears. What would I do without Nancy Litke's hand at my back? Thanks for the many hours of reading and laughter.

I am indebted to the Ashe County Historical Society and Molly Rawls of Digital Forsyth in Winston-Salem, North Carolina. The Board of Architectural Review in Charleston, South Carolina; the community of New Point in Beaufort, South Carolina; and the Congress for the New Urbanism were more than helpful in solidifying details of "Rich as Pluff Mud," as was Charleston history buff and writer David Farrow.

Many thanks to the International Federation of Red Cross and Red Crescent Societies along with the Queen Alexandra's Royal Army Nursing Corps archives for assistance with "The Penitent."

I am grateful to Professor Susan Weinenger of Roosevelt University and the Metropolitan Museum of Art, both responsible for my falling in love with Vermeer and his tiny, neglected painting *Girl Interrupted at Her Music.*

The National Snow and Ice Data Center—who knew it even existed—was most helpful in allowing me to understand the power of earth-altering avalanches.

Hats off to Sam Hook's wonderful cover design and to Kelly Finefrock-Creed for her bionic eye in editing the interior.

Thank you to Marcy Moody for reading and to Matt, Emma and Ginny and all who have attended Wine, Women and Stories for listening.

www.ingramcontent.com/pod-product-compliance
Lightning Source LLC
Chambersburg PA
CBHW020103180626
46812CB00006B/2444